W9-CIH-827

HEYDAY

DISCARDED

heyday

MARNIE WOODROW

TIGHTROPE BOOKS

2015

Tightrope Books
#207—2 College Street, Toronto, ON M5G 1K3
www.tightropebooks.com

Editors: Natalie Fuerth and Deanna Janovski
Typography: Carleton Wilson
Author photo: Janette Piquette

We thank the Canada Council for the Arts and the Ontario Arts
Council for their support of our publishing program.

Printed and bound in Canada

LIBRARY AND ARCHIVES CANADA CATALOGUING IN PUBLICATION

Woodrow, Marnie, 1969-, author
    Heyday / Marnie Woodrow.

ISBN 978-1-926639-90-1 (paperback)

    I. Title.

PS8595.O6453H49 2015   C813'.54   C2015-904877-X

For Janette, with big love,
and in memory of Tiff.

I Know I Am But Summer To Your Heart (*Sonnet* XXVII)

I know I am but summer to your heart,
And not the full four seasons of the year;
And you must welcome from another part
Such noble moods as are not mine, my dear.
No gracious weight of golden fruits to sell
Have I, nor any wise and wintry thing;
And I have loved you all too long and well
To carry still the high sweet breast of Spring.
Wherefore I say: O love, as summer goes,
I must be gone, steal forth with silent drums,
That you may hail anew the bird and rose
When I come back to you, as summer comes.
Else will you seek, at some not distant time,
Even your summer in another clime.

—Edna St. Vincent Millay

We met after the man Ferris invented his wheel and before time-share villas on Mars. It was hot for June. You came dashing down the ramp of life, all boots and hope. In the sun we made promises, plans to conquer the world outside the one we'd had named for us. We designed a wild world of cotton candy dreams and cold drinks and always the decision of whether to spin or coast, soar skyward or rush downward. Do both, you tell me now. And when night comes, autumn—keep your promises, no matter what.

That one day the carbon stench of scorched wood and charred canvas drifted over the harbour. Silver tendrils of smoke rose still from the devoured skeletons of roller coasters. Before even reaching shore I could see and smell the destruction. It was necessary to shut my ears to the comments of gawkers riding the ferry, out for a last good look at the fall-out of a wayward spark in a wooden kingdom. Our world. Their heartless curiosity was nearly unbearable. Talk of insurance and arson and none of it mattered till I clapped eyes on you again and knew that another girl had been taken away from someone else.

She was the healthy one, everyone said. If anything, I should have been the one to get cancer. Me with my long love affair with cigarettes, my big fat appetite for everything decadent and bad for you. And then there was my dishonest heart, loving elsewhere but with cowardice. Loving you through time. You must be this tall to ride this ride…

We'll go to Coney Island, it won't matter. No crying. Girls died every day. *Not mine.*

1.

The first thing she did after Bianca died was pour herself a drink and close the blinds. Never mind that it had been ten years without a single sip. The steadiness of her hand as she poured surprised her. The sequence of events had actually been: Bianca's final hour at the palliative unit, a teary haze of paperwork, a taxi ride to the grocery store nearest the ferry docks. Groceries procured in an exhausted blur—she had happened to have string bags with her at the hospice—why? And whereas Bianca had always loved a good Merlot, in moderation, Joss opted for a stockpile of cold boxed white and a carton of cigarettes.

Back at their cottage on the island side of Lake O, she lit the first of a dozen indoor cigarettes and glared out at the green-blue water. She had promised Bianca she wouldn't spiral, back when the news was all bad and they were chilly with pragmatism and plans. Get your already immaculate life in order had been the decree. Now the business of death would take mere days. Their *affairs* were in order. Bianca had been tidy about everything, even her affairs, even during her illness. Promise me you won't start drinking again when I'm gone. I promise. Promise me and look at me at the same time. I promise.

Tonight was the annual goddess party for solstice. Bianca's timing had been impeccable too. No one but Maxine, who found everything "healing," would expect Joss to attend. Against island custom, she locked the door. Cold boxed wine. Cigarettes. Why not a top-volume play of some of the music Bianca had hated most? Grief had made Joss surprisingly spiteful. By the time someone came carrying a consoling casserole, she would be completely open to suggestions about what to do next. Or just exquisitely drunk.

2.

The trick to tying a bow tie perfectly was to close your eyes and think about shoelaces. "The very last thing you want to do is look in a mirror," her father said, his fingers deftly moving the silk into a tight bow before he snapped his crisp shirt collar down. He always smelled like lemons, and he always looked like a perfectly wrapped present when he went out to one of his meetings. Never a speck of lint on his suits or a lustrous black hair out of place on his head: he was handsome and took the burden of his good looks seriously.

"*You* might want to look in a mirror once in a while, Bette," her mother said, passing by. "The hairbrush was invented for a reason."

Irving Titus seemed to take no notice of these remarks. He smiled at Bette and patted his pockets to check for his notebook and pen. He was never without the notebook now that he practiced automatic writing, a form of dictation from the otherworld, as he explained it. From his waistcoat pocket he produced a cigarette case. He popped it open, held it out to her. "Take two of these, and you'll feel instantly better." He always carried the brightly coloured Necco candy wafers that tasted of orange or licorice, lemon or chocolate, and she had loved them since she was little. They came in the mail from a candy store in Boston.

"Where is this convention, Papa?" she asked, sucking happily on the first of the two candies. Licorice.

"IRVING, we are LATE!" her mother shouted from the landing a floor below. She could be heard stamping down to the first floor, muttering under her breath.

"Ottawa—I think—your mother has all the tickets and things. Now listen," he said, leaning in to whisper. "Don't keep sitting in

Grandie's room, all right? Get out and do something. Get your sister to take you someplace."

"Yes, Papa. Have a good time. I hope your speech goes well." She leapt up and kissed him quickly on the cheek just as he moved toward the bedroom door. Before the shouting could resume. Never keep a bluestocking waiting.

"Goodbye, Momma," she called down the stairs, watching the top of her father's head as he descended.

"Goodbye, darling!" her mother called back with shocking warmth. There was never any telling, though she did tend to become sunnier whenever she was about to leave the house for a journey. "Brush that HAIR!" her mother added before slamming the heavy front door.

She had no desire to spend the day with her sister Margaret, whose recent marriage had rendered her incapable of conversation that didn't revolve around her husband, a milliner with the giggle-inducing name of Clarence Clackum. Before meeting her sister's fiancé, Bette had been unable to imagine what a Clackum looked like. And while she wanted her older sister to be happy, it was close to impossible to understand where exactly the marital bliss sprang from: Clarence Clackum was quite possibly the dullest man alive. In person or as Margaret's perpetual topic. Thankfully he was unable to come for Sunday dinners because of a severe (and rare) allergy to paper: the bookish Titus household, stuffed to the rafters with pamphlets, newsletters, dusty encyclopaedias and Theosophical manifestoes, was unbearable for Clarence. Once a month Bette and her parents trudged over to Margaret's house a few blocks away to have supper. It was almost always an exercise in torture for all present: Margaret couldn't cook, her parents weren't allowed to smoke, and Clarence was all too passionate about the rising cost of ribbon—every time. Bette considered announcing a powerful allergy to petrified roast beef in an effort to be exempted from such meals but doubted it would work.

When her parents' departure was assured (they often returned to the house three and four times to retrieve forgotten items before actually leaving) Bette went straight to Grandie's room and sat on the bed. In the three weeks since her beloved granny had died, she had been unable to read, paint, or consider her own future. Next to insisting that she care more for her appearance, her suffragette mother was adamant that Bette consider her future as an independent woman. Plans, what were her plans? The lecture seldom abated for long. There was an unspoken fear that Bette would never marry. In fact, she had promised Grandie she never would. "There are other ways to find kisses," was all she would say when Bette asked why marriage was to be avoided.

Her granny had been the centre of her universe, even when bed-ridden. And although she could hear her now, cajoling Bette to go and have some fun, the world outside the tiny main-floor bedroom held little appeal. What awaited her? Some boring man like Clarence Clackum who wanted her to have one baby after another? A job teaching dimwits how to add and subtract till her eyes glazed over and she threw herself in front of a streetcar? At seventeen she knew damned well there was nothing to look forward to. Her mother could hand out all the pamphlets she liked, but being a woman was a curse. She hoped that next time—Papa insisted there were many next times for the soul—she would get to be a boy.

A terrible banging on the front door startled her from her gloomy yet somehow pleasurable descent into full-blown despair. Bereavement was a constant ache; self-pity offered a wider range of emotions, like sweets in a variety box. She tried to ignore the hammering, mindful of the fact that her father told her to never answer the door unless she was expecting a visit from Margaret. The banging grew more insistent, and the caller had also located the door-chime, which he now pulled with gusto, alternating between knocks.

Bette grabbed the poker from the iron stand next to the fireplace and marched toward the front door. She had been crying and looked like it, so wiped her eyes with her fingers and tugged the door wide to confront the unwelcome visitor.

"Oh my!" the young man standing in front of her exclaimed, backing up a little. He wore a striped jacket and a straw boater and smart white flannel slacks. Some sort of salesman, she decided, still brandishing the poker. It seemed to be working: the fellow still hadn't spoken further.

"Yes?" she demanded. He had a sheaf of bright yellow papers clutched to his chest.

"Is that your Egyptian look?" the young man ventured, gesturing timidly at her face.

"Pardon?" she snapped, glaring into the mirror positioned next to the front door for the purposes of considering oneself *before* greeting visitors. "Oh, gracious," she muttered, about to slam the door.

"No, please! I like it!" he shouted, grinning to reassure her as he held the door open with one hand. "It's all the rage in Paris."

She had two long black smears of ash, one on each cheek, where she had wiped away her mourner's tears, and her hair was as frightful as her mother had suggested. She could have easily posed for a portrait of Medusa. There, Momma, she thought, I finally have a plan for my life…

"I just wanted to make sure you had one of these," the young pitchman said, holding out one of his goldenrod-coloured advertisements. "You won't want to miss out on the finest summer in Toronto history!"

She studied the piece of paper, which shouted in large letters about amusement rides and diving horses and musical entertainments. Fresh lake air and delicious treats and ferry passage complimentary to holders of this very bright yellow piece of paper. "Why me?" she grunted, remembering the soot on her face and her father's warnings about slick young devils who posed as salesmen. "Why shouldn't I miss out?"

"Why not you?" he asked, winking. "Bring a friend, have a perfect day! I'd take you myself, but I'm working today, as you can see." Another wink. She noticed then that he had bright red hair and freckles. Small teeth. It was true: she would never marry. She decided this as she gazed at him. He was pleasant enough, but probably had a name like Stuart or Donald.

"Goodbye," she announced, slamming the door in his face. It was a horrible thing to do, but then she was horrible. People were always telling her as much; sometimes it felt good to act on her reputation. She could hear him retreating down the front steps, likely glad to have escaped a beating.

She looked at herself in the oval mirror once more and laughed out loud for the first time in weeks. Like an illustration out of one of her father's books on tribal customs with her smudged cheeks and wild snarls of curls. She replaced the poker daintily on its rack and carried the advertisement for Hanlan's Point to the kitchen. Washed her hands in the basin, rummaged till she found her father's stash of ZuZu ginger snaps, and sat down to study the promised location where one could have a "perfect day."

"COME JOIN US FOR THE 1909 SEASON!" she read at top volume, addressing the empty kitchen, enjoying herself. "RIDE THE FIGURE 8! FRESH LAKE AIR AND WONDERFUL FOOD!" She pounded on the countertop. "Every day is PERFECT at HAN—"

"Bette?" a voice said behind her.

She whirled around, wishing she still held the poker, to see her sister Margaret looking worried.

"Father said to check in on you and see if you wanted to go out for tea. What are you doing? And what on earth have you got all over your face?"

At this, Bette burst out laughing again. She had washed her hands but not her face. Her gales of laughter seemed to worry her sister, which made her laugh all the harder.

"Should...should I get Dr. Thomas?"

Bette stood up. Stopped laughing immediately. "Dr. Thomas who killed Grandie? No, I don't think so. And I don't drink tea, Mags. The whole family knows I don't drink *tea*."

"Clarence and I think you should come for supper," Margaret ventured.

Since she had already been querulous once that day, Bette decided to control herself. It would be so easy to keep going, but she didn't dare. Margaret's gaze had travelled to the countertop where Bette had tossed the advertisement for Hanlan's Point Amusement Park. She knew her little sister well and shook her head. "No, Bette. I forbid you. That isn't a good place for unmarried ladies."

Bette nodded solemnly. "I know. That's why you're going to take me, Mrs. Clackum."

"It's too far, Bette. It'll take an entire day, and I have to make sure Clarence has his supper."

Folding the piece of yellow paper, Bette tucked it in the sleeve of her dress and shrugged. "Mother has instructed me to think of my future as an independent woman. My destiny is sealed and my tomorrow is planned for. Now if you will pardon me, sister, I have a thousand things to do."

"What time shall we leave?" Margaret said, sighing.

3.

Joss hadn't picked up her camera since Bianca's diagnosis. When Tess came bearing coffee from the café at the docks, she pointed this out. The gear bag had a patina of dust on it. She did not make note of the empty wine cartons or the overflowing ashtrays. She was too good a friend and assistant, and the source of the wreckage was obvious.

"How was the solstice party?" Joss asked, making room for them to sit in the screened porch. She had been going through back issues of *Food & Wine*, looking for a lost recipe for tomato jam. It seemed very urgent to do so.

"Same as it ever was. Donna was Lakshmi—again—and Maxine wore everyone out with her ritual moon dances."

"What card did you pull?"

"Mahwu, the earth mother, again."

"It's all that recycling work you do," Joss managed to tease. "The rinsing, the fascistic sorting. You're an environmental remedy on legs."

"So, you. Jokes aside."

"Yes?"

"You gonna be okay?"

Joss smiled through a puff of smoke. "I have some plans."

Tess looked encouraged. She held out her hand and waited till Joss gave her the cigarette, from which she took a conspiratorial drag. "You might want to know that Maxine suggested a group smudge of the house when you finally answer the doorbell."

"It's the day after," Joss said blankly. "She can wait to heal me." She sipped her coffee and groaned as the doorbell rang and a knock came soon after. "Tell her I'm lying down."

Tess went to the door and after a prolonged exchange, one long staccato murmur, she returned with a goddess card in hand, pulled from the well-worn deck the island women used at all their parties. "Maxine pulled this for you this morning, and she wants you to come by for dinner." Joss made a face. "I told her you weren't ready for dinners yet." Joss looked at the card meant for her. Isolt. Undying love. She rose from her chair, rushed into the kitchen as if to check on something.

"Is this temporary?" Tess asked when Joss returned with a full glass of wine.

"Absolutely."

"Want me to stay for a few days? Keep the goddesses from your door?"

Joss shook her head. "I'll be fine. I'm going out to shoot later."

Tess smiled. "Music to my ears, that. Call me when you need me."

4.

Margaret agreed to venture to Hanlan's Point, but only on the condition that Bette didn't tell their father about the voyage. And that they have tea first. Just in case the tea clause was some sort of trap to upend the mission entirely, Bette laid out the teapot, one teacup for her sister, and some cookies. She then sat down with her copy of *Tennyson's Birthday Book* in an effort to determine which verse would apply to her first niece or nephew.

"It might come early," Margaret said nervously, pouring tea. "That runs in Clarence's family."

Bette looked up from the birthday book and, without cracking a smile, her voice sugary with concern, asked, "How early could it possibly arrive? I've never heard of anything like that running in families, Mags."

"There's a lot you don't know about the world, Elizabeth," Margaret said shortly. "Being sixteen and all, there's a great deal you don't know a thing about."

"Your *math*!" Bette smiled. "I hope you don't do Clarence's bookkeeping! I'm seventeen. But you're right about me not knowing enough about the world. Which is why I am so thankful to you for taking me out into it today. Now let's see, you married in November—that was a strange choice, wasn't it?—and the baby is to come in August, yes?" She stuffed a Fig Newton into her mouth and smiled as she chewed, knowing she had Margaret right where she wished for her to be.

On the ferry over to the islands she tugged off her gloves and threw them overboard into icy blue Lake O. Margaret was clearly disgusted by the utter waste of such a gesture but said nothing. She was in a foul state of mind because the trip to the ferry dock had been long and uncomfortable, involving a taxi ride (she loathed horses), a long wait for the crowded streetcar and additional walking (not the same as strolling). Out on the boat the sun was high, the wind heavenly hot, like mischievous fingers through Bette's hair. She wanted to remove her hat as well and throw it to the fish, but decided not to press too far. After all, it was a Clarence Clackum original. The best thing she could say about it was that it stayed on in any weather.

The pushing, jostling crowd excited her as they disembarked. Paradise awaited. Machines of some kind roared in the distance, promising exquisite experiences. *Thrills.* Somewhere a crowd cheered: the stadium. Everyone moved along the pathway with a gaiety Bette wished could be the constant way of life. The bright yellow advertisement folded in her pocket hadn't lied. The day was already perfect.

So this was Hanlan's Point. She could barely catch her breath as she took in the whirl of candy colours, greasy food smells, blasting horns and rumbling, smoky engines. And there *it* was: the mesmerizing Figure 8 roller coaster. The mention of it on the advertising flyer had preoccupied her for hours. Now she stared for a long time at the ride, as in awe as an Egyptologist finally faced with the pyramids. Shrieks erupted from the train as it flew along a wooden track like a runaway streetcar high in the air. It was better than anything.

"No," Margaret said, pinching Bette's arm.

The sun pounded their shoulders as Bette stood speechless. Margaret opened her parasol and grunted. She should not even be out here parading her swollen belly in public. Another peal of screams from the Figure 8 made her shiver, even in the heat. Bette had that look. The whole family knew enough not to bother fighting that expression, the source of it always immovable no matter what.

"Go on, if you insist on killing yourself!" Margaret said, heaving a sigh that resigned itself to Bette's early demise. Worse than witnessing the carnage would be explaining how they happened to be at Hanlan's Point. On a Monday. As if there weren't far more important things to be doing than riding machines designed by murderers. Unless of course their father suddenly approved of such things; one never knew. It was hardly fresh air if you could smell coal burning and meat frying at every turn.

Before Margaret could change her mind, Bette sped across the grounds, unaware of the grass passing beneath her feet. After buying a ticket, she joined the line. And though she had always been the most impatient person she knew, Bette grew tranquil in the waiting. Solemn almost, as she slowly moved toward the final gate. Margaret sat scowling on a nearby bench, shading herself, marking her sister's mad progress along the creaking ramp. Her death imminent, Bette turned and waved and smiled and waved harder. Margaret did not wave back.

Thanks to pure ignorance, Bette felt joy, and very little fear. All around her in the queue, before and aft, were pairs: couples, duos of boys. It was hot there in the sun, fancy-hatted, gloveless and garnering stares. It seemed that everyone in the line-up had a partner in the endeavour. Bette was alone in her pursuit of excitement. Her deep need for titillation was unsavoury, said the eyes of the men and women around her. The sign above her head promised thrills, spills and chills. A faint loneliness crept in as she approached the docking platform where passengers finally boarded their trains. Seats for two, and Bette all alone, yet she couldn't imagine turning back or being turned away because of it. Pride pushed her forward, and when she clumsily took her solitary seat, arranging her skirts around her, a ride attendant rushed up alongside her and shouted for all to hear.

"SINGLES? Anyone else all alone?"

It was an eternal humiliation as she waited, eyed by the crowds who stood impatiently behind the gate. She busied herself making sure her hat was firmly fastened to her head, a little rougher with the pins than she needed to be. What she feared most was expulsion from the Figure 8, which seemed to insist on twos for the shared pursuit of death. The man's face lit up, and then he grinned, and Bette was soon joined by a working boy in a cap and apron. He slipped into the seat without hesitation or effort, revealing his comfort with the procedure.

"Hello," he said softly, with a crooked smile. His front tooth jagged sideways ever so slightly in the most charming manner. He smelled of popcorn and taffy; his apron clanked with coins.

"Cap off, Freddy, you know the drill!" the ride attendant scolded, and Bette's seatmate pulled off his cap with a good-natured swipe of his hand.

The boy became a girl. Faint spatter of freckles on her sunburned nose, fiercely red lips, golden tumble of curls. The girl revealed by the doffed cap gave Bette a happy, bright blue look then stared straight ahead, her smile never fading as the train lurched, grunted and squealed forward—then upward in herky-jerky motion.

Bette had never felt pure regret before. It was a feeling much worse than grief, and it expanded rapidly as the train shuddered hideously up the narrow incline. She worried she might weep aloud from sheer terror. Her riding companion seemed completely at ease, looking gamely down over the edge of the cart before she closed her eyes in some form of rapture. And when she suddenly took Bette's hand in her own it startled them both. But the girl's grasp was warm, dry and somehow consoling. As if she knew. Freddy, the ride attendant had called her. Freddy?

Long pause.

Headlong downward plunge!

In the sea of screams escaping mouths, Bette's scream, the other girl's. Her stomach soared and flipped; she screamed all the harder, against death; against weeping or madness, no time to determine which, unladylike, no time for anything but screaming. The girl let go of her hand in favour of clutching the iron bar that was meant to hold them in—would it?—and they continued to swerve along the tracks, thrown hard against each other by force of physics. It was over too soon. Bette stole an admiring glance at her seatmate as the trolley sailed back into the dock. The older girl grinned at Bette and wiped wet curling tendrils of blond hair away from her forehead. Bette was able to laugh suddenly, drunk with after-fear and delight.

Legs wobbling, they strode down the exit ramp. The girl's coin-filled apron made music, and she restored her cap to her head, tugging it down over her bright blue eyes. The craziest blue Bette had ever seen, like aquamarines and smoke together, nearly hard to look at for too long unless you were brave. She felt brave. At the bottom of the ramp Freddy turned to Bette and squeezed both her shoulders as if they were old chums. She suggested they go again, this time as chosen partners. But Margaret was waiting at the bottom of the ramp, shaking her head. She could test the limits of her sister's generosity, she thought, but it might mean never coming back, and Bette wanted to come back, and said so.

"Oh, come back another day then! Tuesdays are better, I don't work in the daytime!" the girl whispered, squeezing Bette's shoulders again. "Say you will!"

"I will," Bette said, smiling.

"*Tomorrow's* Tuesday..." The girl had a deep dimple that appeared like a star in her cheek.

"Next Tuesday?" Bette hoped the girl's smile wouldn't fade. Coming back tomorrow would not be possible with her parents returning from Ottawa.

"I'll count on it! Going to ride once for me and once for you!" She darted back into the line, amazing Bette with her indifference to the insistence of pairs. Who will she ride with next? Bette wondered with envy and something else. *I wish it were me.*

"Imagine riding with a common working boy you don't even know!" Margaret clucked, watching the departure of Bette's companion.

Imagine! Bette didn't answer as she followed Margaret back to the ferry dock. It had been a long ride out to the island for a very short visit, but there was no point in complaining. She would be coming to Hanlan's Point again, and soon. Next Tuesday. She'd promised. Her shoulders tingled.

Undressing for bed that night, Bette found a small patch of taffy stuck to her dress sleeve, right around the shoulder area. The sight of it pleased her so deeply she almost cried. She touched the tip of her tongue to the blotch, tasted salt-sweetness, then blushed even in the full privacy of her room. No one else was home: she had refused to stay at Margaret's, insisting she had to tidy the house before their parents returned from their silly convention the next day. And, whereas she had lately cried herself to sleep missing her Grandie and hating her parents for killing her best friend, she fell straight to sleep thinking, *June 21, a perfect day, at last.*

5.

Their biggest fight had been about New York. Not *in* New York, but about it. About not going and the seven hundred good reasons to stay put on the island. How pointless it was for the citizens of one large noisy city to pay good money to fly to and sleep in another huge noisy city. Tell me you want to go camping north of Wawa— that makes sense to me. It does? Something other, I mean. It makes no sense to go to New York. It makes all the sense in the world and always has, she said under her breath. But the fight—actually a loud, tense discussion—was over. There was no need to go to New York, so they were not going. Not even during the air show that deafened the island populace every Labour Day weekend.

"Don't you have a friend there?" Tess had asked when Joss mournfully mentioned Bianca's refusal to love New York as she did. "Why don't you just go?"

"Without her?"

Tess had smirked and shook her head. "Are you as innocent as you seem?"

6.

Today there was a girl. Usually the solo riders were boys. A beauty from the city—that wasn't so unusual. Her clothes weren't posh but they weren't careworn either. She smelled good, like expensive face cream. Freddy envisioned a big house filled with China vases and flowers. Why envision her house at all? She laughed at herself. They had made plans to meet again, with no real arrangements properly established. They never came back again anyway, those pretty girls from across the water.

The cot was hot and itchy after a long day, but luxurious too just for being there to stretch out on. Norma snored indifferently across the room. In every other cottage, workers slept in groups of three or four, but Norma had clout and she had chosen young Freddy as her cohabitant. Freddy had no idea why Norma had such influence over the midway boss, but she seemed able to have her preference in matters large and small. The only way in which this benefitted Freddy was having a half cottage to herself. And Norma, over six feet in stature, was an imposing person, so none of the male carnies tried coming in to visit after dark. Sleep did not come easily to Freddy, who had of past necessity developed a habit of dozing with one eye open and fixed on any door leading into a room where she lay abed.

The girl kept coming to her mind, and Freddy gave in and thought about her some more. It chased off the usual catalogue of worries. How frightened the girl had been and then how exalted. How curious it was that she rode once and went off—a long way to come for just one turn. But maybe she was one of those carousel lovers, preferring to go round and round all morning long, showing off her hat. She had enormous brown eyes that shone. There was a kindness emanating from her, although it might just have been pure innocence. Something else made Freddy long to see her again, but she could not pin down what it was. Well there was no point pining, as it did no good, she knew. It gave you a stomach ache and almost always led to a sour mood.

I will, the girl had said of the idea of returning, and Freddy had not held her to a promise beyond that. Promises were not to be trusted. She had made some herself and broken them: the promise to write to her mother when she landed safely in Canada, for one. There was nothing good she could write in a letter, she decided after mere weeks at the Knapp farm. Nothing she wished to have her mother know about the way her days played out. She could, she supposed, have written "Landed safely" because that much had been true: the ship carrying her and a few hundred other children had not sunk. The train that took them west to Stratford had not derailed. Landed safely, yes, she could at least have offered her poor mum that much comfort.

But the farm was not worth thinking of, and too-late letters could not be written in the dark. Norma forbid lamps after 9:00 p.m. She wished to think of the girl and only of her. Freddy turned to the clapboard wall and closed her eyes and conjured up the sweet, grateful smile that would cancel out the memory of her mother taking her by the hand to where they rounded up the "lucky" children who were to be sent to Canada to work. The girl had had no such twist in her life, Freddy decided. No hardships. A life of whimsy, of jaunts here and there wherever she fancied to venture. Ease. The one thing Freddy Montgomery could only dream of. She wanted to be near it, that feeling, if only once more.

7.

The working boys across the road were at it early, banging their shovels and calling to one another about soda pop, the Maple Leafs ball team and Coach Joe Kelley's return, how hot it was going to be that day. She woke languidly into this chorus of summer noises thinking of the girl called Freddy and wondering what should stop her from going back to Hanlan's Point herself. On her own. Was the world really so very dangerous as everyone was always insisting? How was anyone to have a single moment of joy if an escort was required for every outing? Did boys enjoy life more? She could only assume yes. Her brother would have enjoyed life more than she—had he lived. Or not, because he was too weak to make it past the age of ten, maybe he'd have hidden himself away, wasting his chance? His passing was not to be mentioned when her mother was around, although Papa enjoyed talking about Oren, almost as if he had merely gone on a trip and would be back again. He was named after Grandie's husband, and as a result, she had an easy, automatic fondness for her grandson. But he'd told Bette that their grandmother showed obvious signs of being a witch. She figured Oren had no stomach for Grandie's rather electrifying readings of Pinocchio, for which she did all the different voices as if channelling the actual characters. Maybe he'd been born with a guilty conscience from his previous life?

Bette's mind began to race unhappily, and as she knew where that could lead, she rolled over and returned her thoughts to Freddy, whose crooked smile and stellar dimple had seemed all the more enchanting in early-morning review. It was rare to have a friend who hadn't come from the weedy garden of childhood. The feeling of knowing someone beyond the neighbourhood and her own family was fresh and invigorating as the cool side of the pillow on a hot night. Nothing was known and there were no old grudges dating back to the nursery. It seemed a hundred years till next Tuesday.

She decided to find an outlet for her energy and tore out of bed, intent on cleaning the entire household before her parents returned. Ambitious, yes, but she felt anything was possible that morning. If they were lucky, she might even cook supper, which she hadn't done since Grandie died. Whereas her sister had trouble navigating a pot of water and a spoon at the same time, Bette was doubly blessed in the culinary realm, being good with stovetop and oven, stews *and* cakes. Thinking of Freddy put her in such a good mood, she decided to make scones for her father and the potato pie her mother liked. There was no point in making bread, which only turned out when she was in a foul temper. *Might never make bread again.*

Unable to face a bowl of hot porridge, she would make coffee instead. Her father had ordered a wonderful contraption from England that could percolate two cups of coffee at a time. As the only member of the family who drank coffee, the machine was considered to be hers, a distinction she enjoyed very much. He'd even managed to find a tiny French coffee cup and saucer for her birthday after she expressed concern about the probable criminality of drinking coffee from a teacup. So fond was Irving Titus of ordering things from all over the world (especially cookies, candies and contraptions) that Bette only needed to express a passing fancy for a flavour, texture, sound or novelty item, and it eventually turned up in the mail. "You're helping my stamp collection immensely," he would tell her with a wink.

Opening the upper kitchen cupboards was always an act of temerity since Felicia Titus, scholar and bluestocking, was unable to contain her papers to her own roll-top desk. Along with coffee and biscuits, there might be three pounds of cascading pamphlets, a bouncing box of pencils, even a wayward bannerette now and then. An ink pen had tumbled out and very nearly stabbed Bette in the eye mere weeks before. "Life of the mind," Grandie used to scoff, "surest path to a filthy kitchen!" Now Bette whipped open the cupboard and held her breath. When the usual avalanche didn't greet her, she was strangely disappointed. Being angry with her mother had become such a habit, she was aware of being robbed of any opportunity to freshen the fury.

Whenever her parents were out of the city, which she hoped would happen more and more often, Bette drank her coffee in her father's study and listened to music on his Victrola with the volume turned up just a little extra. It was a bit of heaven to be alone in the house, drinking coffee and singing along to Ada Jones, her favourite singer. Her current favourite was "See Saw" and she never tired of playing it. Ada Jones was a soprano, and Bette most definitely wasn't, but that hardly mattered. She loved to sing. Some of Ada Jones's songs made her weep and others made her laugh. The love songs might as well have been in a foreign language, but she liked them anyway. She wondered if Freddy knew of Ada Jones and Billy Murray. The recordings never left her father's study, and she was warned repeatedly to handle them carefully. She imagined inviting Freddy over for a cup of coffee, sitting in Papa's study listening to music.

At half past ten and mid-way through a fourth reprisal of "I Remember You," Bette snapped from her reverie of impossible scenarios and got to work on tidying the chaos and then on to the scones and the potato pie preparations. Before doing so, she went first to the coffee can she kept under the kitchen sink, then out to the vacant lot across the road where the boys were working with scythes and shovels.

The tallest of the boys stopped working and grinned down at

her, his face gleaming with sweat. "Hey fellas, look here, a Gibson girl just walked right up to me!"

One or two of the other boys whistled. Bette was hatless and wearing her plainest dress, the one she wore for housework. Her brown hair spilled from a loose bun on top of her head, and although anyone would have been pleased to be compared to a Gibson girl, she was on a mission. Not to mention she knew when someone was full of lard. Bette knew full well her sister was the pretty one.

"I'd like to buy your cap," she told the dark-haired boy. She held out a five dollar bill, and the boy's eyes widened with amazement, then narrowed with immediate suspicion. Behind him his cronies hooted and chuckled.

"Not for sale," the boy grunted, sad to look away from the five dollar bill. But it had to be a kind of trick or she was loony or both, and he wanted no part of being teased all day.

"How much more would it cost?" Bette demanded quietly, ignoring the other boys. It was a hot day, perhaps he was reluctant to go without a covering for his jet-black hair? "I can't pay more than five, but I'm baking right now, and I'll give you a half dozen scones if you sell me that cap."

He glanced over his shoulder quickly and shrugged. "All right. But how about a date thrown in?"

She gazed at him blankly. Then understood. And frowned. The whole population of working boys stood watching them now in silence. The bread-man's truck squeaked past, his horses keen to get out of the sun. This was one of those moments, Bette thought, where she wished she was living inside an Ada Jones song and had all the right words to put this fellow in his place. She'd thought five dollars and a half dozen scones a pretty fancy deal for a lousy used cap. Now here he was making her part of the bargain. Did she need a cap that badly? Couldn't she ask her father to get her one more easily? The sun poured down, and she wondered if her impulsive nature was always going to get her into scrapes like this one. Call it off, she told herself, but she couldn't seem to retreat.

"Some other time then," the boy said, but he surprised her by holding out his cap, his other empty palm held out for payment.

"Thank you, my brother will appreciate this very much," she said in a gasping voice, handing him the five dollars from the grocery budget, thrilled by the damp feel of the cap in her own hand as she rushed across the road without even looking. Indian Road wasn't a busy thoroughfare, most days, but she ought to have been more cautious. The boy watched her without smiling as the other boys gathered around to find out who on earth would buy a dirty old cap for five whole dollars out of the blue like that.

"She's been watching you, Bill!"

"Yeah, Billy, she's sweet on you!"

Bette locked the front door behind her and caught her breath. She would have to toughen herself if she was to make a solo trip to Hanlan's Point. A trip across the road was hardly a voyage to the dark side, but it had rattled her, as had the boy's peculiar green eyes. She could feel them on her even as she climbed the porch steps to the house.

But she had the cap. It was something like Freddy's or close enough to it. She ignored the damp, stained inner band and gathered her hair up under it, tucking and tucking before turning to face the hall mirror. The Gibson girl was gone. In her place, the happiest version of herself that Bette Titus had ever seen.

By the time her parents returned from their Theosophical Society conference in Ottawa that night, the household gleamed and a potato pie waited under a clean cloth on the kitchen counter beside a full dozen currant scones.

Bette lay fast asleep on top of the quilts on Grandie's bed, looking more seven than seventeen.

"Why's she wearing that cap?" Felicia wondered aloud.

"She's her own girl, is all," he said, smiling as he ushered his wife toward the kitchen.

8.

A week into grief it finally rained. She took her bicycle out of the shed and rode it down the old south-facing boardwalk where the waves crashed over the breakwater. She was mildly hung over and the spray of lake water and drumming rain felt good on her too-hot skin. Her camera bag thudded against her back as she ped-alled. Past the only decent restaurant on the island, past the fire hall. A children's day camp marched by on the road, singing one of those annoyingly cheerful songs they would likely remember all their lives. There, in the petite nursing home, more singing, similar ditties with an excess of glee driving the melody. Joss rode faster to escape the snatches of sound, the ill-tuned piano. At the con-clusion of the boardwalk she veered onto a dirt path and glided through a thicket of tall weeds. Birds exploded from the shrub-bery. A red-winged blackbird scolded from the tip of a pine bough. She pumped harder till she was back on the public road that, for now, did not welcome cars other than those in service to the island community.

Bianca had grown up on the island and returned after establish-ing herself as a social worker for at-risk youth. She had loved how everything she needed was on the island, or within a ferry ride. When they were first together it still seemed glamorous and sexy to ride across to the city and attend the opera, have a quick bite at Shopsy's with the tourists, see a Saturday night play and have a drink at cavernous C'est What. But then, upon announcing her early retirement, Bianca had refused to go across to the city side for more than groceries, and even that became Joss's chore after a while. When asked why she never wanted to visit the city anymore, she simply replied, "Why? I know it well enough" and the matter was settled. The more she hunkered down, the more restless Joss became, inventing reasons to ride the ferry.

With Bianca gone, was there any point to staying out here except that the house was paid for and she had no idea where else to go? She pedalled on to Centre Island, noisy with children in spite of the now-light rain. The tiny rides would not be operational in this weather, but still the kids flocked, decked out in bright plastic ponchos. She stopped to watch a young mother with her brood, checked herself for lingering pangs of personal regret and, feeling none, pushed her bike away from the throng. They had not wanted children. Everyone around them was starting a family, via fertility clinics, wild arrangements, adoption agencies. You could do it now and no one blinked. We're too old, Bianca had reminded her. If we had met when we were younger, maybe. But we didn't.

9.

Once a week, sometimes more often, since opening day, he would turn up at the taffy booth. Never at the box office wicket of the theatre, for plays and films were the devil's handiwork. Everyone teased her that he was her beau, which she could see he liked. His favourite taffy flavour was strawberry, and he would ask if she knew why that was the case, and then he would laugh and leer when she refused to answer. He waggled his thick eyebrows at her when he said the word strawberry and called her "Honeybun" within ear-shot of the other customers. Most of his jokes made no sense, but everyone at the park thought he was charming. A clean shirt and jacket went a long way with some folks, she decided, for there was nothing she liked about him at all. Whenever she would hand him his change—he always paid with a ten dollar bill, as if to prove something—he clutched at her fingers for a few seconds longer than was proper.

One day he came and paid with a dime and told her that if she refused to go on a boat ride with him on her break that heaven would elude her and he would have to stop coming round. Hiding her glee, she managed to squeak out a semi-mournful, "I'm afraid I do have to refuse, sir."

"I will rescue you from this life any day I choose to, little girl," he said. "It's really not up to you how it all works out." He wiped a smear of melted strawberry taffy from his mustache and looked sol-emn. "God has a plan for you, dear one, and I am part of that plan."

The mention of God gave her a chill. In her experience, people who invoked God's plan often performed dark deeds in His name. If this lecherous man, who had been coming to her taffy booth since the season opened, had decided God was his trusty accomplice, she might not stand much of a chance of escape. And so she did what countless girls before her have done: she offered a compromise.

"If I agree to the boat ride this afternoon," she said quietly, looking around to make sure no one else could hear, "will you consider leaving me be? I'm betrothed to someone else, you see, and God does not like broken promises."

"You are a beautiful angel," he said. "But a terrible liar. I shall see you at the boathouse dock at three o'clock, the time of your next break."

And so it began that Darius Peacock took her out in a rowboat once a week on her breaks between jobs. Or rather, Freddy took him out, as she did all the rowing. While out on the lagoon he recited not the Holy Gospel as she had expected, but some of the most tiresome original romantic poetry in the history of literature, all while squeezing Freddy's knees and removing her cap and trying to kiss her as she rowed as hard as she could to counter the wind blasting in off Lake O. And Darius Peacock was handsome in his way but by no means tiny; it took all of her efforts to keep them from drifting toward New York state.

This week his visit was close to intolerable, as he had dressed his bulk up extra nice and looked like he had something he wanted to say but had lost the nerve for. He had also doused himself in enough eau de toilette for three men. Freddy feigned a stomach and head ache, but he was not to be put off. Out into the sun-dappled waters of the lagoon, she rowed.

"Will you consent to be my wife?" he finally asked. "I will give you to summer's end to make a decision." He leaned in to caress her knees, as if that would increase his chances of a happy verdict. When she showed no emotion, delight or otherwise, he folded his hands in his lap. "Upon hearing the word yes, and on promise of engagement, I will make you a present of five hundred dollars."

Freddy narrowed her eyes. "On promise of engagement?"

"Indeed. You look tempted to say yes right now!" he cried with pleasure. "If you would make me the happiest man in all of the city today, I'll write you a note when we dock."

"I'm not for sale," Freddy said, wholly offended by the turn things were taking and wanting to put him off while she did mull over the possible ways in which five hundred dollars would ever come her way again all in one lump.

"It would be a present to express my gratitude," he pleaded. "And a woman should always have her own money."

This sounded dubious and in sharp contrast to his poetics, riddled as they were with references to the Ten Commandments and obedience in love.

"I'd want to see out the summer here at the park," she said cautiously. "I've made them a promise as well, you see."

"Naturally. And with your promise to me sealed, there would be no rush. I have matters to attend to before I become domesticated for good."

"May I ask, Darius, why me? Of all the girls on the island, in the city? Why me for your wife?"

"You? Because you need saving more than most."

10.

"I'd like to go over to Hanlan's Point," she told her mother and father on Saturday morning after a few days of careful planning.

Her parents were seated at the dining room table enjoying the first of many cigarettes. A pot of tea, a platter of toast and several stacks of books were arranged between them.

Irving stopped leafing through a giant volume, *Margins of the Oversoul,* and gazed at his daughter as if she spoke another language.

"No," her mother replied neatly, without looking up at all. This response was expected. Bette was prepared. This time, she would remain calm.

"When?" her father asked, exhaling a gust of smoke as he spoke.

"NO," her mother said louder, finally looking up from the more important topics contained within *The Female as Spiritual Conduit.* She looked at Irving, not at Bette, as if he was the person requiring an answer.

"Why not?" he asked, and as had happened many times before, the debate soon excluded Bette, who stood helplessly on the sidelines, listening. It often began badly and occasionally ended in her favour, but patience was essential to victory.

Each of her parents lit a fresh cigarette and pushed the books they were previously engrossed in out of the way. It was hardly an interruption since the key themes—of soul-happiness and the rights and freedoms of women—or one young woman in particular, their youngest daughter—were at stake. Especially soul-happiness, she wanted to say, but didn't. Grandie had taught her that *she who speaks first loses the argument.*

"Why can't she go to Hanlan's Point?" her father repeated.

"There's no point to it, for one thing. That sort of place is for sluts and dipsomaniacs." She did not look over to see Bette wince at this shocking description of her desired destination. Instead, she pressed on, citing a numbing array of reasons sociological, physiological and psychological why such a place was unsafe for a young woman of her sensitive temper. *Overstimulation* was the last word Bette took in before drifting off to let them joust and parry on.

She had always hated the dining room, its walls papered with William Morris vines on a blood-red background. Her parents had installed it soon after they all moved into Grandie's house seven years before. Without asking Grandie if she even cared for William Morris or the colour red. Lack of consultation likely started the quiet war between Grandie and Felicia. At her father's end of the room (as she thought of it, for he never changed seats) hung a portrait of toad-faced Helena Blavatsky, his Theosophy heroine. At her mother's end of the room glowered an even larger portrait of Susan B. Anthony. The hanging of these portraits, again without discussion with the actual owner of the home, one Doreen Titus, was the final straw.

Bette remembered the very night when Grandie made her way into the dining room for dinner and saw the portraits on the red walls. She carried a lamb roast, which she promptly dropped to the floorboards.

"That face will curdle the dairy," she said, pointing to Blavatsky's portrait, "and that one," she jerked a thumb at Susan B. Anthony's grim visage, "will turn the meat right on our plates. What next, children, vegetarianism? I shall eat in my room."

Which she did, from that night onward, till she died. And vegetarianism was next for Irving and Felicia, she hadn't been wrong. She also made her feelings all the more clear by hanging a portrait of the great temperance activist Carry Nation on the hall-facing side of her bedroom door. She of axe-wielding, saloon-smashing infamy. It was well known that Grandie liked her beer and sherry, and her statement on household hypocrisy was loud and clear. She lived for another six years, drinking herself quietly to death in her room with Bette as her helpless companion.

The thought of her tragic death recharged Bette's determination, and she turned her attentions back to the conversation between her parents, who were still happily sniping back and forth. Somehow, the topic had shifted from her request to something called Raja-Yoga and Lomaland.

"I AM GOING TO HANLAN'S POINT! YOU CANNOT FORBID ME!"

Her parents looked startled, not by the volume of her announcement, but by the fact that she was there in the room at all.

"Who will accompany you?" Her mother had sweetly performed one of her maddening turnabouts, and Bette knew better than to rage about it. "I can't see Mags going out there with you in her condition." She calmly struck a match and puffed delicately on her cigarette. As if there had been no initial resistance to Bette's request.

"A boy invited me," Bette said quietly, pursuing her original scheme. "His name is William, and he works across the road. On the lot." Sensing no signals of outrage from either parent, she continued. Their libertine attitudes would come in handy: a working boy was an appealing suitor. "He has a married sister out on the Toronto Islands who will have us to lunch after we ride the Ferris wheel." She didn't have much experience with lying but found her talent for it exciting in the moment. Everything she said now felt entirely true, and her parents' expressions were entirely trusting.

"When is this outing to take place?" her mother asked. She gave a longing glance at her stack of books. A crisp unread newspaper beckoned as well.

"Tuesday," Bette said.

Her father shook his head. "I don't believe it."

"You don't believe what?" her mother asked, again ignoring Bette and turning all her attention to Irving.

Bette's heart thudded. Her father was too smart for this. No one asked a girl to lunch on a Tuesday. Her father had been a lawyer before turning to spirit worship. If only he'd become a drunkard like his father and mother, worshipped liquid spirits instead. The sort that made you forget things. Having to defend this peculiarity of timing would expose her ruse. Bette's mouth was drying up. The room was too hot and smoky. *Please, Papa, be dumb for once.* To steady herself she thought of the Figure 8 ride and of Freddy's smile. Of the ferry ride and the sunshine and how this time she'd stay all afternoon. Maybe she would ride the Ferris wheel, too, for the sake of veracity.

Her father buried his face in his hands, and Felicia went to his side, murmuring something Bette couldn't make out. She sorely regretted her decision to tell a tale and was on the verge of confessing when her father looked up, red-eyed and smiling.

"I can't believe the time has come to lose you to a boy," he said. His expression was completely loving; Bette felt instantly sick to her stomach. Was there anything more awful than deceiving, with full success, someone who adored you so much they could weep at the thought of your happiness?

"I want to meet him, of course, before he takes you half across the province on a boat," her father said, collecting himself a little.

More lying. It was like slipping down a tunnel a foot at a time. "He's got to work right up till we go," Bette explained, aware that she hadn't imagined actually making it seem as if she and Bill were off on an outing together. She'd assumed she could just tell her parents. They were always busy, either reading or lecturing or working. Seldom home, in fact. They attended a minimum of two lectures a week, and one or the other of them was always rallying for some cause or other.

"We'll say hello and see you off," her mother said, eyes back on her suffragette bible.

"He's a lucky fellow," said her father with an even more heartbreaking smile. To no one in particular he asked: "Are we meant to go to Margaret's for dinner tomorrow night?"

Bette leapt in. There could be no dinner with her sister right now, it was too dangerous. Margaret was a terrible liar, not to mention a worrywart. "She's not feeling up to it this week, Papa. And they can't come here, either. The baby—"

"I suppose they plan to have a whole batch of them, rushing like that," Felicia said flatly.

"How long did you and Papa wait, Momma?" Bette turned to her mother. There was some mathematical creativity surrounding her eldest sister's birth date, too. Bette wasn't supposed to know this, but of course after a third or fourth sherry Grandie had been a willing informant on all kinds of family topics. Her question was saucy and out of order and her mother's forehead vein bulged in anticipation of new combat.

"Another Ada Jones recording came for you," her father cut in, eager to change the subject. "It's in my study. Think you'll like it more now that you're being courted."

Bette ignored the last part of his remark and moved around the table to give him a kiss on the cheek. "Can I listen to it now, Papa?"

"Of course—"

"Not loud enough to rattle the cabinet," her mother groused from behind the *Globe* newspaper. Bette fought an urge to stick her tongue out at the newsprint fortress her mother now hid behind.

She rushed into the study and closed the door. The record lay on top of the Victrola cabinet, and she unwrapped it with cautious excitement. She set the needle down carefully on the record and waited for the thrilling crackle and the opening bars. There was Ada's lovely warble but—NO!—she was singing about a sweetheart named Bill Brown! The coincidence was appalling. Pure accident but of all the names, and she used *Bill* in a verse! If she listened to it more than once her parents would accuse her of being in love with that creature across the road. She rushed to the phonograph and silenced the music.

Through the door she heard her father's voice rising. "'Sluts and dipsomaniacs?' That's pretty rich, coming from *you*."

"Let's not start this, Irving," her mother shouted back. "You're in a bad mood because your soulmate won't be at Lily Dale this summer. I wonder why we're even going, you'll be pouting the whole time—"

"LOWER your voice!"

Bette could almost see the sneer on her mother's face. But her parents usually duelled about intellectual topics. Was there a God, were there several of them, should women smoke (clearly she'd won that battle), how would the world change if women could vote at last, what was death really, and so on. There was anger, but it was about the topic, nothing more. Her father had always said it was because they were both born under the same sign of the zodiac, which was Libra. Oh yes, they also fought about astrology, astronomy and something called dream theory. Though neither of them drank alcohol very often, they argued about the temperance movement, too. Yet their ire this morning was alarming, because it seemed to have shifted from matters of the mind to those of the heart. Eager to drown out their feud, Bette rushed to select any other Ada Jones record. In her haste she dropped the new recording, which shattered as soon as it hit the hardwood floor. Up went the volume on the replacement selection while she raced to collect the shards that had been "Whistle and I'll Wait for You." She dumped the broken pieces into her father's waste paper basket and hoped he would understand that it had been an accident. Brought on by an attack of lover's nerves, she'd say. *Not in this lifetime!*

She moved to the window to look across and see if Bill was out there working. Poor unsuspecting Bill. He was out there slaving away on the lot, swinging his scythe in the tall grass, earning his way in the world. They worked six days a week clearing the lot where the Davis family's house had been till the fire. If not for his terrible peering eyes he was probably a nice enough person…

The Victrola cabinet was vibrating as "Don't Get Married Any More, Ma" poured from it. Bette hadn't noticed her selection till the study door banged open and her mother, scarlet with anger, snatched the needle up off the record and silenced the song.

"I'm not sure what I did to you in our previous life, Bette, but I am terribly sorry to see you again, never doubt that!"

With a slam of the door she had just burst through, her mother was gone again and Bette wrapped her arms around herself. She sat down on her father's swivel chair and closed her eyes. It was no fun at all living in this household with Grandie gone.

I just want it to be Tuesday.

11.

As a twenty-first century, North American widow she wished for a black arm band or the custom of such things, something to warn people that tears might erupt at random. Only there were too few tears, not too many, and the guilt that came of the drought was immense. She rode her bicycle as before, all over the island, all hours. Sleep had never been a pal, and it definitely eluded her now. Alone was not something she wanted to be, and Joss fought it by staying outdoors for exactly fifty percent of the day, and indoors for the other half. Outdoors she was a healthy specimen, dashing to collect the mail and power-walking to the canoe rental kiosk and back. She managed waves and good mornings and not much more, but those who knew of her loss were respectful and expected little. Indoors she guzzled coffee and smoked pot and sipped cheap wine, all the while listening to records that had brought a frown to Bianca's lips. Come to think of it, most music save for Italian opera had annoyed Bianca. It felt a little good to crank up The Guess Who and sing along, to strum an imaginary guitar to the roar of a faceless crowd situated somewhere in the tiny backyard.

The wine would stop very soon. She had not lied to Tess, she did have plans. Things she planned to not do, and then of course the to-do list was even longer. She had no plans to resume being an alcoholic, for example. Grief-drinking was to be contained to a set time period and would not be allowed to turn into fifteen years. There would be other plans, too, just as soon as she found the courage to make them.

12.

In a way it was like a savings account and much safer than hiding cash in a tin. She had agreed to marry him at summer's end, and to her amazement, this eased the intensity of his courting profoundly. In fact, as he left her a few safe yards from the theatre box office he apologized for not being able to come at all for the next few weeks and hoped she would understand. The promissory note she held for five hundred dollars would be swapped for cash in hand upon his return from a spiritual retreat in eastern Ontario. His career as a Bible salesman was taking off, he bragged.

Five hundred dollars would buy *a lot* of freedom, even if she would have to leave town as soon as she got hold of the money. By now she had memorized the train schedule to New York City. She would be set, if not for life, then for a good long stretch while she got her bearings in Brooklyn. And her flight was not just from Darius Peacock, the relatively harmless poet-evangelist who would be out of pocket but still fine, overall. She knew that until she fled the city and the country as well, she would never stop looking over her shoulder for Knapp Jr.

Once, walking back from her shift at the theatre, she had been sure he'd been there in the shadows. She'd had to reason with herself the whole way back to her cottage. He was afraid of the dark. He would never have inconvenienced himself by camping out overnight on the island, he was not that mad. The hotel was too expensive for even one night's stay: he was cheap. He had not, she reminded herself, really had any idea where she had gone to when she fled the farm. Her wages, held in trust by Mr. and Mrs. Knapp, were foregone in favour of escape, and she had only managed to salvage enough money for the train. And then thanks to the discovery of a two dollar bill in the dirt outside a tavern on King Street, she had enough for the ferry. If there was a God—and she no longer believed in one—he had slapped down that two dollar bill at just the right moment, along with the arrival of Midway Charlie, who saw her and had the good grace to overlook her digging in the dust. It was Charlie who had invited her to come work on the island, insisting they needed good hardy farm girls, fresh off the train and capable of handling the long days and nights at the amusement park. "Free food sometimes, too," he had whispered, sealing the deal.

The days were long and so were the nights. But the carnival people were essentially good hearted and a little bit lost, so she fit right in. She could see straight away there was a choice to be made: you could drink your wages up and fritter away your future, or you could be prudent. She had come from a family of drinkers and waste, so the choice was quite easy: she would save what little she made, plan for the cheapest winter accommodation possible in Brooklyn and wait for springtime and work a full season by the seashore. The plan to go to New York was still in place in spite of her agreement to marry Darius Peacock. What he didn't know wouldn't harm him, and he could as like as not easily earn back the lost five hundred dollars, more easily than she could afford to give up her most passionate dream. Disappearing was easier than most people suspected. If she found it necessary to flee before summer's end, it might be for the best anyway.

She had a cousin in New York and a picture postcard of the Brooklyn Bridge, and now that she was settled someplace where she could receive mail, she had regular letters from Cousin Lorna. The first one had been a thrill. Just seeing her name and the American postage stamp and the return address on the back of the envelope had made her want to run and hide in the boathouse and read each word aloud to make it more real. She had never had a letter before and read it so many times it grew thin in her hands, the light paper almost transparent as it was. Her cousin had beautiful, flowing handwriting, and she knew how to seduce an outsider into thinking she had come to the greatest place on earth. She applied the word delicious to things that were not edible and saw mystery, adventure and opportunity in every quarter in spite of the fact that she worked in a café. It was so far from any description Freddy could have offered that she was shy writing back, but did manage to, since it was important to keep herself uppermost in her cousin's mind when it came time to run away. To seem cheerful and enterprising and, above all, brave.

The Tuesday morning shift at the concession was slow, and she managed to compose a letter in her head while cleaning, re-stocking and trying to look as busy as possible in case the midway manager came along. Only she found the letter she was thinking of was not to her cousin at all, but to the girl from the city who, if she kept her word, was to come across the lake later today and take another turn at the Figure 8. She did not know anything about her, not her name nor her address nor her age, and so it was a relatively short letter. *Dear Beautiful Miss, I hope you will keep your word and come back to ride the Figure 8 with me. I have no idea how I can miss someone I barely know, but I actually prayed for your return last night. I hope you will not hate me for admitting that I do not pray to God. Behind the cottage where I live…*

"Hello, dreamboat!"

She started and looked down to see Charlie with what looked like a letter in his hand, and for a brief, crazy moment she imagined it was for her, from the girl. That wishing could make it so. But what if it was a letter explaining why she couldn't come? It would still be a letter from her, but one bearing bad news.

"Are you all right?" Charlie demanded to know. Her facial expressions had apparently changed as rapidly as her thoughts had moved from elation to despair. "I've a favour to ask of you, my girl."

"Yes?"

"On your break today, would you mind handing these out?" He held up the sheaf of what she could now see were flyers, not a letter at all.

Charlie was awfully good to her and always brought her leftover fried potatoes and fish from his dinner, and she knew she should jump to help him but of all the days! The girl was not coming, she reminded herself—they never did. The rich ones were the worst, but there was something about this one, and she hoped—

"*No* would be sufficient," Charlie said peevishly and rolled his eyes at her. "Got a date with your preacher?"

"No," Freddy said carefully, not wanting to excite his curiosity.

"No you won't do it, or no you haven't got a date?"

"Both," she said finally.

"Well at least the cat let go of your tongue," he teased. "How about a mallo-roll for my good heart and understanding nature?"

She glanced about, smiled and fixed him up the ice cream treat without hesitation. You could get fired for handing out free food and drinks, but Charlie was also a rather close friend of the midway operator's and, as a result, had carte blanche when it came to dining at the park. He even had his own weekend cottage on the far side of the grounds, a fact he did not keep secret from the young ladies employed at Hanlan's.

"Any news?" she asked as he lapped at his ice cream.

"Gonna be a hot one today," he said, smirking.

"I said news, not weather," she parried.

"Extra motion pictures have been ordered for the Dominion Day celebrations. You'll be working overtime, my precious."

"That's what I like to hear, Charlie," she said with a smile.

"With all that money you make and never spend, you might find yourself wanting to take me out for a steak dinner in the city."

"One day, Charlie," she said smiling, "one day."

13.

She had long ago shot all the dazzling, city-facing sunsets she cared to, had celebrated the look of the wee cottages on Ward's from every angle, inside and out. Joss knew the archipelago from tip to tip, through her lens. And though she was "free" now to go to the city whenever and for however long she desired, she stayed put. Maxine continued her parade of concern, marching to and from the cottage and trying all manner of solicitations to coax Joss back into the world of the living, as she called it. I'm living, she had assured her old friend, accepting yet another meal in a pot or pan before closing the door as gently as she could. Maxine was not a bad person; she simply did not know what it was like to lose someone. There were such people. People whom death seemed to spare until much later in life when attending the funerals of ancient parents and friends became a social ritual. Joss had lost frequently, to the point where she ought to have been awarded a badge. A very close friend in high school, her photography mentor, her mother, three university friends, now Bianca. Well, there were people far less lucky than Joss, she knew, people who'd lost entire swathes of family and with cruel frequency. But Maxine, she simply kept knocking and kept insisting. The passion with which she attended to Joss would have been suspicious to anyone but Joss, who never would have imagined someone using death as a dating opportunity. It was Tess who kindly and firmly warned Joss that Maxine had always had her eye on her. But now? This soon after a loss? It wasn't possible. It wasn't happening.

The scariest symptom of her bereavement was the renewed desire to take photos coupled with a complete inability to actually do so. It had been a dry spell since the diagnosis, but this was different. Darker. Bianca's old pat "Why?" now haunted Joss's every fleeting inclination to press the shutter. She tried doing set-ups on the kitchen table, just something simple to get the sound of the camera back in her heart. Oranges in a bowl, so what? The light would always be just so, and the shadows would always tell a story of their own. Joss did not need to be the one to capture the moment. Venturing out on her trusty bike brought no further inspiration. It wasn't as if she failed to find people and things interesting or beautiful, but that she no longer felt compelled to trap them in her viewfinder. Instead she carried her camera with her like a mandatory appendage that she had become used to over time.

Sometimes, to the quiet amusement of the ferrymen, she rode across to the city side and waited and rode right back. The rocking boat soothed her, and she often rode the boat headed to Hanlan's Point, assigning herself the lengthy walk back to her house no matter what the weather. Naturally they were having one of the finest summers on record, dreamy with blue skies and just enough heat to make the Canadian souls on the beaches purr with relief. Every day seemed tailor made for enjoyment, and while she did force herself to spend the bulk of each day walking and trying to shoot— something or anything would do—she found herself unable to lift the camera as needed. The very act of lifting the Canon to her face triggered immediate nausea. Bitter, effortful tears came next and then a wave of loneliness so pernicious she felt she might actually collapse from the acuteness. She had liked it better when the tears had remained elusive.

Today there was a boy on the boardwalk. He wore a ball cap yanked sideways and no shirt, and when she came upon him he was dancing and making elegant little tap moves with his sneakered feet. His stomach was a thing of beauty, flat and smooth and carved with muscle, hairless and sleek. More striking was the absence of visible tattoos: he was completely unmarked. She pretended to gaze out at the bay, her arms resting on the stone breakwater. He danced and shimmied, eyes closed, but soon she realized that he had tears streaming down his face. It was all at odds with his youthful grace and carefree mop of hair, his dancing, his general aura of self-assurance. She found herself longing to know the cause of his tears, but such conversations never happened. Make one happen, she willed herself as he continued to dance and weep. High on something, she decided, turning away, though she would be haunted by him and her inability to take his photograph for the rest of the evening.

At midnight, convinced he was still out there, she took a flashlight, left her camera behind—why bother?—and crept down the boardwalk to confirm her suspicion. The boardwalk was empty save for the odd skittering raccoon, and yet in her mind he was still dancing out there, somewhere. She became afraid that he had jumped into the lake, and cast her lamp out onto the waves. Nothing.

I need to get out of here, she decided as she stomped back to her house, her unlaced boots hammering the boardwalk. But where? She turned on all the lamps in the cottage and went to fetch a box of wine from the refrigerator. This time her hands shook as she poured. Self-loathing awoke in the pit of her guts. Just this one more night, she told herself. This is not, after all, the life I had in mind.

14.

Irving was in his study preparing for a séance that he and Felicia would host that evening. Felicia was up in their bedroom practicing a speech she was scheduled to deliver at the Women's Christian Temperance Union across town the following Monday. She might even be counted on to not emerge in time for Bette's departure, but there was no knowing for certain.

Bette wiped droplets of condensation from the sides of the glass and carried the lemonade down the front steps across the road to where Bill worked stacking the bricks dug out of the tall grasses. He had a new cap on and seeing her, he tugged it possessively down over his eyes. A boy whistled from across the lot and Bill waved him off. Aware that her mother might look out the upstairs bedroom window at any time, Bette decided to keep it calm and cordial.

"I brought you some lemonade." Her tone was friendly but far from flirtatious. Lemon syrup, shaved ice, water: close enough.

"Uh-huh. And?" The boy kept his dusty arms folded across his chest.

"An offer," she continued. "Drink up. I just made it this morning."

Something in her tone or demeanour must have worked. He took the glass and drained it. To her surprise he took a hanky from his pocket and wiped his mouth. No back of the hand swipe, no sleeve-wipe. Her father had friends who could learn from this chap.

"That was delicious. Thank you. Now what do you *want*, Miss?"

"I need your help." He nodded and suppressed a smile. "There's money to be made, worry not. Ten dollars, in fact. All you have to do is walk me a few blocks and make it look as if we're going some-place together. The only thing is…"

"I have to marry you after?"

A chorus of snickers broke out behind the brick pile. Bill grabbed a brick and tossed it over the heap. Someone cried out.

"Two things," Bette went on. "You have to walk with me, but you can't come back to work here for the rest of the day." She felt her face reddening. If he said no she was going to miss her chance to see Freddy and ride the Figure 8 again. "Does that cover your wages for the day?" she asked hopefully, opening her hand to reveal a folded-up ten dollar bill.

"Are you being mean?" His eyes narrowed. Did she really not know he made a dollar a day? "Those the two things, or is there something else?"

She swallowed. "You have to meet my parents and tell them you're taking me to Hanlan's Point. To see your sister."

"My sister lives at an amusement park?" More giggles erupted behind the brick pile. This time Bette picked up a brick and lobbed it into the peanut gallery. "Nice arm," he said with a grin. She blushed.

"We're going to the amusement park, and then we will have lunch with your married sister. They won't ask a lot of questions. They're very preoccupied."

He took off his new cap and scratched his head as if reconsidering the offer. "I don't know," he said. "It's a bit of a hard sell, Miss. I doubt they'd believe me."

Bette was losing patience. Her back-up plan, to run away in the night and steal a boat to cross to the island, was more dramatic but less appealing. "Why wouldn't they believe you?"

Bill replaced his cap. "Because if I have to say my 'married' sister I'm going to laugh."

"Why?"

"You haven't seen my sister, Miss. On a good day she might win a dog show."

At this the boys behind the brick pile exploded with laughter and Bill did, too. Bette stood red-faced in the sun with her hands on her hips and waited for Bill to regain himself. It took some time, and when he sobered he looked at her with something close to pity. "You must really want to get to Hanlan's Point." She nodded. "All right then, I'll do it. I don't look much like someone who's going on a date though," he gestured at his sweaty, dusty clothes.

"They're socialists," she said, "you're perfect." She gestured at the empty lemonade glass in his hand. He gave it back. "Come call at half past ten. Walk me a few blocks and I'll give you the money."

"Uh, well, where do you live?" he asked. A lousy liar. She rolled her eyes. "Okay, okay, Miss Smart, well what's your name then? I ought to know that sort of thing if I'm so sweet on you that I'll take you all the way across the lake."

"Elizabeth," she said, turning to go. She really needed to fix her hair before it was time to leave for the island. "I'll see you in an hour, Billy."

He laughed then and turned to his crew. "She remembered!"

"Ohhhhhhhhhhhhhhhhh!" they all cried in unison.

Bette slipped in the front door intent on getting to her room without encountering either of her parents, but her father waited in the hall. The ten dollar bill was tucked up her sleeve, but the lemonade glass could not be as easily concealed.

"This seems a rather serious romance," he said, taking up the glass and inspecting it with a stern expression on his face.

"Papa, don't joke. I have to get ready." She caught a glimpse of herself in the hall mirror and knew it was urgent that she get back to her toilette.

He smiled and rummaged in his waistcoat pocket and withdrew a rumpled five dollar bill. "Just in case," he said, holding it out to her. When she took it he patted her on the shoulder. "It was in the mailbox anyway. Perhaps the postman is tithing for some reason?" Though he said nothing more she felt he wished to. It was agonizing. Bette felt like a wild pony in a paddock. And Bill had obviously put the money she paid for his cap in the mailbox, which bothered her.

"Papa, is there something else?" She looked up at him and felt bad all over again for lying to him repeatedly.

"Just have fun, my darling," he said, caressing her cheek. "Always have fun. That's what I wish for you. You are divine."

"Thank you, Papa." With a quick kiss she darted upstairs. His sudden sentimental mood made her feel guilty. If she gave in to it she would confess all lies and never see Freddy or the Figure 8 again.

A half hour later her father's booming voice travelled up the staircase to her room, "Here comes your union man! All hands on deck, Felicia! The swain approaches!"

Bette opened her bedroom door just as her mother opened hers.

"You look lovely," her mother said. Bette smiled. Compliments about her appearance were rare. Before descending the staircase, Felicia added, "Don't let him touch you. You'll end up like Margaret. I know you don't want that."

Bette could barely breathe as she watched her mother's chignon bob down the stairs ahead of her, the clack of her high boots ominous till she reached the landing and the doorbell sounded.

15.

Freddy adjusted her cap and gazed out across the park to where her secret beach waited. It was one of three sanctuaries she treasured. The smell of boiling sugar and burnt molasses had at first been unbearable. Delicious, then sickly, then the cause of a constant, low-grade headache. Now she was used to it all, except for the bees and the burns. But she much preferred the happy afternoon hour when she walked over to the Little Gem Vaudeville Theatre. There she worked till eight o'clock selling tickets, ducking into the darkness when she could.

She had never seen a motion picture before coming to the island amusement park, and now she was hooked to the degree that she could watch the same one three dozen times and still be enchanted. The projectionist was a gruff American-born man named Whitehead who smoked cigars and cursed under his breath continuously but nevertheless let her sit in on as many screenings as her work schedule would allow for. He sometimes even invited her to come view the newly arrived selections so she would be able to sell more tickets, but those summonses were rare.

Between the secret beach, the theatre and the Figure 8, Freddy reasoned she was as happy as she could ever hope to be. Though she dreamt of escape, it was mainly to put more miles between herself and any chance that Knapp Jr. would hunt her down. And with the exception of the unwanted attentions of Darius Peacock, she went about her days in relative peace. She had no friends, it was true, but there was little point in making any when she planned to live out her days in New York. A little hungry—she would not spend extra money on food, seeing it as a waste—and quite often lonesome, she would have a whole different life in New York and was prepared to wait. Fewer friends meant fewer farewells when the time came to disappear.

But the girl from the city. She did so hope she would see her again, and she could not fathom why this girl meant a fig more than any other. If she even turned up, which Freddy grew more doubtful of as the afternoon clocked on, and as she found herself heading for the roller coaster—just in case—she made a deal with herself. If the girl was true to her word, Freddy might make an allowance for just one true friend in her otherwise lonesome world.

16.

Once she did go by herself to New York, and she still thought about that trip. Her old friend Laura had offered up her empty apartment for a week and it coincided with Meryl Streep starring in *The Seagull* in Central Park. Tickets were free, provided you lined up all night the night before to get them.

"I don't know about you sleeping in the park for tickets," Bianca had said as Joss packed like a fleeing refugee for the potential campout. "Is Laura really not able to be there?" This was generous of Bianca, who couldn't stand Joss's long-time friend and former paramour.

"No, she's working in LA." Joss had wanted to shout, "The only reason I am going to Laura's apartment is because she isn't in it." That was how it worked with Laura, always at a remove, in absentia. She could count their actual hours together on one hand in recent years. But there was no need to shout, just as there was no *need* to go to New York. She did go, however needlessly. It was a trip to remember and savour for always, a secret high-point. Laura, as it happened, came back from Los Angeles two days early, citing Meryl Streep as her motivation. Far from being hurt or alarmed, Joss was overjoyed. And although it had felt like an ending of some kind, it was never quite over with Laura.

Camped out on Central Park West with other theatre fanatics, there had been the awful revelation of how much easier it was to breathe away from Bianca. A lightness she did not feel at home had invaded and carried her through five blissfully self-directed days. Did all couples feel this way when apart? The Mary Ellen Mark show, the solo Mexican dinners, heavy on spice and noise and cilantro and everything she had missed. She basked and savoured and did nothing with the revelation. She flew home, back to comfortable, if unremarkable, love and continued taking the same sorts of photographs she always took. Her style, people called it. Privately, she knew it was a rut.

17.

Even though she had paid him. Even though they had an agreement that all he had to do was walk her out of the neighbourhood and a little further so that her parents would truly believe he was her escort. She now wished they weren't so liberal: a chaperone was usually mandatory for any first date. Now she was alone with this fellow, blocks from her house. No wonder Margaret married so quickly, she fretted.

"I'm fine from here," she said, peering out from under her parasol, hoping no one from her street would pass and witness the discussion.

"I have the day off now. Can't think of a better way to spend it." Bill was intent on joining her for the whole expedition, and that had not been the plan at all. He cracked his knuckles and peered down the road. "So what next, do we take a cab or walk or?"

Bette urged herself to remain emotionless. "I'll go the rest of the way myself, Bill, like we agreed. You know I'm not interested in a date." The sky was clouding over and that was worrisome: what if it rained just as she arrived at the ferry dock? Would they still let people go across to the island? Don't be stupid, Bette. Don't panic. She didn't suppose they operated the Figure 8 during a storm of any kind. A light rain was nothing. He's talking, pay attention.

"I'm happy to accompany you, dear," Bill said, trying to loop his arm through hers. A lady passed by with a little dog on a leash.

"Bill. You already know I'm going to Hanlan's Point to meet someone." His sparkly green eyes bore down into hers. She could smell carbolic soap and realized he must have washed up someplace before coming to her house. He was going about this all wrong. Or she was. He was moving forward, and if she didn't stroll alongside it would seem as if he were dragging her.

"Who are you going over to meet? Surely not my married sister?" He laughed at his own joke, a braying sound that agitated her further. *Ada Jones, Ada Jones.*

"Not that it's your affair, but I am going to meet my cousin." He raised an eyebrow and shook his head in disbelief. She broke loose from his grasp and turned to face him, standing very still. "I happen to have a cousin whom no one likes except me. I'm forbidden to see her, and I have to come up with all sorts of stories to have any time with her at all. She's very sick. The poor thing has no one in the world but me, and I can't believe you're going to make me late for the ferry, Billy, after I paid you ten full dollars to help me out. What a rotten rogue you are turning out to be." To punctuate her sentiment she stamped her foot.

"I'm sorry," he stammered. "I thought maybe you'd changed your mind about me."

"Well I have, and not for the better. Now go on and don't say a word to anyone or I swear I will haunt you for life, you awful boy." Another foot stamp seemed in order. A little cloud of dust whirled up from the warm sidewalk.

"Enjoy your day," he said weakly, crossing the street, shoulders rounded. Where had the villain in him gone? Now he looked only pathetic.

A pang of sadness for him, yes, but she was free and planned to enjoy it. You have to have a plan for your life, Bette, wasn't that what Momma was always saying? She knew the plan should extend beyond riding a roller coaster with a new friend—oh please let her be there as she said she would be and make the sun come back out—but larger plans could be made later. After she located a cabriolet and got herself to the ferry docks.

A cab came along the main thoroughfare, and she waved frantically at the driver, who made a dismissive gesture at her until he noticed her pronounced limp. It had come on rather suddenly, but he didn't know that, and so he stopped out of pity a few feet away from her.

"I was on my way home, dearie," he said as he helped her into the cab.

She informed him of her intended destination, and he looked worried. "I hope you have someone to help you get around over there! A girl alone! There's a lot of no-goods living out there, you know."

"My cousin lives out there," she said tartly.

"Beg pardon," the driver said, speeding up ever so slightly.

When the cab finally reached the ferry dock, a ride that seemed eternal, Bette paid him and let him open the door for her, but waved off any further assistance. The poor man stood amazed as she bolted for the ferry, hat ribbons flapping, no sign of any impediment to her gait slowing the sprint.

"That's enough for one day," she warned herself as she sailed through the gates above which HANLAN'S POINT was painted in large, exquisite letters. It might as well have said *This way to heaven*.

18.

Joss flattened the avowed last-and-final wine carton and tucked it in the recycling box on the front steps. Gave the remaining weed to Tess with best wishes. She would live without crutches, without numbing agents. She had done so before. The cigarettes were harder to dismiss from her daily diet—a love-hate thing wherein love trumped hate more often. Tomorrow, she would go for a run.

She sat down with a mug of black coffee and a stack of magazines. The estate lawyer had called that morning and their finances were all settled. Everything transferred and tidied, no snags thanks to a thorough will and a marriage certificate. She did not want to think about their wedding, which had been as matter-of-fact as a tax return. Now there was nothing more to do except decide where to sprinkle Bianca's ashes. No small decision but no rush to make it either: the urn had been delivered the day before. It now sat on the dining room table where Bianca's place always was. Former partner arrives via FedEx. Joss flicked through old copies of *Vanity Fair*, issues that pre-dated Bianca's illness. Had the world continued on while they rushed from doctor's offices and labs to treatment rooms? It seemed to have, if *Vanity Fair* was representative of life's continuation. The cruelty of everything could get to you if you let it, so she refused to let it.

She went across on the ferry to the market and bought a fifty dollar bottle of red wine. This time I mean it. Last one.

When Laura called, Joss was digging through the trash looking for cigarette butts she could still salvage. Rehabilitation wasn't going so well. She was three quarters of the way through the bottle of Ripasso and barely able to talk thanks to a combination of drunkenness and shock. They hadn't spoken in long months, and the last "conversation" had taken place via email. Priding themselves on a low-maintenance friendship, months *could* go by. And did.

"Are you all right? I just heard. Why didn't you call me?"

The warmth and immediacy in her voice perked Joss's hopes. Not in terms of a full reunion, but perhaps a visit would be in the offing? And why did they spend so little time together? Laura had an apartment in Toronto, she wasn't always away. It was such a wasted opportunity, their old love.

"Joss?"

"I'm here." She would not ask, she would not put herself in the position of asking. Will you come and see me? Will you let me come and see you? The last Joss had heard, Laura was shacked up with a classical musician in Topanga Canyon.

"What can I do?" Laura asked, her honeyed rasp too painfully gentle now. Had she been crying? Shouting? Joss pictured her then, singing at the top of her lungs on the back of a motorcycle, her arms around the latest man.

"If I think of something, I'll call," Joss said finally, flooded with guilt that this soon after losing Bianca she could be turned on by the voice of another woman. That other woman.

"Why don't you come to New York? You always feel better here."

It had not occurred to her. New York. But *why don't you come to New York* had a different ring to it. *Here* meant she was there. She didn't dare ask.

"Thank you, I might," Joss said, regretting her now-failed attempt to quit drinking and smoking all in one day. She eyed a wasted cigarette butt with longing. It was soaked in coffee grounds, beyond repair. Was it salvageable? "How have *you* been?" It was a question that would look after a good hour of the day. Their mutual favourite topic would be covered in detail.

At the end of the conversation, Laura announced that she was celebrating three months of sobriety thanks to AA. A near-miss car accident had woken her up. "How are you doing with the not-drinking?" she asked, and Joss glanced at the empty bottle of wine at her elbow.

"Fine," she said with a resolute nod. "I had a little wipe-out, but everything's back on track now."

19.

Hot as a vaudeville spotlight, the sun came out just as Bette exited the Hanlan's side ferry dock. She told herself that Apollo worked for her exclusive personal benefit, blessing the day's events with his yellow glow. She didn't open her parasol, and after a short struggle, removed her hat. It would have been delightful to pitch them both in a trash basket, but she decided against it. Nothing could be held against this expedition in order that she might make it again.

She wondered what a Saturday must be like if a Tuesday was this crowded with pleasure-seekers. A Saturday night must really be something to behold, all the electric lights glowing and the dark cool aroma of the lake washing over the dance pavilions. There were hotels out here, and she could hardly stand the gorgeous idea of sleeping overnight in a place like this, and waking up first thing in the morning with the seagulls crying overhead…

"Your mother know you're out here solo mio, crumpet?" a man said as he passed by too closely. Close enough she could smell stale cigar smoke on his breath. His ridiculous moustache made him look like a baby walrus, and she longed to tell him so. She decided to keep moving, relocate the Figure 8 and, with any luck, lovely Freddy. It was a shame they hadn't chosen a precise time or even a meeting place. Had she meant the invitation? It only just occurred to Bette now that she might not have. Oh! The crowds made concentrating on landmarks a little difficult; Bette's jumpy nerves began to cloud her reason. She realized too that her breakfast had been too small to carry her through a full day of travel and confusion.

"Lost, buttercup?" Another man, this one kitted out much like the man who'd brought the flyer to her door in the first place. Red hair, small teeth. "Well hello!" He tipped his hat and winked. It was the very same man. "You made it! On a Tuesday! You must have been desperate to see me, cherie!" He had a kind twinkle in his eyes, but thanks to Bill she wasn't in a trusting mood. A fuzzy green feeling rose up in her belly and the world grew spinny. He caught her by the arm just as she began to swoon and guided her toward a lakeside bench on the boardwalk. "Which ride were you on, dolly? You don't look so good! I mean you look pretty as a picture, kiddo, but one done with a lot of greens and blues!" Bette laughed, she couldn't help it. He talked like Billy Murray sang. She wondered if she should just let him talk on till she felt better, or whether she should ask for directions to the Figure 8 outright. But there it was, right through a stand of trees: the screams of people enjoying the ride pealed overhead. He followed her gaze and clapped his hands and stood up. Holding out his arm he said, "Ah, so you're a coaster girl! This way, madam! In my experience there are two distinct groups of people in the world: spinners, and coasters. You my dear are a coaster and should therefore never board a ride that spins. Know thyself!"

Again, she couldn't help but laugh as he led her along the path toward the gate of the Figure 8 roller coaster. He then pressed a bundle of bright red paper tickets into her gloved hand. "I'm supposed to hand them out to the kids, but I can see you'll make better use of them."

"Thank you!" Bette was caught off guard by his gift.

"No charge for the advice," he said. He leaned forward as if addressing a child. "You know I sure would like to see you again."

"I—"

"You came all the way out here. A gal who responds to advertising…"

"COOKIE!" a voice shouted, splitting the conversation in two. Bette and the man both looked over to see Freddy standing with her arms thrown wide for an embrace before she charged right at Bette and gathered her up. The hug was so familiar, the man would have had no idea the two girls barely knew one another. Freddy's cap fell off in the midst of the embrace and the man picked it up.

"Friend of yours, Fred?" He held out the cap, which she snatched back but did not wear. "Didn't know you had any feminine chums in your sphere."

"That's right, Charlie." Freddy gave Bette a squeeze around the waist and tugged her toward the entryway for the roller coaster. "See you later!"

Charlie waggled his fingers at Bette, "See ya, Cookie."

Moving up the ramp, Freddy finally let go of Bette. "You came!" was all she said before they were two turns away from riding. After her grand performance on the boardwalk for Charlie's benefit, an unexpected shyness swept through her. She kept her hands clasped in front of her and waited quietly till their turn arrived. She looked smaller without her apron on for some reason. Exposed.

Belted into their seats in the rear car of the coaster, Freddy regained the power of speech. "What's your real name, anyway?" Her dimple reappeared. The train jerked up the hill, but Bette dared to look over at her new friend.

"Cookie," she said. Why not? Freddy had chosen it, and it was nicer than Bette and twice as wonderful as her middle name, Joan, which she loathed. Cookie was a fun name, a secret between them.

Freddy laughed and gave a little shrug and gripped the iron safety bar and closed her eyes, again looking exalted. "Here we GO!" she shouted as they reached the top of the hill before the first horrible-horrible-horrible, fantastic whooshing drop.

And then all too soon it was over.

"Go again?" Freddy asked as they jogged down the exit ramp, elbows bumping.

Bette's prior nausea was all but forgotten. Her stomach was steady, if empty. She showed Freddy the small handful of tickets, and the girl hooted with happiness. They rode twice more and then decided to walk around a little. Freddy wanted 'Cookie' to see as much of Hanlan's Point as possible.

There are coasters and there are spinners, Charlie had said. It made sense, because just looking at some of the other amusement rides, the ones that flew up and spun around or went in circles only made her head swim. She asked Freddy if she ever went on the other rides sometimes.

"Just the Ferris wheel. When I want to see the world like a bird does. But the carousel gives me the willies."

"The what?" Bette laughed.

"I don't like it," Freddy explained. "I don't like the carved horses with their dead eyes. Or the motion of it. And the music's awful. Reminds me of a bad dream." As they walked along it seemed that Freddy was always looking about, her eyes darting over the crowds beside and behind them. She had her cap on again, tugged low.

The golden scent of warm pretzels floated through the air toward them, and something like roasting meat and hot sugar doughnuts came rushing in together on a second breeze. Bette's stomach growled, and she wondered why Freddy showed no interest in the banquet they were passing through. Boiled candy, hot roasted peanuts covered in some kind of sugar coating, French fried potatoes with brown vinegar—one tormenting aroma after another assailed Bette's nostrils.

"Aren't you hungry?" she finally asked Freddy.

"For this?" She looked at the concession booths as if seeing them for the first time. "Oh, this is new for you! That's right. I've had my fill of taffy and nuts, let me tell you. I sell them all day long every day and for half a day on Tuesdays. But you go ahead! The pretzels are good—have one! Have two, Cookie!"

Freddy spooned brown mustard onto Bette's warm pretzel and watched as she nibbled at one end of the twist. "How about an ice cream?" she suggested.

"Will you have one? My treat." Bette had the wrinkled five dollar bill from her father, and though she had planned to make Bill take it back, she knew he wouldn't. They walked to a stand with a bright pink and blue striped awning. Expressing shock at Bette's wealth, Freddy ordered one ice cream for them to share. Everyone working at the park knew Freddy and greeted her warmly, but she continued to look guarded. The ice cream was packed in a conical waffle biscuit you could eat when you were done lapping at the ice cream itself, and Bette marvelled at this fact as they took turns licking, passing the ice cream back and forth as it dripped in the warm air.

"Let's go by the water," Freddy said.

"I can't walk and eat at the same time!" Bette said, proving her point as a gob of strawberry ice cream splatted down the front of her dress. "Have the rest," she said, handing Freddy the coronet. To her amazement, Freddy finished it in three quick bites.

"Over this way," Freddy instructed as they moved away from the screams and music and humming motors. Following along, Bette saw now that her friend wore boots a few sizes too large for her feet, men's boots. Out on the lake a small regatta of sailboats tackled silvery-blue waves, their captains calling good-naturedly to one another as they raced. It seemed painful to even think of riding back to the city, leaving any of this behind. Freddy motioned for Bette to follow her down a narrow track leading behind a sand dune to a tiny beach sheltered by a willow tree. The noise from the midway could still be heard, but faintly.

"Is your name really Freddy?" Bette asked when they were stretched out on the sand.

"I don't know, Cookie, what do you think?" Freddy teased.

"Bette."

"Short for?"

"Short for nothing. It's just Bette. I'm only called Elizabeth when someone's mad at me, but that doesn't count." She rolled onto her side to face Freddy, who was sifting sand through her fists hourglass style, watching it form miniature, sugary mountains.

"Fredelle," said Freddy. She kept her eyes on the sand. Her lashes were the colour of spider webs.

"That's beautiful! I've never heard that name before. It's really lovely. Are you French?"

Fredelle didn't answer. She sat up and removed her too-large boots and shook them out. Her bare feet glistened with angry red blisters as she rubbed her heels with her hands. "I prefer Freddy," she said, glancing at Bette. "That's what everyone around here calls me anyway."

Bette tried not to show how sad the sight of Fredelle's feet made her. They looked sore from the boots that didn't fit right. She was a chipper girl, probably a little older than Bette, not by much, but her feet revealed something else about her life. "Have you worked at Hanlan's Point a long time?" Bette asked. She had so many questions, so much she wished to know.

Freddy nodded. "Since May. I work concession during the day, as I said, and I work over at the theatre selling tickets six afternoons and four evenings."

"And you like living out here? It's awfully beautiful. Not to mention fun!"

"This is my special spot," Freddy said. "My getaway. The rest of it's all right. The people are good to me."

"Where do you sleep? I suppose the hotel's for rich people."

Freddy threw her head back and laughed. "You're funny, Bette." She rolled onto her belly and rested her chin on her fists. "How do you know I'm *not* rich?"

Bette covered her mouth with her hands, and Freddy laughed even harder. She reached over, tickling Bette's ear lobe and underarms till she fell sideways and screamed, "You're rich, you're right, you're rich!"

"I've no time to spend my money, so that helps," said Freddy when Bette had recovered herself. The wrestling match over, they both sat upright, facing the lake. A single swan bumped up and down on the waves, no mate in sight. "I'm saving for something," Freddy said as they watched the bird.

Bette felt a hot ache in her chest when she thought of riding back to the city on the ferry. Sitting in silence with Freddy, a fantasy spun in her head of curling up on the beach right there for the night, disappearing into life on the island, working a taffy booth just as Freddy did and having the other workers as family. Seeing Freddy every day…a poke in the ribs roused her from her reverie. Aquamarine eyes stared intently at her when she turned. Those eyes dove into her thoughts, scattering them like leaves in a windstorm till there was no one thought, only a pleasant, hazy blur.

"Penny for your thoughts," Freddy said, poking her again, which made Bette jump. No answer forthcoming, Freddy leapt to her feet, shuffled cheerfully into her miserable boots and slapped her brown plaid cap on. She jammed loose golden strands of hair beneath it and said, "C'mon, let's use up those tickets! Who knows when I'll see the likes of you again!" She held out her hand and shook her fingers till Bette grabbed hold. That there was any possibility of there *not* being a next time frightened Bette as she ambled up the dune path behind Freddy.

On the Figure 8, as the train climbed skyward, Bette looked bravely out over the park, over the treetops and lake and up to the clouds. She forced herself to keep her eyes open, taking it all in just in case Fredelle was right and she could never manage to get back out here. She had done it once, sure, but it would become trickier and she did not want to involve Bill anymore. He had strange ideas. She so wished her brother Oren had lived. She could have paid him *two* dollars a trip and left out the unpredictable working boys and strange men who spoke to lone girls riding through the city...

Freddy grabbed her hand hard just as they plummeted downward, and Bette lifted right up out of her seat. Her heart pounded with terror: they would fall straight out of the train, they would crash to the ground. Freddy squeezed her fingers harder as they flew back up the next hill. She was laughing, and no one had fallen to her death, and it was grand, she kept shouting it was grand, eh? Wasn't it grand, eh? Bette's ears played tricks. Grandie, she heard, and tears spilled down her cheeks. People cried when they laughed, too, so Freddy didn't think anything of it.

Freddy's voice was hoarse and hopeful as they eased back to the platform. "Do you have time for another ride?"

"I don't know, what time is it?" Bette dabbed at her eyes with her handkerchief, the one Grandie had embroidered with tiny musical notes. The thought of leaving made her grumpy.

"Time for another ride!" The sun wasn't due to set for ages. Freddy could see the clock on the hotel behind Bette and knew she wasn't late for her job at the box office and said so. She pointed to the clock.

"How about the Ferris wheel?" Bette asked. "I've never been on one. It scares me a little but I want to."

"Let's save it for next time, then. That way you have to come back!" She reached out and squeezed Bette's shoulder. There would be no taffy left behind this time, as it was her afternoon off and her hands were clean. She was an interesting girl, Bette thought. Ever so affectionate and comfortable one minute, then quiet and inscrutable, then warm again. They had wrestled on the sand, but even so Bette hadn't been sure she should tickle back. But Freddy was so beautiful it made Bette's heart do somersaults.

The lineup for the Figure 8 was slower to advance this time. A group of schoolboys in dark blue uniforms plugged up the gangway.

"If you could eat anything at all, what would you choose?" Bette asked brightly. She had decided to push past Freddy's quiet streak and barge on to knowing her as well as possible in the next few moments.

"Roast beef sandwich."

"Butter?"

"NO! Horseradish, salt and pepper."

"What day were you born?" Bette decided that if she made it sound like a game she could get lots of answers out of Freddy.

"Don't know. What about yourself?"

The queue moved ahead slightly. The boys started singing a hymn at top volume until their teacher made them be quiet.

"You don't know your own birthday?"

"That's right. I came over from Scotland, and they lost my papers. I think July was the month, though. My mother complained of the memory of heat the day I was born."

"Well when do you celebrate it?"

Freddy shook her head. "I don't." Bette looked shocked. Freddy gave her arm a pat. "One day I will, but not yet. When I have something to cheer about, you'll hear me all the way from New York, you can count on that." She removed her cap in anticipation of their turn. Bette now recognized the soft burr when Freddy spoke. It was barely there but for the music it left behind. New York?

"All right," Freddy said as they began their favourite ascent. "This time, eyes open the whole way round, no cheating! No cowardice! Brave soldiers!"

Bette poked Freddy in the ribs this time. "How on earth will I know if you've closed your eyes? I'll be too busy screaming to notice!"

Freddy was solemn. "NO screaming." Then she cackled and squeezed Bette's hand as the hilltop approached. She stared straight ahead. "I like you, Bette. I hope you'll come back again and see me."

There was so much screaming and rattling of wood that Freddy didn't hear Bette's answer: *Try and stop me.*

Freddy walked with her back to the ferry. "I wish you could come Thursday. It's going to be a spectacle. Fireworks, hot air balloon rides, everything. Dominion Day, can you come?"

"I can't promise. My parents are rather strict…"

Freddy laughed. "How'd you get here today then, all alone?"

"I lied and said a boy was bringing me to the island to meet his sister. It won't work again. I'd have to think of something else." The ferry horn sounded in the bay as it approached the dock. *No, no, no.*

"Say you'll come anyway, and I can look forward to it even if you don't end up being able to."

The logic of the approach made no sense to Bette. She had a strong feeling she wouldn't be able to return so quickly to the island, and it seemed wrong to imply otherwise. "You'll be working though," Bette reminded. "Won't you?"

"That's true. Say you'll come next Tuesday then."

The ferry blasted again. *No, no, no.* The crowd churned river-like around them. Bette realized she'd left her parasol on the beach and cried out. Her mother would scold her for being careless.

"I'll run back and get it, don't worry," Freddy reassured her. "I'll keep it in my room at the cottage where I stay. Promise." She gave Bette a little push toward the ferry. "See you in July."

"Next week!" Bette called out as she eddied amid the other moving bodies. "Tuesday!" An old woman admonished her to watch where she was going and to put her hat on like a proper lady. She fought to keep Freddy in her line of vision, but a moving forest of parasols and hats got in the way.

20.

She pulled the prime rib from the oven and set it on the butcher block. Let stand for thirty minutes or some such nonsense. It was too expensive a piece of meat to slice before it was time, but her stomach was insistent. She broke the end off of a stale baguette and dunked it in the pan juices. The heat in the lake-facing kitchen was oppressive but good smelling. It wasn't exactly a summer menu, but it was her old standby and she was standing by it.

The Yorkshire puddings would be done at the last moment, now that the oven had been liberated. Everything else would be cooked *à la minute* to guard against latecomers. Someone was *always* late, just as there was always a potluck somewhere if you didn't want to eat alone. Joss wondered if her future would include chronic attendance at those church suppers where you came carrying your own plate, cup and fork. She half thought of hunting one down just to get it over with, for it symbolized a gameness, a kind of moxie that she longed to have. Will go anywhere alone, anytime.

It occurred to her, as she guiltily opened a bottle of wine, that there was nothing heroic about how long they had been together. There was a photo on the false mantel that showed them with beaming smiles, no evidence of the malaise Joss felt deep down. She went to the living room window and gazed out at the tiny front yard. Bianca had loved tending the Rose of Sharon. My baby, she called it. A dangerous wave of memories threatened to crest, and Joss downed a hefty glass of wine like it was mother's milk.

She had purposely invited three people who self-identified as introverts. Introverts always self-identified, at soonest opportunity she found, and she figured a dining room filled with them would be a peaceful affair. One that ended early. If Melanie stayed on, Tess could deal with her extroversion.

The rule of someone always being hideously late also dictated that someone would be inappropriately early. Due to the ferry schedule, which baffled landlubbers, one could almost always count on being torn from an illicit nap or late-running shower. When no one burst in on her to claim the title of early-bird, Joss was afraid for the overall success of the party. Tess swung through with an armload of flowers borrowed from neighbouring gardens, and Joss arranged them swiftly. They shared a glass of the Amarone and fussed with seat cushions instead of talking, and Joss considered it a rehearsal of sorts, not a sign of anything wrong between them. But when the clock chimed eight and still no one had turned up, when the oven had been shut off for reasons of conservation, Tess slammed a cookbook down on the counter and glared at Joss.

"What?" she asked, genuinely shocked. Tess wasn't usually a slammer.

"This was a bad idea. Honestly, why didn't I stop you? Why did I let you type an email all by yourself?"

The idea of having a sixtieth birthday dinner for Bianca had been someone's. It hadn't seemed macabre till now. A reason to gather, some form of tribute in place of a funeral, but now it looked ridiculous, all the more so for being out at the island house instead of in a neutral restaurant on Front Street. Joss had been creative in her selection of guests, or so she had imagined. Bianca's ex-husband, Mack, was slated to come. Bianca's former dragon-boating coach, Melanie, a couple from Madrid who seemed to be invited to everything that summer, though no one really knew where they had joined in, and Tess. Always Tess, whose patience for such experiments in human behaviour had come to a halt. As Joss's long-time assistant, she could get away with a certain amount of honesty.

"Are you *trying* to have a lousy dinner party?" she asked, looking around for cigarettes. Finding none she was even more furious. "Did you quit again?"

To placate Tess, Joss went to her laptop and re-checked the email and found that she had typed September 11 on the group invite. It was now July 11. For a panicked moment she couldn't remember Bianca's actual birthday. Today, she reassured herself. She had never enjoyed her own birthday, but made a habit of feting Bianca every year. "How could I forget?" she wondered aloud.

"Shit happens," Tess said, suddenly warm and cheerful. "I could never stand Mack anyway. More prime rib for this mamacita!" The already-sliced beef was in a warmer, and she helped herself. "Remind me I am busy on the eleventh two months from now, k?" Joss fired up the oven and made the Yorkshire puddings and tossed the salad as if everyone who'd been invited was bustling around the miniscule dining room. The table, set for six, was easily transformed into a table for two, and Tess took that on as well.

"You're practically radiant over my faux-pas. Do you really not like Mack that much?"

"He never talks unless he's telling you about software! But it was the dragon boating dragoness I feared most," Tess admitted. "ALL she talks about is BMIs and Isogenics and race training. AND she's hot to boot, which makes her all the more annoying."

Joss laughed for the first time in weeks and felt instant guilt.

"Normal," Tess said, re-filling her glass with a fresh bottle pinched from Bianca's private "cellar" in the shed. That Bianca had been something of a high-end wine bootlegger on the island was widely known. If you needed a decent bottle, not just a plonk-de-plonk, you could come see Bianca in her beloved potting shed.

Joss and Tess sat on a tiny bench in the backyard and sipped in silence.

"Is a Mensa meeting always this noisy?" Joss asked. Tess yowled with laughter and nearly slipped off the end of the bench.

"I love you," she said when she had recovered herself. Her hand rested on Joss's knee, and it was one of those worst moments in life, pushing that young hand away, gently but still away. Tess took it well and suggested that they go in and clean up.

"I'll do it," Joss said. "I don't sleep anymore anyway. You probably have somewhere more fun you could be."

"Oh yeah," Tess said, stacking dishes.

21.

Mr. Whitehead didn't scold her for being five minutes late to sell tickets at the Gem. He would have, but the look on her face told him she was a kindred, and lovesick. He waved as she hurried to her post in the wicket, mopped his ample forehead then went back to reading his copy of *Madame Bovary*.

Five people were waiting to buy tickets to the new feature, *The Country Doctor*. Freddy had been allowed to see it once, without music, and quietly vowed again that she would one day meet Miss Mary Pickford in person. But the sweet feelings in her belly that the actress aroused now paled by comparison to how it felt when Bette looked into her eyes or brushed her hand. Mary Pickford had been the first cause of such inner pandemonium, but now there was a real-life girl making it that much harder to think of marrying anyone. She wondered if Bette would also like Mary Pickford and if she'd dream of kissing her. That was a dark thought; Freddy wanted Bette to want to spoon with her. Did she have such thoughts? Was there any simple way to find out? Freddy began to feel blue and after selling the last ticket, crept to the back of the theatre and watched the final moments of *The Country Doctor*. She would keep her sights and affections trained on Mary Pickford, who was clearly going to make a million pictures and would always be there for Freddy.

22.

Streetcars home, no taxi cabs. The return must be as slow as possible, as agonizing and hard won as could be. She lollygagged instead of walking briskly. The séance crowd would soon be arriving at the house. The thought of it made her blue. What Bette wanted most was to sit in Papa's study and listen to one record after another. No singing along, just wide-eared listening till the ache ate itself up and faded away. This method had worked before, although this time the melancholy was far more mammoth. She understood love songs at last and it frightened her.

The boat ride back to the city had been anguished, and every shriek of laughter around her only made her mood all the more self-pitying. She missed Freddy so fiercely she almost wished— almost—that she'd never met her. There was a new loneliness in her she could hardly stand, and it confused her. The anticipation of getting there and being with Freddy and riding the Figure 8 had been so immense all week that now she felt herself tumbling down a dark tunnel of ingratitude. She should be glad of the day, appreciative of the sunshine, thankful for the free tickets given to her by strange Charlie; she should block out any of the moments that were alarming or tedious and think only of those searching blue eyes that studied her like a textbook and knew so much about the world that she didn't. Grandie would have reproached her sharply for not paying attention to the goodness of her day. For the remaining blocks, Bette lectured herself without mercy.

It was almost six o'clock as she turned onto Indian Road toward the three story brick house she had once loved the sight of when they were visitors. As a little girl she had run up its front walk with glee. Her grandparents had always stood very close to one another, and Bette liked to play with her paper doll and list the amazing number of endearments they used. Being a child had been such pleasant work. Now, perhaps because of the longer summer hours of daylight, the boys still laboured in the lot across the street. To her horror, there was Bill, swinging his scythe as per usual—going against their agreement! Out in the open, working when she herself had yet to return, right where her father could see him. She wanted to march over there, have a word, but it was too late, her father stood on the porch smiling down at her as she came up the walk scowling.

"That's quite a face to wear after a beautiful day at a park," he said. "I see you ate something pink."

She quickly exchanged scowl for smile and kissed his cheek on the porch. "Hello, Papa. Sorry I'm late. It takes quite a while to get there and back from here. When are your spiritualists arriving? Are we feeding them?"

Her father said nothing and stared across the road at the lot where the boys were packing up their shovels and other equipment. He smoked and watched, and Bette's dread increased with every second of silence.

Finally she couldn't stand it anymore. "I'll go in and make the tea, then."

When she closed her hand on the doorknob her father asked, "For whose benefit are you lying? Not mine, I assume?" She froze in shame. "You might consider a career in the theatre, Bette. You've a great talent for fakery."

Oh, what a day! From the greatest bliss to the deep sorrow of disappointing the one who loved her most. Her shoulders slumped and she couldn't make herself turn around *or* go into the house. Helpless.

"Evening, boys!" her father called to Bill and his crew as they passed by on their way home. Bette's ears burned scarlet. Her father's hand landed gently on her shoulder. "Let's go inside, Bette."

"I'm sorry, Papa," she whispered, finally able to meet his eyes. "I felt certain you'd never let me go if I said I was going by myself."

Her father considered this. "You're probably right. But you succeeded!" His generosity of spirit made her feel worse. "Next time, you had just better bring me some candy. I bet they have some interesting comestibles out there! Come now, we're late again."

She wanted to tell him about Freddy, about the rides and the exquisite smells and the little beach and midway barkers, of how she longed to go back at night to see the lights, stay at the hotel, but there was no time. The spiritualist group they hosted twice monthly always made a collective, noisy entry, and Bette preferred to eavesdrop on them from the upstairs landing after she'd laid out the tea. She wasn't entirely sure they weren't just a batch of lonesome lunatics. The first time they had gathered in the dining room, she and Grandie listened in from Grandie's big bed and Bette was scared. There was a great deal of knocking, and one of the women kept calling out to Isis.

"Misfits. No worse than church people," was Grandie's pronouncement. "Fetch my Harvey's from under the bed, would you, duckie?" The bottle of cream sherry was always in one of four hiding spots, the location of the cache sometimes temporarily forgotten, but never for long. Dr. Thomas made sure the supply never ran out.

Bette wondered whom the spiritualists were so determined to bring forward. She was concerned they might end up with someone like Bloody Queen Mary or Ivan the Terrible smashing through the house, but aside from one man's obsession with bringing Joan of Arc to tea, it wasn't all that exciting. Her father said each person had a different someone they were keen to connect with again. Someone they missed, or someone they had 'unfinished business' with. Isis was invoked each time. Bette was invited to join the circle—young women often had great success with channelling—but she declined. There was no need to join hands with eccentrics to summon spirits when she could talk to Grandie any time she liked just by closing her eyes.

There was a great racket of chair legs scraping floorboards and too-loud greetings between the women and men of the group as they settled in the dining room. Bette had set the tea out on the sideboard and made as little eye contact as possible as she flew up the staircase to her room. Always, before the unsettling opening rituals began, Bette retreated. She wished her father's phonograph player was upstairs with her so she could play her records and imagine herself back on the Figure 8. Instead she lay on her bed in her ice-cream stained dress and squeezed the fingers of her right hand as hard as she could with her left, just as Freddy had. She closed her eyes to bring her friend closer. Half-aware of chanting one floor below, she slipped into a gauzy half-sleep and dreamt of Freddy waving to her from the top of the Ferris wheel, which grew steadily larger, wider and taller.

A loud bang followed by the sound of glass breaking and a series of shrieks snapped Bette to attention. She jumped from bed and ran to the top of the stairs and looked down. Half a dozen spirit-chasers filled the downstairs corridor and Bette smelled smoke. She hurried down the stairs in her stocking feet and searched for her father or mother.

Her father beat the dining room table with his waistcoat, and the flames were all but extinguished. Her mother stood with her arms folded across her chest, watching with an expression on her face that Bette couldn't decode. There was a strong smell of wax and scorched cloth, but no one appeared to have been injured. Bits of glass glittered on the floor.

Bette gave her mother a questioning look as she moved toward her. "One of the oil lamps exploded," she said. "Mary Agnew was startled and knocked over the candelabra. Nothing to worry about, Bickie." The pet name for Bette had been coined by her Grandie many years before, and Bette looked at her mother with amazement. It meant biscuit, and no one else really called her that except Margaret and Grandie. In fact, her mother had always claimed to despise pet names.

Lamps did crack from time to time, although they didn't shatter with such force very often. And Mary Agnew was a rather large, clumsy woman with terrible nerves. If you startled her by opening a door unexpectedly it took her three days to recover, so it was no surprise to Bette that she had made such a mess when surprised by a small explosion. Bette wondered who they had been trying to channel when she glanced at the Susan B. Anthony painting to see that one of Susan's eyes had been slashed. She quickly looked away, hoping her mother's gaze wouldn't be drawn to it. How had it been damaged?

"Why did you just call me Bickie?" she asked instead, herding her mother toward the dining room door in an effort to get her away from the vandalized portrait.

Her mother laughed. "I have no idea. Isn't that funny? I never liked that name for you."

"Yes, I know." Bette felt a little shiver run up the back of her neck. "I'll go back to my room if everything is all right, then." She began to back closer to the door, keen on exiting as soon as possible.

"Bette!" her father shouted gaily just then. "Quite the fracas we had here for a moment or two! Have you come to join us?" He shook his scorched jacket out and surveyed the charred table once more, then shrugged. He seemed to be enjoying himself. "What's the matter, Bette?"

"She's got nerves like Mary Agnew," her mother sniffed before moving into the corridor to attend to the guests now crowding the vestibule.

"What happened, Papa?"

He looked around and drew her close to him so he could speak softly. "I think Grandie came to visit." His excitement showed that he didn't see any menace or warning in the shattered lamp or table-top blaze. Bette pointed discretely at the gouged eye of Susan B. Anthony, and her father's mouth dropped open, then promptly closed. "Oh no," he murmured.

"I'm going upstairs," Bette said firmly. "I don't care for any of this."

Her father's normally robust complexion had become very pallid, and he moved quickly into action, gently announcing that the summoning would have to happen another evening. There was a faint buzz of protest, but Felicia assisted in the polite but firm expulsion. Bette noticed that some participants had fled voluntarily. Mary Agnew clung to the newel post and played her role to a dwindling audience.

"Such unhappiness," she sobbed, though no tears leaked from her eyes. "I saw the lamp rise from the table!"

"Good night, Mary," Felicia said, steering her directly toward the front door.

"I saw the eye torn out of that portrait!" Mary shouted as she went down the front steps. "And if thine eye offend thee, pluck it out!" Bette's heart sank. Although it was inevitable that her mother would see her heroine's mutilated picture eventually, she had hoped it wouldn't be that same night.

"She should be in a facility," Felicia muttered as she stomped upstairs to her bedroom. Ironically, the slamming door often promised some hours of peace ahead. Her father had retreated without another word to his study, his door closed against further excitement.

Bette slipped into Grandie's bedroom and closed the door ever so gently. Nothing seemed out of order. She sat on the plump mattress and wondered if Grandie really had come to visit or if her father simply wished to see his mother again so ardently that he imagined she had come. Did he feel guilty for taking over her home when his father passed? Had his remorse led him to imagine she had caused the explosion as a display of her enduring displeasure? They had been meant to come and keep her company, but she ended up in exile in her own bedroom partly because of enmity between her and Felicia. But was that all that had driven her to withdraw from the household? She was an awfully strong-minded lady; the decision to not put up a fight never did make sense. But Bette was starting to understand how much Grandie had missed her husband.

On a whim Bette looked under the bed to see if the Harvey's Bristol Cream bottle was still safely stowed. It was not. She checked the somnoe cabinet, the secret shelf in the clothes cupboard and the final hiding spot, on the floor behind the heavy window drapes: nothing. Someone had obviously found it and removed it, just as the picture of Carry Nation had been removed from Grandie's door the day after she died. Bette had refused to speak to either of her parents for many days after Grandie's death, especially when the portrait was so swiftly relegated to the fruit cellar. As if they couldn't wait to be rid of her comment on their audacious tributes to what they believed in.

She looked around the room and wondered if there was anything she might give to Freddy next time she saw her. Some small item that might please her when she wasn't busy selling candy or tickets. Shoes were an obvious choice, but Grandie had been a tall woman with long narrow feet that required custom made slippers and boots. The bureau was laid out just as her grandmother had left it, all the simple items of her toilette arranged neatly on an embroidered cloth. Dusting powder, hair combs, hair brush, hand mirror.

She opened the top drawer and rummaged till she found what she sought: a tiny hand-carved wooden cribbage board and the well-worn deck of Union Jack cards they had played with. If Freddy didn't know how to play, she would teach her. It had been a game that consumed Bette and her grandmother for hours at a go, especially when it rained or snowed. They had become quite competitive in the final year of playing together, and if Bette played a good hand, Grandie wasn't above calling her names and shouting her indignation. It was all in fun, and Bette had only become good because Grandie was such a fine player with a very quick mind for mathematics. She was willing to bet that Freddy had the same knack for numbers and tucked the tiny board and deck in her apron pocket before reluctantly leaving Grandie's room.

The matter of the disappeared sherry was solved when she paused at the door of her father's study, now ajar. Without knocking, Bette pushed the door wide and found her father sitting at his desk with the sherry bottle at hand, a half-filled glass beside it. Seeing her, he raised a finger to his lips and motioned for Bette to come sit.

She had never seen him take a drink of alcohol before. It worried her a little. His tie was crooked, probably from trying to extinguish the dining room fire, and his hair, usually smoothed into place, hung limply in his eyes.

"How was your day, Bette?" he asked. She could hear the sherry under his words. He looked weary and sad now, nothing like he had a half hour before.

"It was wonderful, Papa. I hope to go back."

He sipped the sherry and shuffled some papers on his desk. "Oh? Why's that? What was so wonderful out there?" He leaned back in his leather chair, folded his hands and seemed genuinely interested. "Tell me all about it. I want to picture what you saw. Be vivid, now, don't leave anything out!" He closed his eyes and she stifled the urge to laugh. She loved him so. The sherry was meant to soothe his nerves after the séance went awry, she guessed. She reached across to the glass and dipped her finger into the amber liquid and pulled it out, realizing too late that her father watched her with narrowed eyes.

"You're becoming something of a bandit, Bette. I'd watch that urge. You want to get to Summerland, after all. Go ahead and have a proper sip, but don't be furtive." He motioned at the glass and waited for her to pick it up and drink. As she did so, the smell made her stomach turn over. She thought of the spinning rides at Hanlan's Point and gagged.

"I can't bring myself to," she said, setting the glass down.

"Good. Because it killed your Grandie," he held up his hand when she began to protest, "as it kills everyone who touches it. Besides, it's not womanly to drink alcohol. Your children will all be born without brains if you drink that stuff."

This made no sense, since all of Grandie's children had been extremely bright: a lawyer, a doctor and a scientist among them. She reminded her father of this.

"She took up sherry *after* we arrived," he said and waved his hand. "Your day, please, in full detail and with any embellishments that you deem necessary. For colour."

"Today you've told me not to lie and not to be furtive, Papa, and now you want me to make things up?" He often teased her this way, and she never quite knew which advice to actually follow.

"At the beginning, please."

In the spirit of full disclosure and a clean slate, she began her story with Bill and her efforts to dismiss him on the street. She admitted to having taken a taxi, which was decadent she knew, but she was in a hurry by then. In great detail she described the ferry ride and her emotions when the sun came out as she landed on the shore of her dreamed-of destination like some sort of explorer (she thought he would enjoy the odd allusion). Although tempted to leave out the alarming invitation to visit the private room of the midway barker, she decided not to, since it added to the drama, and even in telling it she felt her heart quicken with refreshed anxiety. She paused briefly in case her father demanded to know the man's name, but he remained quiet. As she neared the moment of the story when Freddy rescued her by calling out, she felt hesitant to continue. She leaned forward in her chair and closed her eyes, squeezing the fingers of her right hand with her left to urge herself onward. The desire to keep something private was new. Her father would be glad she had a friend, but for some reason she could not make herself say Freddy's name out loud or tell a thing about her. Her tongue would not form the necessary words.

A purring sound came from her father's chair, and she looked up to find him sound asleep in his chair, hands still folded, lips parted, the abrupt end to his cherished evening of spirit communion a memory. Whereas thoughts of her day would keep her awake all night long, she guessed. The nervous excitement of it was still very much with her and telling about it rejuvenated the details.

Bette collected the sherry bottle and the glass. She tiptoed to the kitchen first, rinsing the glass as quietly as possible, then moved on to Grandie's room, where she stowed the sherry and the glass on the secret shelf of the clothes cupboard.

Emerging from Grandie's room for the second time, she found her mother standing in the doorway leading to the dining room. The damage to Susan B. Anthony's face had been noted, judging by her mother's dark expression.

"That is truly terrible, Momma," Bette said with sympathy. "And a little bit scary."

"Yes," her mother replied, and Bette saw that she held the fireplace poker in her right hand, close at her side. Without speaking further Felicia walked up to the portrait of Helena Blavatsky and drove the poker straight through the centre of the Russian Theosophy queen's face, chipping the ornate frame as she stepped back with her weapon. "*Fide nominem.*"

Trust no one.

"Goodnight, dear," she said without turning to face Bette.

23.

Summer swaggered on. She thought about dating a man, for counterpoint. It wasn't a completely outrageous consideration, given that she had felt so little carnal passion with Bianca. Maybe a truth was urging forward in her later life, a bisexuality she was too previously prim to admit? She tried ogling various males on the beach and on the ferry, tried deep appreciation of hands and legs and asses, piecemeal, the way objectification should be carried out. Nothing. She gazed at the backs of heads, some bald and others sporting ponytails. She made small talk about photography until the didactic tone of one chap made her want to strangle him. Would she have responded the same way to an omniscient woman? Likely not. Maybe. She gave up on the idea that choosing a man instead of a woman could erase the hollow in her guts. It wasn't who she was.

There were the helpful tips from friends and magazine articles alike: take a class, learn a new language, take a vacation. But she found that her mind circled too much around the topic of who she might meet (or not meet) in a class, whether or not Russian was practical for her to study and, as for travel and trips, summer in Toronto was not to be missed in favour of a steamy all-inclusive resort.

The morning she borrowed Maxine's canoe was seen as a powerful sign of her progress through what everyone else imagined were the tidy stages of bereavement. Except that she had borrowed it with a mind set on paddling till she capsized in the middle of Lake O. She took nothing with her, not a water bottle or even a sachet of trail mix. Paddling to oblivion had been the plan. She had woken up with the suffocating awareness that she would have to do it all over again: meet someone, get to know them, deal with their quirks and foibles, expose her own flaws *ad nauseam*. The whole production. It would be expected and, worst of all, she would expect it of herself when enough time had passed. Unbearable. Maxine had been all too glad to offer up the boat, her hand-hewn paddle, even a brand new life jacket.

"I'll be gone all day," Joss warned her, wondering how long it would take to become exhausted. She was out of shape. The running regimen hadn't taken hold yet. The sun would, she reasoned, likely get her first. Could the sun in southern Ontario actually kill a person? Maybe the blond and the blue-eyed could count on it?

"The boys don't ever use it," Maxine assured her, carrying the canoe to the water's edge with Joss, still jazzed by her friend's seeming initiative. From grief to gumption in one brutal month.

"Thank you," Joss called out as she paddled into the gentle waves in the bay nearest Maxine's house.

Her arms quickly began to throb, and she pointed the canoe back to shore. Skirted it for a good half hour till she reached the clothing optional beach on Hanlan's Point. From the water the naked bodies were Fauve smudges of peach and brown and fish belly white. She coasted in, then climbed out and tugged the boat the rest of the way. To earn her place and reassure the others on the beach, she peeled off her top, unhooked her brassiere and sat facing the water with one hand resting on the pale blue canoe. Oblivion would wait for another day. She would leave when her bones were warm and the sunburn became unbearable.

24.

By late that evening she could barely keep her mind on her work. Tallying the tickets took every bit of her concentration. The only antidote for the yearning in her was the theatre. Happily, a new shipment of Pathé pictures had come in and Mr. Whitehead wasn't sure about them. Would she agree to test them out early the next morning? Freddy was careful not to seem desperate with her *yes*.

She barely slept, and next Tuesday seemed so far away that she considered trying to find a third job to occupy her few open hours. But that was ridiculous, since she would need her breaks for when Bette returned. Bette with the big brown eyes. She felt like singing corny songs and instead lay quietly in bed, lulled by Norma's snores, composing a letter to Bette and planning to send it via Charlie.

Dear One… no… My Darling One… I dream of your eyes and of your laugh and I would spend every waking hour with you aboard the Figure 8 if I could have my way…

What would Bette make of such a letter? Would she think it queer and too friendly? Or write back with equal passion, the way only another girl could? Was it worth the risk? It seemed it was, but then seemed it wasn't, all in a second's passing. Freddy felt mixed up inside and nervous and thrilled, much as she had the first time she ever rode the Figure 8 herself. Knapp Jr. seemed a million miles away, his miserable cold eyes obliterated by the warmth and enthusiasm of Bette's smile. In all the times Darius Peacock had squeezed and caressed her, endearments had never come to mind.

At eight o'clock the next morning she waited patiently in the dark theatre while Whitehead fussed with the projector and finally called out, "Showtime!"

In the flicker of the story, she felt calm again. The urgent, pining feeling subsided and she could once again connect with her resolve to leave at summer's end. She now had to, after all, for Darius Peacock would expect her to make good on her promise, and she had no intentions of doing anything but enjoying his five hundred dollars in a much nicer movie house in New York City. But before then, she would try to enjoy this summer with Bette as if her life depended on it.

25.

After the mutilated portraits were removed from the dining room walls where they had presided for years, meals were strained by excessive politeness between Felicia and Irving. The wallpaper was redder where each guru had stared down, so that now instead of faces there were telltale vivid rectangles of wall untouched by sunlight. Bette didn't quite understand the unspoken war between her parents; she hoped they would resume livelier disputations of one another's ideas. The chilly pleases and thank-yous became distressing after a few suppers.

She was seated at her little work table in her bedroom, starting a new shell painting, when her father appeared in the doorway. The work station consisted of a jar of paste and several glass jars of various sizes containing the numerous shells Bette had inherited from Grandie's own collection. This time she had decided to use the tiniest of the shells in spite of the fact that fine work tried her patience. A beach scene was sketched in pencil on the small square of board in front of her. Grandie had taught her to begin pasting from the centre outward to prevent mishaps, but she was already discouraged. Paste clung to her fingers and she was irritable.

"Such a beautiful day to be indoors," her father said, observing her mood.

"I've got to do *something*," she said, moving a tiny shell into place and frowning. She secretly wished he had come to announce that her parents were off to another of their conventions.

"Well exactly," he said. "How about a trip to the island with your dear father?"

Bette looked up to see if he was teasing. His hopeful expression indicated that the invitation was sincere. But what a mixed blessing, she thought, because it's Saturday. It was awfully fine out and the sudden possibility of returning to what had now come to feel like some sort of pined-for homestead made her giddy. Would her father want to ride the roller coaster? She couldn't picture it. And what if the torment of not being able to visit with Freddy was worse than staying home and wondering what she was doing on the hour? If only it was Tuesday. But then she wouldn't really like to have her father along on the only day when Freddy could join her on the Figure 8...

"A decision by summer's end would be helpful," her father prompted with a grin.

"All right, let's!" She closed up the paste and screwed the lids on her shell jars.

"Your mother thinks it would be an excellent place to hand out flyers for her women's group."

Bette froze. No! The whole day would be spoiled if Felicia came with her pamphlets and her megaphone. The mortification would be permanent. Papa had tricked her into saying yes only to ruin it all with the revelation that it wasn't a purely social outing. How awful it would be if Freddy saw her mother in full suffragette flurry. She'd want nothing to do with Bette ever again! She would have to renege and risk her father's unhappiness. They could go without her if they were going to behave like fanatics.

"She's not coming with us, Bette," Papa said as she stormed around pretending to look for her hat and gloves. "We're to hand them out *for* her."

Well, that was a relief. But there would still be the matter of handing out pamphlets instead of enjoying rides and keeping an eye out for Freddy in the throng.

"But Papa," she began.

"I'll meet you downstairs, all right? Your mother wants us to take our own sandwiches so we don't eat the food over there." He winked. She winked back. It had been a long time since she'd spent an entire day alone with her papa.

Because it was Saturday the ferry was all the more crowded and lively. Irving kept his word to Felicia and handed out a half dozen pamphlets as they disembarked from the boat and then another handful while Bette waited on a nearby bench. His manner was so easy and his smile so charming that passing women of all ages gladly took the piece of paper, some of them barely giving its contents a glance. Others read as if he had handed them the secret to a long and happy life. The importance of the right to vote for women was discussed on the front, and on the back, a list of open conferences that welcomed both women and men to hear a roster of respected speakers on the topic.

"The working day is done," he said, holding out his arm for her to take. "Show me the world, Bette!"

Far from being an expert guide, Bette felt a little overwhelmed as they strolled along. Happy, dizzy, semi-lost. But her father seemed right at home and was soon tugging her toward a very high platform where a sign promised that a full-grown horse would dive into the lake on the quarter hour.

"I can see why you wished to come back!" He admired the crowds of people of all ages. "Your mother would hate it. The only crowds she cares for are those that are seated and facing her in rapt attention." He tapped Bette on the shoulder. "Who're you looking for, daughter? You haven't heard a word I've said!"

It was true. She'd been scanning the crowds for Charlie and, half-heartedly, for Freddy, although she knew she was busy working at the candy counter at that time of day. She suggested they walk over to the Figure 8 so she could show her father why she loved the island so much. It loomed above their heads, and he shaded his eyes to get a better look.

"You rode that?"

"That's right. More than once!" There was pride in her voice although he stared at the ride with what she believed was disdain. In fact, it was fear. His beloved daughter. Someone had allowed her to climb aboard that terror train?

"Alone, on that contraption?" A wave of screams tore across the sky overhead and he frowned. The only time her father didn't look handsome was when he worried. An unsightly row of deep lines appeared on his forehead and stayed there.

She supposed her idea of riding it with her father wasn't to be realized. Could he be talked into the Ferris wheel and would Freddy be disappointed if Bette rode for the first time without her?

"Let's give it a try," said her father suddenly, and he began to march toward the Figure 8 entry ramp like he was in some sort of trance.

"But Papa," she called after him.

"Don't dissuade me!" he shouted. "Come now or I'll never have the nerve again."

"You need a ticket!" Bette rushed over to the little booth by the gate her father had already reached. The ticket seller told her five rides for twenty-five cents. She would save the remaining tickets for another day, she decided as she hurried to escort her father onto the roller coaster.

The man operating the ride that day insisted that all passengers remove their hats, no exceptions. Her father reluctantly handed the man his derby and waited for Bette to remove her elaborate satin Clackum creation. Someone blew a whistle twice and the operator shouted, "All clear!" and the ride juddered forward. Irving Titus gripped the safety bar so tightly his hands were nearly grey. Bette didn't dare touch him. The ascent was more worrisome than thrilling. She appreciated her father's determination but missed Freddy all the more.

"The lake smells good," her father muttered through clenched teeth, just before the train plummeted southward.

"This way Papa," Bette said, leading her ashen-faced father toward the little beach Freddy had shown her last time. He staggered a little as they moved away from the cause of his discombobulation but seemed grateful to his young daughter. She had helped him to retain his dignity as they exited the ride, and now she seemed to have a further solution. "Mind your footing," she instructed as she led him down the sandy path between the dunes.

And there was Freddy, seated on a blanket with a young man. Freddy and Bette looked at each other with equal surprise. *What are you doing here?* The man had his hand clasped over Freddy's, but she pulled it out from under his grasp as soon as she saw Bette. Her cap lay on the blanket between them; her blond hair hung loosely around her shoulders.

"Hello, Bette!" Freddy said cheerfully, moving toward her friend as she pulled her hair into a bun. The suitor brushed sand from his trousers and stood up, a disgruntled expression on his face. His face was sunburned—or flushed from annoyance, Bette couldn't quite tell. She felt badly for having imagined it would be all right to bring her father to Freddy's secret retreat and was flooded with regret. Behind her, her father cleared his throat.

"My father's not feeling too wonderful just now," Bette explained.

"Please come and sit down, sir," Freddy said, gesturing at the blanket on the sand. She smiled tenderly at Bette and seemed oblivious to her male companion, who now stood with his hands clasped behind his back. Bette's father loosened his tie and fanned himself with his hat. Everyone else stood mute, watching his recovery, till the young man spoke up.

"Would you like some water, Mister? Or a lemonade?" he offered.

"Oh, yes," Freddy said, "Go and get him something to drink! Would you like that, Mister—?"

"Titus," Irving said. "That might be a good idea. But I think I ought to walk a bit and get something to eat as well."

Freddy made a gesture at her male companion as if to say, *Well go then, take him with you!* The young man made an unhappy face, but relented when he realized Bette was staring at him.

"I'll bring you a hotdog," he told Freddy. Now it was her turn to make a face, and Bette tried not to laugh. They watched as the two men made their way up the path back to the boardwalk.

"What are you doing here today?" Freddy asked happily, holding out her hands to take Bette's.

"I feel awful, coming to your secret spot without you," Bette apologized. She had trouble meeting Freddy's gaze. It was clear that she and her father had intruded on a date of some kind. A private meeting. The fellow had not looked at all pleased, and Bette felt a mix of sadness and anger. Who was he?

"That's my stepbrother," Freddy said. "He came to see me without writing to tell me first. My boss gave me a little bit of extra time for lunch so we could visit. He came all the way from Stratford." The more she talked the tighter her grasp on Bette's hands got. She spoke quickly, nervously, and Bette wished she would be quiet. There was something untrue in her explanation. Too many details, yet she didn't say the man's name. And why would her stepbrother sit so close to her on the blanket? It seemed odd even to Bette, who had limited experience of the world but a powerful instinct all the same. Finally, Freddy fell silent after explaining that he was actually the son of the German farmer who had adopted Freddy when she came over from Scotland. She had been a juvenile farm worker right up till coming to Toronto. Not quite a stepbrother, then. Bette tried to think of something cheery to say. Her mind was blank: a rare occurrence.

"I'm happy to see you," Freddy said, squeezing her hands once more before letting go.

"My father was of the mind that he wanted to see Hanlan's Point. Only it seems he's not as fond of amusement rides as I am."

"A hotdog will either sicken him further or make him feel right as rain again," Freddy said with a laugh.

"Oh! Take these," Bette said, pulling the sandwiches her mother had insisted they bring along from her beaded handbag. Freddy received the brown paper packages with delight and gave them a good long sniff.

"Mustard and ham," she surmised. "Thank you, Bette! But will you eat? Come sit down with me on the blanket."

Bette hesitated before moving to join Freddy, who had already unwrapped one sandwich and was eagerly biting into it.

"I'll bring roast beef next time," Bette said as casually as she could. "What's your stepbrother's name?" She dreaded his return for some reason, although it would be good to see her father restored to his usual vitality. There would be no more rides today, she supposed.

Freddy chewed slowly and swallowed. Bette waited for her answer. Seagulls shrieked above them and the din of the motors from the midway lent a pleasing buzz to the atmosphere. Freddy did not want to answer the question—that much was clear. She took another bite of sandwich and kept her eyes on the water.

"Look what I've got!" Bette's father shouted behind them. The girls turned to see Irving gambolling down the dune with a paper cone of pink cotton candy in each hand. His natural colour had returned, and he looked extremely happy. He held a cotton candy treat out to each of the girls and waited for them to sample it.

"Papa, Freddy doesn't—" Bette began, but Freddy silenced her with a feathery tap on the arm. She plucked a large wad of the pink fluff and popped it into her mouth to be polite.

Bette asked where the other fellow had got to. Not knowing his name, she had no choice but to refer to him as her father's new friend. She hoped he would know the man's name and use it, but there was no such luck.

"He said he had some business on the mainland and he'd see you another day," Irving told Freddy. It was then that Bette realized she hadn't offered a proper introduction either.

"Papa, this is Freddy. She rode with me on the Figure 8 the very first time I tried it. They make you ride in pairs and so we met."

"Pleased to meet you, Mr. Titus," Freddy said shyly.

"You ride that thing regularly?" Irving marvelled.

"Freddy works out here on the island," Bette explained. "She rides it all the time."

Her father shook his head and stole a handful of Bette's cotton candy. "You girls," he said. They all stood about awkwardly for a few moments, devouring the spun sugar treat and pretending to watch the seagulls frolic.

"I ought to get back to my stand," Freddy said. Why did she look so sad?

"Do you still have my parasol?" Bette asked. Freddy nodded. "May I come get it on Tuesday?"

"Of course," Freddy replied.

"I left it behind last time," Bette explained to her father. "I'll need to come back next week for it. Momma will be upset if she thinks I've lost it."

Irving looked at Bette and then at Freddy. "I know you both just want to get back on that roller coaster! Very well, your lost parasol secret's safe with me, Bette. Nice to meet you, Freddy. Don't be late on our account!"

"See you Tuesday!" Freddy threw her arms around Bette and squeezed hard. "I'll explain better when you come back." Bette could smell burnt sugar in Freddy's hair. She wished she could bottle up the aroma and keep it with her.

"Lovely girl," said Bette's father as they watched Freddy scramble back up to the midway in her too-large boots. "Her friend is a bit strange."

"Oh?" Bette wanted desperately to know his name. She asked her father.

"I asked him," Irving said as they made their own way up the path to re-join the milling crowds. "He said, 'It's not important,' and then he pointed me in the direction of the hotdog vendor and left me standing on the boardwalk!"

"I thought he said he had business in the city," Bette reminded her father.

Irving smoothed his hair and sighed. "Not exactly, dear. I could see your friend was embarrassed. I didn't want to add to it." He settled his hat back on his head. "Don't worry yourself. I don't think he stands a chance."

They walked along in silence for some time, admiring the Hanlan Hotel and the well-dressed guests who came and went through its front doors. Bette couldn't stop worrying but didn't let on. She did not like the man who was not really Freddy's stepbrother. There was something unpleasant about him, and he obviously had bad manners, leaving her sick father alone to find his own way around. Freddy had something to tell her, and Bette wasn't going to let her change her mind when Tuesday rolled around.

She and her father made their way along. The crowd thickened in places where people stopped to watch a juggler tossing knives in the air or a magician performing sleight of hand tricks. A fleet of dancing poodles had everyone in the audience cackling. The dogs wore tiny costumes, and Bette and Irving both agreed it was unkind.

"You haven't eaten," her father observed. "Why don't we stop and you can have one of the sandwiches?"

Bette flushed a little. "I gave them to Freddy."

"Of course you did," her father said, giving her a little hug as they walked on. Yet again she felt a sudden sorrow as they approached the ferry dock. It was as if she was bewitched by the very air of the place. A man marched past playing a children's song on a tuba. A breeze off the lake brought the sweet smell of fish and seaweed; they passed a wheeled cart full of roasting peanuts and cashews. Hot aromas constantly met with cool perfumes out on the Point. To sit on a bench for the rest of the summer and just breathe seemed somehow heavenly. But flights of fancy were useless. She had to be practical, she decided, jerking herself back to what was.

"Don't tell Momma I'm coming out here on my own next week," Bette said on the deck of the Bluebell. "Say you're coming with me. Or that Bill is taking me again." Her mother wouldn't notice if Bill was across the street working when he was said to be with Bette.

"You're developing quite a talent for fabrication, Bette," he said. "No idea where that comes from." He popped a saltwater taffy into his mouth, offered her one. "Now, if we could just sort out where your death wish comes from!" He gave a theatrical shudder. "Next time let's go on that whirl-a-gig machine instead, the one that goes round and round in a dependable circle. All right?"

They spent the remainder of the crossing arguing about whether there really were only two kinds of people in the world.

26.

Lift your camera. Risk tears. Do it. Do it. And it was as if she realized: I am a hunter who cannot shoot. Joss restored her lens cap. Popped it off again, just in case she mustered the nerve.

Everything that had once mattered had fallen away from her grasp. She had portraits hanging in esteemed galleries across Canada. She'd had a vocal champion in her late mentor Hank Carver, which meant something to certain collectors. Come on, lift that fucking lens. Cradle your girl and get on with it. Her agent had all but given up, except that certain of the photographs kept being used by permission. Neat deals, little infusions of cash that would be even less noticeable now, rich as she was in her widowhood. Tess had been on a kind of generous, if ill-advised, retainer for the past two years. Free to work with other photographers, she chose to waitress at the island bistro until Joss pretended to need her for something. Usually their meetings were about having coffee and very long talks about movies they had seen and loved.

If asked to go anywhere without that camera bag ten years ago, even five, she'd have refused. Now just moving her tripod from one end of her office to the other triggered a panic attack. What was really going on? Why this paralysis?

Money wasn't an issue. Bianca had believed whole-heartedly in life insurance. There would be no need to buy vegetables from the nearly-spoiled rack at the grocery store. Not yet. It was all surplus, this money she seemed to have inherited. The trade-off was being left behind and she wasn't fine with it. Being alone sucked.

The moment to capture was gone. A couple, embracing on a picnic table submerged in the water. They were oblivious to her, it was perfect. Only their torsos rising above the surface of the lake, their lower bodies hidden by water. It would have been a beautiful shot. It wasn't that she feared crying. Tears she could handle, now. But the feelings that flew in under the tears were a problem and she was not giving in. If that meant never taking another photo again, well…

She jerked the camera upward and snapped a mediocre version of what had just happened. The click was loud as a shotgun in her ears. Again, she willed herself. But no. She deleted the shot immediately, as if it never happened.

She should go home. They had boxes and boxes of photos of their life together as a duo. Bianca was a handsome, confident woman who enjoyed being photographed. For a couple that seldom travelled, they had an awful lot of pictures. For a photographer she was hopelessly disorganized about her personal images. Joss would dedicate herself to organizing them for the rest of the summer, she promised herself, pushing her bike out of the dune. That counted as work, a kind of editing.

One box into sorting snapshots, her hands began to shake so insistently she stopped sorting. She had purposely run out of wine and a trip across to the city seemed a major bother. The shakes were a new thing. Unwelcome for what they suggested. This relapse was going on too long.

"You going into town anytime soon?" she asked when Tess picked up.

"I can do. What do you not need that you're going to ask for anyway?"

Joss chewed her lips. Considered her options. Said nothing.

"Are you putting me in this position?" Tess asked quietly. "Because I'd rather not be in it." She waited. "I'll bring some hot and sour soup. You'll sweat and feel like shit, it'll pass. You were doing really well."

"I was?" Joss whispered.

"You are," Tess promised.

27.

He hung about and made her late for her shift at the theatre. He had not gone back into the city on business at all, for he had no business in the city. His clothes indicated as much: he still had dried manure on his trouser cuffs. She wanted to ask how he had found her, since she had told no one at the farm where she was headed. When the Tituses had left, she felt sad, but also glad because she knew that Knapp was still creeping around. The look on Bette's face when she saw Knapp's hand clamped down on Freddy's was almost as awful as the feel of his callused paw.

She had long ago memorized the look and feel of his gnawed-at fingernails and scabby red knuckles. He was not interested in having her hand in marriage, for he felt he possessed her already. But "love" acquired by holding a hunter's knife to the delicate throat of the beloved was not love at all. This they both knew, and the filth that had occurred between them made her eyes water to think of, so she didn't. But now he had found her, and she had no idea how, except that his animal instincts had always been keen. He knew precisely when he could get away with his acts of depravity, and he knew when his father, Knapp Sr., was close at hand and might catch them. She would never speak of the things he had done to her, not even to Bette. Especially not to Bette, with whom she felt clean and bright and cared for, even already. Like a new person, without the grime of her recent past on her. And though she felt a curious yearning to tell Bette every last thing about herself, it wasn't this part of her history she wished to talk about. With time she had hoped it would wither away in her mind and disappear, but the nightly terrors suggested otherwise. Knapp Jr. was alive and well, and he had found her, again.

"What do you want?" Freddy asked when he approached the taffy booth.

"Nothing you've got," he sneered. "You look ugly and tired, living out here."

Freddy continued winding cotton candy around a cardboard baton and did not meet his eyes. His eyes, lit by hatred, were worse than his hands.

"Why don't you come back? Mutti says she'll put you to work in the house if you do."

She stopped twirling the spun sugar and bristled at the mention of Mrs. Knapp. The matriarch had actually caught her son with his hands around Freddy's throat in the barn one afternoon. She had said nothing and he had gone unpunished. This added layer of betrayal only increased the confidence of Knapp the younger. His attentions escalated mightily, and Freddy could not believe Mrs. Knapp would stand by, letting a girl be harmed, but so she did.

"Meet me by the theatre at five o'clock," Freddy said as she handed him a cotton candy. "I'll let you into the pictures for free." Her plan was to get him into the theatre, and then slip away from her post at the wicket before the program let out.

"I've got no time for pictures," he said, glowering. He held the cotton candy awkwardly away from himself, and she tried not to smirk. He had to go to the theatre, it was her one chance.

"The main show is about a champion racing horse," she coaxed. "Oh?"

And so, because he loved horses more than he feared the dark, she managed to get him seated in the theatre in time for the early evening program. She would flee during her one-hour break between programs and hide in her cottage and pray that he would give up and leave the island. Her arrival at the cottage would surprise Norma, who never saw Freddy except at bedtime. But she would simply tell her she had a ladies' complaint and needed to lie down.

It was a gamble, and as she waited in the wicket, selling no more than three additional tickets to comers, she shivered with panic. On most occasions, Freddy was known for her calm temperament. But the sight of Knapp Jr. loping toward her on the boardwalk, as if he had been transported there by devils, was too much. He was the one person she had encountered in her brief life that could inspire such trembling and ill-health.

On the stealthy path back to her cottage at break time, he popped out from behind an outdoor water closet. "Headed home?"

"No, just dropping in on a friend," she said, sounding as nervous as she felt. "You've missed the racehorse picture now."

"I didn't stay for any of it," he confessed. "It's not safe in there. Too dark."

And she could see, beyond his gruff dismissal of the pictures, that they had frightened him. The darkness, the flickering images: what she loved most had terrified her tormentor. She hid her pleasure at the thought of something on this earth striking fear in his puckered little heart.

He rummaged in his suit jacket pocket and brought out a news clipping. Her heart sank, seeing the photograph. How he'd found her: opening week, the *Toronto Daily Star* had sent a photographer to do portraits of the carnies. They had actually published the one of Freddy holding a cotton candy baton aloft above a picturesque tornado of sugar. He waited for her to return the clipping, but she tucked it in her apron pocket.

"I have to go back," she announced, turning to go past him in the direction of the Little Gem.

And of course he grabbed her. His roughness was not the surprise, but rather how nervous he seemed. As he dug his damp fingers into her arms, his usual arrogant sneer was absent. He tried pressing his mouth in the direction of hers, but the advance was arrested by a loud slap from Norma, who stood towering over him.

She had come from the nearby outdoor water closet and now, with her hand on his neck, gazed directly at Knapp Jr., as if Freddy were invisible.

"And what do you think you'll do next?" Norma hissed at Knapp.

"Nuh-nuh-nuthin, Mister," he stammered. When she shook him a little he realized his mistake and gasped, "Miss."

"You are on your way home, as I understand it," Norma said, now winking at Freddy. The girl took her cue and began to walk in the direction of a cottage not her own, where she would hide.

"Hey!" Knapp cried out, foolishly. "You'll come back to us, you'll see."

Norma's large hand landed firmly over his mouth and stayed there, blocking his nostrils too, till his eyes bulged, pleading. Her other hand remained fastened to his neck, lest he should think he was slated for a quick escape.

"I don't know who you are, besides a friend of the devil himself," Norma whispered at him as his face reddened and headed toward purple and blue. "But I don't want to see you out here ever again, most especially not near my girl." When she released him, she pushed him backward a little so he would struggle for balance. He gasped and pawed at his neck, where Norma's fingerprints glowed white. He looked like he planned to say something, so she raised her fists as if about to strike him and he fell silent.

"Git," she growled, watching with satisfaction as he trotted away from the cottages.

Back in their shared room, Freddy tried to express her gratitude. Norma held up her hand. "No need to say a word, my girl. You're not the only one, is all I can tell you. In fact, rare is the girl who hasn't been."

The urge to clean herself up in the eyes of Norma was fleeting, as she could see the older woman had no wish to discuss it further. And anyway, why exert the energy required to lie or tidy the story? Norma would only narrow her eyes at the deception. She sat quietly on the edge of her bed and wondered where he had scurried off to, and if he was lying in wait someplace across the island. Having come all this way, he must have been desperate for success. Norma had thwarted him, but Norma would not be with Freddy every moment of the day or night.

"I'll walk you back to the theatre," Norma said suddenly, stabbing out a cigarette in a tea saucer on the table. "Make sure the little fink doesn't get any ideas."

The projectionist Mr. Whitehead was waiting on the front verandah of the theatre when they arrived. His omnipresent cigar dangled and bounced as he spoke to Norma and Freddy.

"Got a bunch of new Yankee pictures in today," he said, not looking either of them in the eye. "You ladies want to stay on after the evening program and tell me what you think?" He stole a shy but affectionate glance at Norma, whose imposing stature and mannish hands did not usually generate admirers. But clearly, here was Whitehead's chance to strike up an acquaintanceship with the object of his desire. Norma blushed and, surprising herself, Freddy knew exactly what to say.

"I won't be able to," Freddy said, "but Norma, you should definitely take Mr. Whitehead up on his kind offer."

"I will if you stay too," Norma said with great meaning behind her words. "You need me to walk you home."

"I'll be fine," said Freddy, moving toward the box office. "I feel a summer cold coming on and really ought to go to bed straight after work." For good measure, she yawned and pretended to stifle a little cough.

"All right, Sarah Bernhardt," Norma said softly as she half-heartedly looked for a way out.

"Come on in now if you like," offered Whitehead. "Let her on in for free, Freddy."

"My pleasure, Mr. Whitehead," Freddy piped up. Her sense of romance piqued, she focused on her work at hand—the evening program was busy—and nearly forgot about Knapp for a while. At the end of her time in the wicket, she locked up her booth, took the cash box in to Mr. Whitehead and wished him a lovely evening.

And then she ran like Tom Longboat all the way to her cottage.

28.

Standing with the closed parasol held like a soldier on the march might hold a rifle: solemn, upright. Her blue eyes zipped through all the people, and when she found Bette, Freddy smiled.

She had a full day planned for them. She said nothing as she grabbed Bette's hand and dragged her toward the first of many stops. The sky was plump with dark clouds and an afternoon storm was inevitable, so they couldn't risk pausing for too long. Freddy was in a mischievous, secretive mood and even went so far as to cover Bette's eyes with her hands as she pushed her toward the first of many of the day's attractions.

"What about tickets?" Bette fretted, half-heartedly pulling at her friend's fingers.

"Got them already! This way, Miss! *I'm* treating today."

They rode the miniature steam train along the boardwalk beside lagoons. They plunged down slides wet and dry, stumbled through the glittering Crystal Maze, the House of Fun and the Old Mill ride with its man-made canals and murals. Freddy seemed to have an endless supply of tickets and energy this Tuesday, and Bette had to work to keep up. She even agreed to a turn on the Circle Swing ride, but only after insisting they ride the Big Scream and the Figure 8 twice each to erase the queasiness brought on by too much spinning. They skipped the carousel and opted instead for the Royal Gorge aerial tram and two turns on the Switchback Railway.

When the first thick droplets of rain fell, Bette felt certain their day together was over. She would give Freddy the roast beef sandwiches she had made at home and reluctantly board the ferry, or perhaps they could take cover in one of the picnic gazebos...

"Bette! I said come quick or we'll miss the start of the program!"

Freddy was several feet down the boardwalk now, and the rain was coming harder. Bette opened her parasol and sheltered them as they thundered in tandem along the boardwalk planks.

By the time they took their seats inside the Little Gem theatre their clothes were quite damp. Bette placed her sopping parasol in the coat room in the lobby and now set her wet hat on the empty seat beside her. The audience was small given that it was a Tuesday, and Freddy only had time to offer the briefest explanation of what they would see—"It's a cinematograph show!"—before the auditorium lights were extinguished and a screen in front of them began to flicker in the dark. Behind a purple velvet curtain down near the front of the stage, someone played a piano. The words THE THIEVING HAND appeared on the screen in bold, fancy lettering. Bette felt almost more frightened than she had the first time on the Figure 8 and sunk down a little in her seat. There were photographs, but they were moving like real people did. She had heard of this invention but had never seen one, and her eyes could hardly take it all in as the story unfolded. Beside her Freddy was as calm as could be, chuckling now and then in spite of the disturbing nature of the story. The man on the screen was missing an arm. He purchased a new arm from a store that sold arms—this was distressing enough—and the new arm did what it liked, including unlawful things. Freddy didn't seem frightened in the least, while Bette watched with one eye closed, as if to lessen the influence of the strange events unfolding in front of her. It was make believe but felt all too real. When the words THE END came up, she was relieved and reached for her hat, but the lights did not come back up, and Freddy tapped her arm and shook her head. "There's more!" she whispered happily. "We can sit here till it stops raining!"

The next story was called *A Trip to the Moon*. It was much less upsetting, and Bette found herself enjoying it. She glanced over at Freddy whose profile was lit up silver and white in the dark, shadows flashing over her face at intervals. She is exquisite, Bette thought. Freddy turned to look back and smiled, and reached for Bette's hand as she had on the roller coaster. Only there in the dark Gem Theatre there was no urgency in her grip, and she simply entwined Bette's fingers in her own. It was peaceful. A heavy rain drummed on the theatre roof, and the pianist struggled to keep up with the score that matched the cinematograph story.

They watched two more stories, and then the lights came back up. "Rain seems to have slowed down a little," Freddy said as she shook out her still-soggy cap and put it on. "I think we should've had some lunch by now!"

Outside everything gleamed from the rain, and the lake was choppy with waves and residual wind.

"Where shall we eat? I brought sandwiches."

"I was hoping!" Freddy grinned. She put out her arm like a gentleman, and Bette took it. All day she had been nudged and led about by her chum, and she liked it. It was what she imagined a date ought to feel like with the right fellow in charge. This was even better, for your virtue could hardly be questioned. They strutted along the lakeside, arm in arm, and it was then that Bette realized that Freddy was wearing new boots. Her stride was smooth and she didn't limp or shuffle in the slightest, and the new boots didn't slop all about on her poor sore feet. They were shiny, dark brown leather with smart black laces.

"You got new boots!" Bette cried, stopping in the middle of the boardwalk.

Freddy shot one out from under the hem of her skirt and posed with pride. "I did so. A friend brought them back from town." In fact, they had appeared on the doorstep of her cottage via an anonymous donor. Instead of fearing their source, she wore them with pride—and comfort. She was pretty sure the gift had come from Norma.

"Those must feel ever so much better!"

"By a mile," Freddy said. "You'll never beat me in a race now! You'll have to call me Freddy Longboat!" She tore off down the boardwalk. There was no choice but to follow her although it was revealed to be a pitiable no-contest after a moment's chase.

Freddy waited, barely out of breath, outside an empty picnic gazebo. They set up their lunch on the small pedestal table inside and watched as the rain intensified again. It had been a wonderful day, running from one ride to the next, nothing else in mind but fun and more of it, racing against the rainstorm and then finding sanctuary in the Little Gem. And now, eating roast beef sandwiches together, watching stragglers seek shelter from the downpour. Bette hoped with all her being that no one else would come to the gazebo to duck the rain. It was a selfish thought, but she couldn't help it: she liked being alone with Freddy, and besides, she wasn't leaving till Freddy told her what she had promised to on Saturday.

"I could eat these sandwiches every day!" Freddy eyed the second uneaten half of Bette's roast beef sandwich. The bread was fresh, and Bette had dolloped just enough horseradish on and just the right amount of salt and pepper. "You'll be an excellent wife, Bette!" she teased.

Bette pushed the remaining half of her sandwich toward Freddy, who only pretended brief protest before lifting it to her lips. "I'm never getting married," Bette said when her friend's mouth was full of sandwich. "I promised my grandmother I wouldn't and I won't."

"That won't be an easy one to keep," Freddy pointed out when she could speak again.

"Why not?"

"Because. Someone'll ask you and eventually you'll have to say yes."

"Just because someone asks doesn't mean I have to say yes." Bette wasn't sure she believed her own words. She wished she hadn't brought up her promise to Grandie in case it made her seem ridiculous and naive. A boy ran past chasing a little black and white dog with a stick and shouting awful things at it. Someday he'd be someone's husband.

"Thank you for bringing the sandwiches," Freddy said, offering the easy gift of a change of subject.

"You're welcome." She folded the brown paper wrappers from their meal very slowly, very precisely. "What…had you wanted to tell me?" Freddy looked at her without comprehension. Bette's heart thudded a little. She pressed on. Three days of waiting and wondering bolstered her courage. "The other day you said you had something you wanted to tell me. Tuesday, you said. It's Tuesday…"

Freddy nodded and looked around as if to make sure no one had his ear pressed to the screened walls of the gazebo. She leaned in closer, arms folded on the table top.

"The day we had today, riding all the rides and running around laughing and watching motion pictures?" Freddy looked excited, her eyes now lit with some new sparkle Bette hadn't seen before. She nodded to egg Freddy on. "I'm going to live that way every day soon. Oh, I'll still work, but I won't be selling candy or tickets, that's certain."

"What will you do?" Bette asked, grabbing Freddy's wrists, leaning ever closer.

"It's more a question of where!" Freddy nearly shouted it. She unlaced her boot and took it off, then pulled a folded piece of paper from inside. She held it up. "My dream is coming true. I wanted you to be the first—and only!—person to know, Bette. You can't tell a soul. Promise me." Bette nodded solemnly as they shook hands. Freddy handed Bette the folded paper. It was a letter and Bette felt shy about reading it, but Freddy insisted. "I have a cousin who lives down in Brooklyn." The handwriting was ornate. Bette pretended to struggle to decipher the words beyond Dear F. She very plainly saw the words 'job' and 'treat' and 'soon' before her eyes filled with water and she couldn't go on. And given the sick feeling in her stomach, she supposed she had the gist of what Freddy was telling her. She was going away.

"I'm going to Coney Island!" Freddy hammered the table joyfully with her fists. She reached over and took the letter from Bette and read it aloud without the slightest effort, almost as if she had committed it to memory. To Bette's heartbroken ears the words came as if shouted down a dreary mine shaft, though her friend's face showed nothing but happiness, and she tried to strain forward to hear something she could find delightful, too. Freddy's cousin had a job for her and a rented room in the middle of Coney Island, right in the middle of it all. Someone named Mr. Wannamaker was going to make them famous, and he knew someone at Vitagraph Studios, and they might even meet Thomas Edison himself. Freddy was to write as soon as possible and let her cousin, whose name was Lorna—a name Bette knew she would never like again—know when she would take the train to New York City to start her new life. It all sounded rather grand and impossible, but Bette didn't say so. Freddy was practically shaking with joy.

"You must be over the moon," said Bette, stating the obvious as she willed herself not to cry or even look as though she might.

"Oh I am, Bette, I am! You've no idea what this means!" She folded the letter carefully and tucked it away again. When she'd re-laced the boot, she stood up and peered through the screen wall of the gazebo in the direction of the clock tower down the way.

"When will you go?" Bette asked.

"I've got to go now," Freddy said, somewhat flustered. "It's past four already. Walk with me back to the theatre."

"I meant when will you go to Coney Island?" Bette said as they hurried out of the gazebo. She was working diligently to keep her expression bland, her voice even. It had been a lovely day, and she wasn't going to sulk and spoil it. That could wait till she boarded the Bluebell.

Freddy stopped mid-step and turned to Bette. She peered into her eyes without smiling and took each of Bette's sleeves in her hands, shaking Bette's arms ever so gently. A wilful tear welled up and slipped down Bette's cheek before she could squeeze it back. Too late. Freddy looked surprised. She wiped it away with her thumb and murmured, "What's this?"

"Oh, it's fine. I get the grippe whenever it rains," Bette said, avoiding Freddy's gaze and praying an authenticating sneeze would come over her just then. "Sitting in the theatre in wet clothes, you know."

"Yes," Freddy said without smiling. "That will do it." They resumed walking, a notable space between them where before they had walked arm in arm or with hands clasped. When they reached the theatre where Freddy was employed, the screams from the Figure 8 pealed with extra poignancy. The rain had stopped and the rides were operating again, though with fewer customers, Bette noted. Blissful one moment, shattered the next: this friendship had begun to feel like a roller coaster.

"I won't be going for a few weeks yet," Freddy said before she went inside the Gem Theatre. "Are you going to stop coming to see me? I know it's a bother for you to get out here... Please come sometimes, though?"

Bette kicked the ground and shook her head. She wanted to be able to say she was never returning to the island and Freddy should enjoy her wonderful new life with her silly cousin Lorna and never look back. Friends could be found anywhere.

"I'm going to be late, Bette," Freddy said softly, "tell me what you're thinking."

"See you Tuesday," Bette said. "I'd like to ride the Ferris wheel next time. If you won't join me, I'll ride it myself."

"See you Tuesday!" Freddy said. Late for her shift, she disappeared into the theatre with a smile on her face.

No one was home when Bette returned. The evening was muggy after the rain. She fixed herself a cold supper of bread, cheese and sliced cucumbers and sat miserably at the dining room table. Thoughts of Grandie flooded in and mixed with her grief over Freddy's news. She then realized she'd forgotten to give Freddy the little cribbage board. The whirlwind of the day had taken over, and something as simple as a board game slipped her mind. And now it might well be a going away present instead, to be enjoyed by Lorna. She felt a bit silly disliking someone she'd never even met. It wasn't charitable, and Grandie would have scolded her for passing judgement. Freddy was ecstatic about going away and maybe there was a reason. Perhaps, unlike Bette, she had made a plan for her life beyond the day at hand. Or maybe she was lonely out there on the island with all those misfits. Apparently the woman who slept in the cottage next door to Freddy's weighed three hundred pounds and there was a sideshow man with a miniature arm growing out of his belly. She remembered *The Thieving Hand* and shuddered. Sitting with Freddy in the dark had been so lovely, but her introduction to moving pictures was unnerving. And yet much like the way she'd felt after riding the Figure 8 for the first time, she found she couldn't wait to go back to the Gem Theatre and see what else the movie men got up to with their stories. Vitagraph was the name of the company that made *The Thieving Hand* and it sounded as if, from Lorna's letter, Freddy would like to meet those famous men at their motion picture studio.

And someone will ask her to marry him, and she'll say yes. Eventually that's what happens, Freddy had assured her. She thought of Freddy's so-called stepbrother with his hand over Freddy's on the blanket. Of the man Charlie suggesting that Bette should come to his room. All of it made her want to disappear into thin air.

Nothing consoled her. She roamed from room to room in the empty, lonesome house. There was nothing Ada Jones could sing that would make her laugh or feel better. No motion picture movie house was close enough that she could venture in and lose herself in flickering stories. Across the lake she imagined Freddy in her ticket booth, handing over tickets and making change, counting the days till she would escape.

She was halfway through washing the seldom-used, good service china when her father returned from wherever he'd gone off to for the evening. He came into the kitchen in a whirl of sweet cigar smoke and night air and put out his smooth cheek for her to kiss as he often did.

"How was Canada's Coney Island?" he asked, peeking in the ice box for something to eat. "Did you bring me any candy?"

Bette stopped washing dishes and asked why he had called it that.

"That's what the people who run it call it. Makes it sound more exotic, I suppose. Canada's Coney Island."

"But you have to know what Coney Island is for that comparison to mean anything," Bette said.

"Well, everyone seems to," her father said with his back to her. "Those who care, anyway."

"Yes," Bette said. Everyone did seem to know what Coney Island was all about. And how to go there…

Irving, obviously hungry, was now in search of the biscuit tin. Before she could remind him to be careful he opened a cupboard and a waterfall of papers rained down on his head. "Damnit!" He knelt to clean up the mess and Bette helped.

"Do you think I could ever go there?" she asked as they gathered stray pamphlets that advertised TEMPERANCE & THE VOTE & YOU.

"Go where, Duck?"

"Coney Island. The real Coney Island, I mean. Is it difficult to get there?"

He sat back on his haunches and pushed hair from his eyes and looked at her with his soft green-brown eyes. "Wanderlust, eh? You can probably go anywhere you put your mind to going, Bette. But it's going to get a little tricky trying to cover up for a Tuesday jaunt to Coney Island!"

The tea kettle on the stove began to sound off, its whistle not unlike the blast of a train coming into a station.

"Thank you, Papa," she said, removing the kettle from the stove before she ran upstairs to her room. She needed very much to be alone and away from the sad curiosity in her father's eyes. The decision was firm in her mind. She would not be swayed. Not even by Freddy. She had known one perfect day, but she was greedy and wanted many more just like it.

29.

Joss was riding in the pitch black island darkness, thinking about Laura, about how there was such a thing as too much chemistry. That was their problem, she felt, and they had solved it over time by never being in the same room together too often. Other people felt it and excused themselves. Joss's partners always despised Laura, and she was powerless to dissuade them: they had been friends forever and always would be. And over time the snap between them had become a pleasant, anticipated hum. Every so often, say once a year, they would have a four-hour dinner and avoid prolonged eye contact or certain topics. But the truth of the matter was imbalance: Joss was in love and Laura wasn't. At one such dinner a waitress had brought them a tiramisu to share and asked how long they had been together.

"Forever," Joss had half-joked at the precise moment that Laura scoff-laughed and said, "Oh, no! We're just really good friends."

And even that wasn't really true anymore.

30.

Sometimes when he was having his vicious way with her in the barn, she would close her eyes and float off to an imagined house that she built with her limited knowledge of architecture and furnishings. There were always paintings of lanes and trees, and flowers in every vase on every table. She longed for a bedroom filled with peonies and daisies and the heady scent of paper whites. Flower scents she knew, from the earliest memories of a garden she was taken to where her mother had worked. Sit there, her mother had warned her, and name all the plants while you wait for me. She was too small to know the proper names of flowers and plants, and so gave them people names, which she then reported to her mother. "As you will," was all she had said before she grabbed her hand and led her back to their council flat.

And now, curled up on her cot, she blocked out the stink of hay and the vivid push of his eyes and ugly mouth coming at her with a fantasy of what Bette must be doing. Bette had a good father, she knew that much, and likely a good mother too, one who would never have sent her off to another country. But it was important to keep the thoughts on happy things, and so she trained her mind toward Bette's big, ample bed and the night breeze blowing in over her as large trees rustled in the yard. She envisioned Bette's strong, warm hand in her own, how peaceful they would be listening to night birdsong and the leaves...

At six o'clock, after a full night awake, she gathered up her boots and a bathing towel and slipped out of the cottage. This was the hour of day when the island seemed a world away from its daily purpose. The air wasn't filled with screams and no motors roared. There was no scent of oil and gasoline on the wind, just for those few idyllic hours. Although she adored the rides and felt life was nothing without the thrill of them, she found herself drawn to the silence of the early hours. The farm had never been peaceful like this.

Barefoot, she walked till she reached her little beach, her sanctuary. And just as she came up over the dune, she realized too late that of course he would wait for her there. His slumped frame looked pathetic in the pale yellow summer light. If she hurried backward like a crab, she might slip away before he woke, but anger kept her in place. Would he not leave her be? She wished for the magical appearance of a knife in her hand so that she might at least frighten him off. But knowing Knapp, he would be quick to turn it on her, and he was stronger by far. He stirred and muttered, and Freddy knew she should run off but could not for whatever reason make herself go. She felt the thing to do was to sit right down beside him and pour sand on him till he roused, and so she did, trickling it straight into his ear.

The ugly word erupted from his mouth as he came to. It was ever on the surface, that rage of his. When he spied her she grinned, a lunatic smile that did the trick: he sat up, but did not maul her.

"The police will give you a ticket for loitering," she warned him, lacing her boots now and gazing out at the fine blue water. She had wanted a swim but was not about to have one with him there. "We've our own constabulary out here."

"You need to come back to the farm," he insisted, much like a cracked musical recording. "These people are not your family."

"I'm to be married," she said weakly, knowing it would spark his temper.

"You? Who would have you? You're spoiled goods! You're good for nothing much now. I'll tell whoever it is not to bother." He continued to pepper her with his usual litany of insults. Tenuously, she clung to the image of riding the roller coaster with Bette, and how the girl looked at her, as he continued on. That he did not lay a hand on her as he berated her was new. She supposed she should feel grateful. His words pecked at her as they walked toward the ferry dock, an unwitting journey she had taken him on without meaning to. He trotted along beside her, belittling and scolding as if a timer was running out and he had to get all his cruelty in. The first ferry of the day blew its horn in greeting, and Freddy waved.

"I'll wait in the city till you come to your senses," he said. "I won't leave till you agree to come back."

"I'm to be married before summer's end," she insisted, gently leading him toward the boat. He grabbed at her arm, but she slipped out of his reach and called a hello to the ferryman. This kept Knapp from dragging her onto the boat, and she used the opportunity to step back onto dry land.

"You'll marry me or nobody," he shouted as the boat sputtered in reverse. "That's a promise!"

"Bit early for such hollering, isn't it?" said the ferry dock attendant to Freddy.

"He can't help it," she said. "He's hard of hearing."

Once the boat was well into the bay, Freddy turned and walked back to her ruined sanctuary and gazed at the indentation of his body in the sand. Kicked at it till it disappeared. She could only hope he had spent a night in torment out there, scared in the dark and pestered by the coyotes that wailed in the forests nearby. The city, if he did choose to wait there, would not be much more soothing to his farmer's nerves.

Freddy checked her battered pocket watch and decided there wasn't time for a swim after all. Her stomach growled and she sat down on a log and debated whether to go get a sweet roll at the workers' restaurant or not. Bette would be having warm crumpets lathered in butter and preserves, her father at her side. Perhaps someone even served them their tea in the mornings, a hired girl.

Freddy had been promised such a job by the Knapps when they first picked her up at the station, a job indoors doing housework and serving and so on. But it was not to be, and as soon as they put her out in the barn to work, he was on her.

No sweet roll, she decided, brushing sand from her skirts. No more thoughts of Knapp Jr. She could be free of him if she just put her mind to it. Hard work would save her. And a ride with Bette on the Figure 8. And Coney Island.

31.

The lagoon was sheeted glass. She crept along the shoreline as quietly as possible. It was a cool morning, the sky verging on a storm. The heron waited on a stump in the middle of the bay, stock still and regal as a prince. Joss's foot slipped and she sunk into the muddy shore, rustling the tall weeds. The heron turned its head ever so slightly and seemed to hold its breath. Pale blue and purple smoke coloured its folded wings.

"Is it you?" she whispered as she lifted her camera. The depression of the shutter in a rapid succession of clicks sent the bird into the air. One mighty push and it flew away from the stump, low over the water, its wing tips grazing but never cutting the water. She captured the mighty sweep of those wings and the brief, disdainful cry that scolded the interruption of solitude.

Since Hank had died she looked for him in animals, in butterflies and, sometimes, in babies in strollers. She was convinced that he would come back and be in proximity to her, pay a visit and let her know everything would be all right. That was what he used to tell her when she would get down about her work not progressing. "Everything will be all right." And he had said the two words all right as separate entities, giving them a grandeur and an imminence. He would place his large, warm hand on her shoulder and squeeze ever so gently. She was sure now that the heron had not been Hank at all, but someone else. Painfully, she realized she was not looking for a visit from Bianca. Was not imagining Bianca peering in the window in the form of a robin, disapproving of her slide into drink and discouragement.

On her way back to the cottage at the other end of the island, she listed the things about Bianca that she missed: her melodious laugh, her blueberry tarts made on special occasions, the way she disappeared into the *Guardian* newspaper for hours. It was not that their relationship had been bad, because in so many ways it was the partnership of someone else's dreams—solid, quiet, devoid of dramatic tantrums or tears. Steady. But it had also been, over the years, a duet of wills, a quiet battle to see whose way of life would win out and define their days. Had Joss known she was winning that battle in the early years, that Bianca had—before the hurts piled up—been in love with her, she would never have slipped into complacency soon after. It was then that Bianca's insistence on complete order, continued tranquility and refined routine began to quietly drive Joss crazy. As it turned out, the seven year itch was real. The sole person who knew that Joss had considered, very seriously in fact, packing a bag and walking away from it all, had been her sister, who voted against it. "Take a road trip, clear your head," she had advised. The fact that Joss did not have a car was no deterrent. "Rent one and get on with it," Roxanne had said in her usual older-sister, matter-of-fact way.

Bianca had been nothing but supportive of the road trip. It was awful, given that one of the purposes of the trek was to decide if their relationship needed to end. New York would have been nice, but Joss wanted to drive someplace, detour and meander.

"How about Stratford?" Bianca had suggested. "You love seeing plays."

"I want to go someplace where I don't know a soul," Joss explained. She had several friends in Stratford she hadn't seen in years, and she hadn't been back since Hank died. His studio was still there, being operated by his partner Philip. It would be too painful and busy there. She wanted to be alone.

"I think Ohio," Joss announced. She had not been to Cedar Point since she was a little girl, and now it called out like a siren. The coaster park was on her list. She had always joked that if she found out she was dying, straight to the thrill mecca on the shores of Lake Erie. It had been a private if childish ambition to ride every roller coaster in the world and Cedar Point had a whole bunch of new ones on offer.

"It's your life," Bianca said with a weary sigh.

On the drive down she listened to "Green Onions" by Booker T and The MGs on repeat. Stopped for cream puffs at a small bakery in Ashtabula, Ohio. Thought of the Dylan song "You're Gonna Make Me Lonesome When You Go." There were important, life-altering decisions to be made, but her mind turned to none of them.

It was not until she was in line for a turn on The Rampager that she regretted her decision to come to Cedar Point alone. Everywhere there were groups of families and couples and kids affiliated with summer camps. When at last she was strapped into her bucket seat, restrained in every possible direction, the train roared forward up a perpendicular incline. It hovered at its apex. Tilted and dropped with such force that death seemed likely.

I will not leave Bianca, she decided.

32.

The streetcar accident delayed everything. Looking out the window, feeling strong and sure, then deafened by a terrible screeching and a bang, Bette couldn't quite see what was happening up at the front of the trolley. The feeling of being trapped came over her quickly, and she knew she needed to find a way out of the squeeze of bodies.

It was an unbearably hot day, and she had been late leaving the house because of a spat with her mother that would have become a full-scale battle had Bette not been desperate to get to the island. Her mother wanted to turn Grandie's former bedroom into a study for herself. Suffragette headquarters was expanding. She made the mistake of using the word shrine. She needed sometimes to get away, she said. Well amen to that, Bette thought, and to her mother's amazement, she let the feud fizzle as she pulled on her gloves (hateful things) and her hat (she soon wouldn't need it) and said a pleasant goodbye. Her calm had completely disarmed her mother to the degree that she failed to interrogate Bette about her plans for the day. The week. The year ahead.

A man closer to the front said the streetcar had driven into the side of a beer delivery wagon. What a lost opportunity to hand out Momma's temperance pamphlets, Bette mused before she spotted the time on a pocket watch the man next to her had flipped open. There was no time for laughing. The walk to the ferry docks from here would delay her terribly. Freddy would think she wasn't coming.

She wasn't proud of lying, but since Grandie was already deceased it didn't seem unlucky to say she was sick in the hospital and desperately needed to see Bette. The conductor finally released her from the compromised streetcar.

The pavestones were covered in sour-smelling foam, and a man in overalls waved his fist at his own horse as she made her way through the muck to the sidewalk. The hem of her skirt would smell of beer. She knew the smell of it from carrying pails of pilsner down the back lane to the potting shed when she was younger. Before sherry, and when she was still mobile, Grandie had enjoyed beer. Until she got the knack of it and built some strength, Bette had spilled a fair quantity of beer down the front of her skirts. Grandie quickly switched to sherry when Bette's parents questioned the mysterious aroma of beer emanating from their young daughter. Besides, Dr. Thomas provided an endless supply of Harvey's Bristol Cream, by "prescription."

Two and a half hours walking in the sun without a sip of water. She took her hat off and put it back on, as it was the only canopy from the blasting orange heat. Her gloves had come off fifteen minutes into the southward hike. It was tempting to stop and eat the sandwich she'd prepared for them to share—there hadn't been enough ham for two that morning—but she trudged on, telling herself that all the great peoples of the world knew what it was to walk long distances for a higher purpose. She entertained herself with thoughts of cool lake breezes and the little secret beach and the impending taste of an ice cream, hard won this time.

Squinting made the lake look like an ocean. The city looked like a quaint village on the shore as the ferry moved her closer to happiness. She practiced her speech to Freddy, the one she had composed and rehearsed at night, stretched out on top of the quilts in the summer heat. Freddy's joyful response, their embrace, it was all as vivid as the motion pictures at the Gem, and Bette played and re-played it. She had started a speech meant for her father's ears but couldn't quite get through it. It seemed likely she would simply have to pack a bag and slip away some night without warning. That too would break his heart, but she could not risk obstacles. She would miss seeing Margaret's first child. That was troubling, although if she were honest, her visits with her sister were fully obligatory since meeting Freddy. Tea was poured and words were spoken and tiny little hand-knit sweaters and blankets were held up for approval, not to mention a half-dozen bonnets made by the baby's genius of a father. One with blue ribbon, one with pink, one yellow, etc. But thinking of not meeting the little sprite sent a deep pang through Bette. How could she be so cold about some things and so completely consumed by the fire of love and adventure?

She dashed down the gangway from the boat and straight for the park gates. You could leave unwanted thoughts at the dock, she decided. It was time to shake off sentimentality, which would only ever be dangerous to larger dreams. If Freddy was going to Coney Island to become famous—for what exactly Bette did not yet know—she would join her. Every day would be like last Tuesday, and she would learn to like cousin Lorna, who after all had facilitated this grand turn of events and opportunities. Escape.

Waiting at the entranceway to the Figure 8, waiting some more. She took her hat off and put it back on. Faintly, ever so faintly, she could smell the stale beer from the earlier accident; it was as if Grandie was looking over her shoulder, standing by. She kept a pleasant expression on her face, but inside she worried. She had been awfully late. Patience, she told herself. People clambered up the ramp to the roller coaster and swooned past after riding it. She wondered if she should check the secret beach but worried that Freddy might then turn up at the ride gate. The sandwich was in dubious condition, and she would not be seen eating while standing up at the foot of a ramp. Some dignity was left.

After a full hour's sentry she was crestfallen. And faint from hunger. She should wait for as long as she herself had been tardy.

They never set a precise hour of meeting, but she had come at noon each time; it was reasonable for Freddy to count on a noontime arrival then. But it was two when she landed, and it was three now.

"Well, my lucky stars, look who it is!" Charlie peered down at her. He had grown a fuzzy russet moustache. "How are you, Cookie?"

"Hello, Charlie. How are you?" She worked quickly to mask dread, disappointment and the unexpected rush of relief that a familiar face of any kind can bring in certain circumstances. The wrong face, true, but for now it would have to do. And he might know something about the whereabouts of Freddy.

He took her in, a trained reader of expressions and postures. A lucky guesser. "You look to me like someone who could use a lemonade. Maybe even a hot dog. Why so glum?" He looked around, up and down, ever the showman, and snapped his fingers. "You're waiting for Freddy!" She nodded. "And you've been waiting a long time, which explains the long face!" Bette fought a smile. It was hard to stay annoyed with this fellow. "Well, honey, I can offer you a salve to your ache: she's not here today. Your vigil is over!"

Not here today? When was Freddy not there on a Tuesday? Why would she make Bette promise to come back and then not be here for their standing date to ride the Figure 8 and whatever else they pleased?

Charlie clucked his tongue. "You girls and your Boston marriages. She went into the city. It's her day off, after all. How about you let me treat you to an ice cream? You look wan. I'll revive you."

Bette turned toward the Figure 8. "I'm not hungry, thank you."

"Suit yourself, kid. But let me tell you, you keep riding those things and you'll addle your brains for good. I've seen people carried off on stretchers. Some of them don't make it that far."

"Sounds heavenly," Bette murmured. "If you see Freddy, tell her I came by."

"Sure, Cookie. Whatever you like. I'll tell her. One of these days you're going to owe me!" He tipped his hat and winked before gliding down the boardwalk in search of fresh impressionables.

She left the flattened sandwich on a bench seat on the ferry back. The day had been a disaster. She felt as though the three-hundred-pound lady from the sideshow was seated on her chest the whole way home.

Felicia was singing when Bette let herself in. Singing? And by the smell of things, she was baking something. Baking? Something was clearly wrong with the world this day. Felicia's idea of time in the kitchen rarely involved more than the boiling of a kettle, occasionally the buttering of toast.

"Momma?" Bette stood at the edge of the kitchen, surveying the bubbling pot on the stove, the large ceramic bowls on the counter covered in cloth. She was making soup. And bread. In July. The kitchen was stifling, although it smelled delicious. What was the occasion? Or was it portent?

"Are you hungry, Bette? I've made potato bread and a vegetable soup."

In July. Bette remained suspicious. She asked how many bowls she should lay out. Two. Where was Papa? Meeting with his old law firm associates.

"Let's eat here in the kitchen," her mother suggested. Bette set the table. When asked about her day she was cautious. Vague, but not too vague because that always rankled Felicia.

"You seem sad," her mother said when they were halfway through their bowls of soup and a half loaf of bread.

"Just tired," Bette lied. "Fresh air makes me sleepy."

Her mother was about to say something but seemed to censor herself with a mouthful of soup and a bite of bread for good measure. They ate in pleasant silence till the soup was gone.

"Oh! Something came in the post for you today," Felicia said, setting down the dirty dishes and hurrying off. She returned with a familiar square package from the musical recordings company her father ordered from each month. "Let's see what he chose this time!" Her mother was so present it unnerved Bette. What was she up to? She usually had her nose in a book and her mind on something else while she read. Her distraction had been especially pervasive since the International Women's Congress in June. Her enthusiasm for a record album was odd. Or maybe she was just lovely sometimes and Bette, being innately horrible and hard to please—she was really beginning to believe it—neglected to notice.

"Open it!" her mother admonished. "You're a thousand miles off tonight."

Bette relented and cut the string on the package. She pulled off the brown paper and sighed, quite eager to get upstairs to her bed where the whole awful day could be played out in the private theatre of her mind.

The water was cold as it hit her face. Her mother shouted her name. Yes, she thought she had answered.

"I'm going to call for Dr. Thomas!" her mother cried.

That worked wonders. Bette turned sharply and yelled, "You will NOT! I'm fine!" She stood up, snatched the phonograph record from where she had dropped it on the kitchen table and stomped toward her father's study. She hated everyone, every single person in the world including her mother and father, cousin Lorna of Brooklyn and Ada Jones. She dropped the needle onto the record, sat back in her father's wingback chair and clamped her eyes shut to keep from crying.

Her father had chosen the song to make her happy. She knew this. Freddy hadn't meant to miss their date: she knew this, too. But the song, "Coming Home From Coney Island," made her mad and sad all at once. It was a ludicrous song, not even remotely sentimental, but it still made her want to bawl. But tears led to resolve, she had lately discovered. She played the record once more, and then slipped it onto the shelf with the others. Thank you, Papa.

Poor Felicia was just as perplexed as when Bette had left her, although now she was at work boxing up Grandie's things and making the room her coveted study. The fury it stoked in Bette was only helpful now. Let her erase Grandie as had always been her wish, Bette decided, watching her. I won't be here to suffer through it for much longer. She stood quietly in the doorway for another moment.

"Momma?"

Felicia looked up. Her expression was stoic, as if prepared for attack. "Yes, Bette."

"What's a 'Boston marriage'?"

Felicia's eyes grew wide. She wet her lips and tried to formulate a reply, but Bette was impatient. "Ask your father," she said finally, looking back down at the crate she was packing. "That man," she muttered as Bette closed the door to what had long been Grandie's lair.

33.

He had rented a room in a boarding hotel on Queen Street, and she was ordered via a wildly misspelled letter to meet him there. The consequence of not doing as he demanded had always been the threat of having her disgraceful immorality exposed. To go to him with such obedience was wrong in every way, and her stomach ached as she rode back across to the island. This time round he had been curiously soppy, but then she realized after one mauling that he was drunk. At ten o'clock in the morning! An overturned beer pail stank in one corner and a bottle of whiskey waited on the wash-stand. She held her breath and pretended to listen as he lamented her absence from the farm. Waited until this weird tenderness returned him to a more familiar, brutal mood. The whiskey aided this hairpin switch, and he slapped her for saying she would never see the farm again. Her mouth bled a little, which seemed to satisfy him, and he did up his trousers and told her to leave. That he would see her again whenever he decided she was worth the trouble and expense. That she belonged to him, and he would make sure that everyone in her new "home" knew she was a whore if she dared speak out or seek help from her mannish friend, the giantess Norma.

She went straight away to the secret beach and, after removing her new boots and dress, walked directly into the water in her undergarments. Plunged herself under the lake's icy surface and held her breath and waited till the urge to scream went away. She wished for soap, a huge cake of it, to lather herself into cleanliness again. But such cleanliness would elude her till she could get away for good, or so it seemed. He had said he was going back to Stratford, to the farm, to explain to his parents that he had not been able to find her. Said that they would all come and beg her, if necessary, next trip. Freddy knew in her gut that the Knapps had no idea he was hunting her down. He could not leave her alone, and never would, he promised, hissing it into her ear as he hurt her over and over. She would, he assured her, never be truly free of his love.

Returning to the cottage in her dampened dress and sopping wet underclothes, she was relieved to discover that Norma was out. Perhaps at the theatre, revelling in the pictures? Whitehead had come out of his shell and was courting Norma full-tilt now. Freddy peeled off her wet clothes and hung them over the back of a chair, knowing Norma would have questions. There were plenty of witnesses who knew she had gone into the city for the day, and it was always assumed a young woman would be shopping on such an expedition.

In her one change of dry clothes, she hurried to the theatre and tried not to cry thinking of her missed visit with Bette. Of course he had summoned her on a Tuesday, spoiling all that was good in her life. The true heartache had been hiding from Bette when she saw her waiting for the ferry back to Toronto. Freddy had lowered her head and, without her cap, was unrecognizable in a wide-brimmed sunhat as she pushed alongside the crowd farthest from where Bette stood. It would be just punishment if Freddy never saw her new friend on the island again.

34.

Maxine came bearing another casserole. But not just any casserole, she was quick to point out. This one was gluten, soy and dairy free, satisfied all the rigours of a vegan diet and contained organic produce. There was no reason it could be turned away. Except for the prime rib, which Tess had helped to polish off, it had been the summer of gratefully eating mostly-vegetarian dishes cooked by others.

"Thank you," seemed a good enough reply, but Maxine was on a mission. She edged her way into the kitchen and scanned for signs of chaos and despair.

"You're still in shock," she announced, finding nothing out of the ordinary but the stench of cigarette smoke and a dish rack piled with freshly washed dishes. "You need to reach out. We'll have a drum circle for you on the beach next weekend."

"That's awfully kind," Joss said, "but I'm going to New York." It was the first she had heard of it, and for a brief second she wondered who had spoken.

"Oh? What's there?" Maxine asked peevishly. She did not host a drum circle for just anyone.

"A friend," Joss said forcefully. "And it's New York. And Meryl Streep is playing Mother Courage." She knew this from scanning a copy of the *New Yorker*. Apparently she was going to see it.

Maxine prowled around some more, looking for a way to prolong her visit. Some needy niche she might fill, some way she could make herself useful.

"Well, I can't very well compete with Meryl Streep now, can I?" she whined. And as if to cement the grave truth of this fact, she cast her eyes on a cut-out photo of the great actress on the fridge. Bianca had put it there as a joke of sorts: Meryl in *Silkwood*, in a magnetic heart-shaped frame. Joss had seen the movie no less than thirty-four times and counting.

"I just need to get away," Joss added. "It's nothing personal."

35.

Bette decided the place had been the person. That once Freddy wasn't reliably at Hanlan's Point, there would be no reason to trek back out there. Not now, not ever. Or maybe it would be like sitting in Grandie's room, amongst her things. There was comfort in that, although that was about to be taken away, too. Contrary to fashion, everything did not have to change constantly, she felt. She liked to count on things, find them where she left them. Small shells in certain jars, as an example. Old dresses. The first hill of a roller coaster, which now reminded her of love.

The lot across the road was nearly cleared. The boys had worked hard, long hot days till it was weedless and ready for a new house to be built to take the place of the burnt-down Davis home. She sat on the porch and tried to remember what the original house had looked like. It had been much bigger than their home, with an impressive veranda and a widow's walk on the uppermost floor. The name for the small balcony had given Bette the willies. The willies—there was Freddy, traipsing through her words.

With the working boys gone, the street was far too quiet and she craved noise. Hollering, banging and sputtering soothed her, or so she had discovered. Freddy would soon be immersed in the roar of machines, housed amongst roller coasters and shouting crowds three times the size of those at Hanlan's. Why must everything, including silence, remind her of Freddy? She thought of writing her a letter but had never had much patience for the activity. And what would she say, anyway! *I miss you, my love. Why are you leaving me, Freddy?* Bette had been determined to tell Freddy she wished to join her on her mad adventure. She had marched resolutely off the Bluebell electrified by convictions, and yet Freddy's absence had been enough to shake her courage completely. It was going to be a long life with such a limited quantity of pluck. It was crucial to gain self-control. She would not give Freddy another thought. It had been a pleasant idyll knowing her, and she wished her well. A more detailed plan than running off to live beneath a Ferris wheel with a pretty orphan from Glasgow was required immediately. There would be no more foolish Tuesdays.

36.

She was being punished for hiding from Bette on the ferry back. Tuesday came and went, and though she lingered by the Figure 8 then hovered by the Ferris wheel, there was no sight of her. Freddy asked Charlie if he had seen her, and he reminded her that he had *last week*.

"You girls need to learn to use the post," he said with a knowing smile. "Besides, I know where she lives!"

"You do?"

"Indeedy-do! Nice big house on Indian Road. Why, you could say I'm why you met her. I take full credit for your blooming affair of the heart!" Now he danced around and clutched at his breast like an old vaudeville star and Freddy laughed. He pantomimed licking the nib of a pen and wrote in mid-air, "My darling lover—"

"Hush!" she begged him and looked around.

"Ninotchka, my darling Nina, my little girl," he said in a falsetto, swooping in and tickling Freddy. "That's your Russian name."

"Oh? And why do I need one of those?"

"Everyone needs a Russian name in love letters, Ninotchka. It is all the rage *a Paris*. Don't you read novels?" He twirled again and Freddy began to see why it was that she was not afraid of Charlie. He could wrap his arm around her shoulders and tickle her and not a whisper of fear went through her. When Darius Peacock touched her, she felt nothing but fury and nausea.

"Now," he said quietly, looping his arm through hers and leading her toward the midway. "Let's talk about this problem of yours."

"My problem?"

He nodded. "That one boyfriend of yours is sweet, if a little too old for you. The other one? Pure trouble. I think I can help with the first one, but the second fella gives me the creeps. Who is he?"

"He's nobody," she replied as they made their way up the ramp to the Shoot the Chutes. "Just someone I met on the train coming to Toronto."

"He seems a bit stuck on you," Charlie said with a frown. "And I don't get the impression you like it."

"I don't," she admitted as they buckled themselves in.

"Maybe he'll get bored and start chasing your friend Bette?"

Freddy turned to Charlie as the ride surged forward with a clang and a splash. "No," she said.

"Want him all to yourself, huh?" As they careered down the first hill he screamed and drowned out Freddy's correction.

37.

It had been three quick and cruel months from diagnosis to death-bed. There was just too much to deal with, too much to do. The tumours kept appearing, they kept finding new ones, and each day was an exercise in keeping the faith when the writing was on the wall: she didn't stand a chance. And worst of all, Bianca had taken Joss's hand and told her, "I'm okay with this. You have to be too." Not even the decency to fight, Joss thought bitterly. There had been no funeral, at Bianca's request.

Now Joss was calling to ask Laura if her offer to use the apartment in New York still stood.

"When are you coming?" Laura asked, indicating she was there now. Joss tried not to feel excited. "Because I leave for East Hampton this weekend. You can have it for a week if you like, or two... I'm so sorry, Joss. I haven't stopped thinking about you since we last spoke."

She was doing a play at Guild Hall, and if Joss could wait, she could have the place for a week. Two weeks if she liked. In reality it was too small a space to share. There was one bed and the minute bathtub was in the kitchen. They weren't kids anymore. Or lovers.

"I'll FedEx you the keys," Laura promised and it was decided that Joss would come next week. She thanked her emphatically and hung up and wondered why there had been no invitation to come see the play or have dinner or even a coffee. She did not allow herself to think that it was because she was, technically, single again. Widowed, no less. Laura was still inclined to flight at the news that Joss might be available, at last. Her own thoughts shamed her. She did not miss Bianca as much as she missed Laura.

Joss hung up and called to book a flight to New York. Feeling angry but not knowing why, she took her camera and power-walked all the way to Hanlan's, to the haunted lighthouse. On the road she saw the artists from the retreat centre and gave a half-hearted wave. The clapboard wooden lodge that housed writers and painters and theatre people for sessions of work was a subject of great curiosity. It snuggled down next to a pretty little beach and was surrounded by regal stands of trees. She briefly considered seeing about a room for rent, just to escape the Ward's Island network of peering eyes and concern.

Walking, she tried to imagine this lush forest as an amusement park and could not. She remembered reading that it had once been known as "Canada's Coney Island" and smiled. There was nothing to stop her from going to Coney Island herself, now. She had looked it up, it was Diane Arbus country, and she longed to see it. In all her previous trips to New York she had never made time for it. Yes, she would do that, and quench her thirst for a roller coaster ride of historic importance. Another notch on the coaster belt. Maybe she would just travel the world, riding her way into lonesome old age? Santa Cruz, Blackpool, that monstrous high-speed contraption in Japan ... Save the biggest, fastest one for last and finish herself off on the first killing drop, age ninety?

As if to spite her, two teen girls wrestled and kissed on the grass near a baseball diamond. She quickened her pace, then slowed as she saw that the horses from the farm were out for a supervised late morning stroll. In the winter they ran loose, retired police horses with a whole new life on Toronto Island. Once, when she had stood on the sparkling, ice-crusted sand in winter, a mare had galloped right past her, brushing her sleeve. Hank had just died the day before, on Valentine's Day. One of those singular time-snaps, like first kisses, that matter only to the people they have happened to. But it had felt like a message of sorts. From whom?

Tess would be waiting back at the house. A German art magazine had called asking for archival materials for a retrospective. They would go through actual negatives and, likely, reminisce. She liked the thought of Tess letting herself into the cottage, making a cup of coffee with cinnamon. Tess, with her dolphin tattoos and ferocious blue eyes, a cleft in her chin you could lose yourself in…

"Fuck off," she told herself out loud, rushing to catch the ferry. She would ride into the city and force herself to take photos of street life. Would call Tess when cell reception allowed and apologize for forgetting their meeting.

"It's fine," Tess said. "I'm going to work on your fridge. There are lemons in here from the nineties."

Joss left the ferry with a cluster of people waving bright red and white parasols. A tour group. The city loomed beyond the exit gates. In the midst of the throng she turned and ran back to catch the Centre Island ferry. Another day, she promised herself.

Tess waited at the ferry dock, her bicycle balanced against her thigh.

"I won't even ask how you calculated the brevity of my absence," Joss said, shaking her head as they walked back toward Ward's Island.

"It was cleaning your crisper. The fumes made me psychic like the Oracle of Delphi."

"You're hilarious."

"I know." Tess stopped pushing her bike and looked at Joss. "I have to tell you now."

Joss kept walking. True to form, she moved away from any source of hurt or annoyance immediately. Tess was forced to catch up.

"I might have another job," Tess blurted, partly to make Joss slow down or stop.

Joss did stop. She held her arms out and open and welcomed a hug. "That's terrific news, Tess. I'll miss you, so much, of course—"

"It's in Paris. Editing."

"Whoa! Fantastic!"

"You're not mad?"

"No, my duck. I would never be mad about you moving on. Sad, absolutely. Gutted, in private. But let's get home and open a bottle of something to celebrate."

Tess shook her head. "We have work to do. And anyway, what the fuck is this business about going to Coney Island without me?" Joss looked startled. How would she have known?

"Relax, you left your browser open."

"It was just a silly idea," Joss said with a half-smile that immediately proved she was lying. "I thought it might inspire some shots."

"All the more reason why I should come with you."

Joss was tempted for a moment, but chased away the notion. "I think I better get used to life without you," she said, tugging Tess's shirt collar. "Besides, you don't even like rides, remember?"

"I'll stay in Toronto if you ask me to," Tess said quietly, putting her hand over Joss's.

"Don't do anything with me in mind." Joss tugged her hand out from under Tess's and made a move to keep walking.

"I do everything with you in mind."

"Don't," Joss said softly. "It's a dangerous thing to do."

"Sometimes you talk like a suicide," Tess said. "Stop it."

38.

There were four beach scenes, one with a lighthouse; one half-dozen roses of varying proportions and positions; a failed attempt at a peony. The picture of the horse was primitive but not without charm, and she'd had a great deal more success with shell pictures of shells. Her bedroom had taken on a cloggy perfume of melted wax and hot paste and there were bits of pasteboard affixed to the Turkish carpet beside her bed. In spite of the July heat, Bette worked on, producing several shell paintings each day. Yet again, her father's fetish for ordering things from mail-order companies came in extremely handy. Upon deciding that she would not return to Hanlan's Point for the remainder of summer—if ever—Bette asked her father to cease ordering phonograph recordings and instead spend that money on sea shells of all available shapes, sizes and colours. As many as they could comfortably afford to purchase. And some driftwood, if possible; she had additional plans to create ornamental frames for her creations.

The shells arrived in two large crates with a letter from The Dolphin Bay Bead and Gift Company president tucked on top of the carefully wrapped bundles inside. "I have dedicated my life to hunting the shells of all shores, Miss," wrote Mr. Linus Libby, "so that you may dedicate life to enjoying them in your parlour." *The closest I may ever get to a love letter.* The treasures had been gathered from the shores of North Carolina, Texas and Florida. They had also included an order form listing rare shells from Mexico, Brazil and exotic islands Bette had never heard of. When she had a spare moment she would consult Papa's globe.

"Are you starting a factory?" her father asked when she came down to the kitchen to make herself a restorative cup of coffee. He had helped her carry the shell crates upstairs and after seeing the rate of production, went out and purchased additional pasteboard, glue and wax. Bette smiled and cranked the hand-grinder, enjoying the dark smell of the freshly split coffee beans. Also ordered from afar. She had a mild headache from being cooped up with the paste pot. "Are you all right, Bette?" Her sudden reluctance to enjoy music was suspicious, as was her disinterest in food, outings or anything but shell pictures. He was either helping her by providing the necessary supplies or adding to the underlying problem.

"I'm fine, Papa," she said with a beatific smile. She did in fact feel a tremendous calm since coming to the conclusion that single-minded pursuit of indoor activities suited her better. The riding of roller coasters had done nothing but addle her, as had been promised. She had become too excited and too excitable.

"Your mother mentioned," her father began a little nervously, "that you had been asking about 'Boston marriages' the other day."

The coffee pot began to burble and huff steam. She looked at him blankly.

"We wondered why." He cleared his throat and watched her tend to the coffee pot. She could feel his discomfort and wondered what the source of it was. Should she bother with a biscuit, or wait to see if the coffee cleared her headache? "Bette?"

"I suppose it's when people get married in Boston," she said without emotion.

The front door knocker sounded sharply, and he gave an exasperated snort. She poured her coffee and listened as her father greeted the caller. There was a muffle of male voices, and she assumed it was the postman come again with more packages.

Her father's expression was inscrutable when he returned to the kitchen. He plucked a bit of wayward pasteboard and glue from her hair and said, "You have a guest." Again she had no idea what he was talking about. Boston marriages, unexpected guests at the door: she wanted only to enjoy her coffee in peace and get back up-stairs to her creations. She'd had a lovely inspiration for a windmill picture while the coffee percolated. Her father gave her a little push toward the front foyer of the house.

Charlie!

"What are you doing here?" she hiss-whispered. "Why are you always prowling around this neighbourhood?"

He laughed merrily. "I'm not *prowling* anywhere, *Bette*," he said, pointedly acknowledging her real given name. "I live not far from here. Sometimes I hand out advertisements for the park on my way to work. Sometimes I'm just out for a stroll like any other gentle-man on a fine summer's day. And sometimes," he reached into his jacket pocket, "I'm delivering mail." He held out a small envelope with her name written on it.

Taking it, she was flustered. "You don't live on the island?" He had just said he didn't, but she needed time to collect herself. The envelope could only be from one person. The one she had de-cided to forget, who didn't seem to care if it was Tuesday or not. The handwriting was beautiful, exquisite feminine loops and curls in thick blue ink. It was hard not to admire it, but he stood there watching her so closely. Her cheeks heated up. She knew also that her father was likely listening in from the hallway.

"Thank you," she squeaked. "Thank the sender on my behalf."

"I certainly will. Hope to see you back at Hanlan's soon, Bette! These lovely sunny days of youth are not to be wasted."

She stood in the foyer with the letter in her hand and wondered what to do. Read it there, immediately, or rush upstairs feigning some urgent matter and then return to the kitchen after hiding it in her room? She wanted to savour it, although a larger part of her dreaded its contents. Today was Tuesday. She had planned to skip her trip the island. Perhaps Freddy had had some good reason why she'd missed meeting the previous Tuesday.

The light in the foyer was too dim. She went out onto the porch into the hot sunshine and closed the front door behind her. Her father would come looking for her any minute, wondering who her visitor had been, why she had not returned to the kitchen. Her hands shook as she tore the envelope open, careful not to rip through the artful scripting of her name.

Dear Bette,
I hope you are not ill. I could not meet you last week. There was an emergency. Come back! The summer goes by so quickly. Charlie said he would remember where you live. There are not many people to trust in this world, but he is one, and he knows how very much I care for you, Bette. More than you know. I will wait for you beside the ride, as usual, every chance I get, afternoons, till I see you again. Come away with me. If you say yes, our lives will never be the same. If you say no, the same will be true.

Always yours,
Fredelle Montgomery

She sat on the front steps of the house she would leave soon. The warm breeze buffeted her cheeks, and she imagined Freddy across the lake waiting for news from Charlie. Had he delivered the letter? Had she read it, was there a message back? Bette wished she had read it in front of Charlie and sent a note back, quickly, to re-assure her. Upstairs her room was a jumble of shells and half-completed pictures and mess. She would go in and tidy everything, find some way to conclude the conversation with her father in a natural way. Unless of course the Fates smiled, and he had gone back to work in his study, scribbling in one of his many notebooks, taking dictation from the underworld and the Oversoul and all his other channels. She shouldn't laugh at what gave him comfort. No, if she wanted life to go well and happily she would have to learn to be more pleasant and definitely more courageous.

"Your friend has found a messenger," her father said when she came back inside. Bette blushed furiously. She longed to race upstairs and be alone in her room. "It's beautiful to see you happy, daughter. I could die right now and be peaceful."

She looked at him with sudden scorn. His peculiar, always tender remarks! "Well, don't!" she shouted before stomping back to the suddenly unsatisfactory solace of her shells. She would go at once, and never mind the mess in her room.

39.

It was a shock to see her coming down the Figure 8 ramp by herself. She had her cap in hand, and her eyes blazed with all the pleasure Bette had come to associate with the ride. For some reason Bette had never imagined Freddy riding without her. Ridiculous, of course, because she had been riding it well before she ever knew Bette and anyway, she lived out there, what else was she supposed to do for fun? But the sight of her bouncing along in solitary delight was jarring.

"Bette!" she cried out when she spotted her friend. Her surprise was genuine. Her rambunctious attitude did not seem in line with the worried tenderness in her letter, but Bette was beginning to see that Freddy had an outer shell she relied on most of the time. They embraced and walked with arms entwined all the way to the secret beach.

"I thought maybe you and your family had gone on holiday. I didn't expect to see you," Freddy said as they removed their shoes and stockings, hoisted their skirts and waded into the lake. It was a blistering day. Children screamed and splashed nearby. The midway noise was magnified by the humidity, and Bette wondered how she could ever have imagined doing without the blare and whine of it all.

"But your letter—" Bette said.

Freddy looked uncomfortable, and Bette decided very quickly to chase the moment away and replace it with something lighter.

"How are your plans coming along?" she asked instead. *Why weren't you here that Tuesday when I came?*

"Let's go back to shore and let me tell you," Freddy said, squeezing her hand. And there it was again, that drowning sensation. Or was Bette being swallowed? It was far too hot. She suddenly envied fish their cool world and stumbled, nearly falling into the lake. Her skirt was already floating on the water's surface anyway, she might as well just plunge … But Freddy had her firmly by the elbow, steering her now to the beach, looking concerned. "Have you eaten today? You look thin. Have you been ill?"

Bette waved off the suggestion, and they went to a log in the shade of the willow. There might have been no one else in the world except for the clunk-clunk of shoes and boots on the boardwalk up the dune. She did feel terribly nervous, and her throat was so thick she found it hard to swallow. Freddy continued to direct Bette along, making her sit with her back against the log, legs outstretched on the sand. She then sat on the log behind Bette, side-saddle, her thigh pressed against Bette's shoulder blades. She rested her hands on Bette's shoulders. "Close your eyes," she murmured in her ear. "I'm going to take you to Coney Island."

Bette leaned happily back. Freddy, often a girl of fewer words, now spoke in a confident, sweet torrent of images and adventures all made possible by the simple choice of Coney Island as a destination and location for the best possible life on earth. Cousin Lorna was not mentioned, which was secretly pleasing. The caper starred only Freddy's voice and the grounds of Luna Park, where at night the streets and buildings and rides were awash in electric lights, thousands of them. There'd be no need to travel the world if one lived and worked there because all of the world's architecture had come to Luna Park, all the towers and bridges and lagoons you saw in picture books. Minarets like those in *Arabian Nights*. Castles with moats, huts shaped like onions and cakes. There was a place called Dreamland, too, but the only thing she knew about it was that it had a boat ride ominously called Hell Gate. There had even been a hotel built in the shape of an elephant somewhere at Coney Island, but it burned down. Freddy supposed firemen set half the fires to keep themselves busy. This was a rather audacious theory, but Bette let it slide by. Rides? More rides than you ever imagined being in one place, there was nothing else in Coney Island but rides, mile after mile of them, and the ocean right there nudged up beside it all. Shoot the Chutes soared high over a lagoon and camels walked the boulevards. It was all named after a ride that could make you feel like you were off to the moon, just like in the movie they saw! And if you got hungry— and you would of course, with all that ocean air blowing and miles of rides—there was every kind of restaurant. Fish and oysters and German fried potatoes. There was hot bread and cold beer, the latter of which they wouldn't drink too much of, being sensible.

At first, it might be necessary to do the same sort of work Freddy did at Hanlan's Point, but not for long, she insisted. There were wealthy people crawling all over Luna Park and Dreamland; she knew this from Lorna (it wouldn't be possible to leave her out of the story entirely—after all, she was making it possible!) and you didn't want to get stuck selling sour pickles or bratwurst sandwiches behind some counter for too long. Only boys got to become oyster shuckers, but that wasn't going to stop Freddy, although the bigger plan was to sing and dance and get noticed and after that, who knew where a person might end up.

"I can't sing," Bette admitted, her eyes still closed. She wished they could be there right now, this July.

"Can you dance?" Freddy tickled her earlobes. "Shuffle your feet?"

Bette laughed, still squeezing her eyes shut tight. She didn't want to open them and remember they were facing Lake O, not the ocean. Hanlan's had been paradise enough until she heard about Coney Island.

Freddy leaned close and sang into Bette's ear: *"We'll take a trip up to the moon/For that is the place for a lark/So meet me down at Luna, Lena/Down at Luna Park."*

Her voice was so rich and steady she could easily have been a recording star, and Bette's eyes flew open. She tilted her head back and sideways to get a better look at her astounding friend who may have been a taffy and ticket seller but had so much magic in her throat she simply had to go to Coney Island or wherever you needed to go to become a singer on a phonograph recording.

"Where's that song from?" Bette asked, scrambling up to sit beside Freddy on the log.

"It's a fellow called Billy—"

"MURRAY!" Bette shrieked, cutting Freddy off. "I have a dozen Ada Jones and Billy Murray records at home!" She could hardly contain her thrill at that moment. Her love. Her amazement. How could she have sulked for a week and nearly missed another Tuesday with this divine girl?

"Let's go ride the Figure 8," Freddy suggested. It seemed so unnecessary to Bette now that she was surprised. It must surely pale compared to the rides at Coney Island and besides, they should sit and make detailed plans. Freddy was obviously destined to sing. How many other songs did she know? Bette wondered. She begged Freddy to sing something else. "Maybe later," Freddy said, stroking Bette's hand. But before she could pull her hand away Bette grabbed it.

"I'm coming with you," Bette said, looking straight into Freddy's lake-blue gaze. "You shouldn't go alone, not anywhere ever again, without me." Freddy's eyes glistened. "I know I can't sing and I might have to work behind a counter, but I'd be happy to learn how. And I do paintings, pictures made of seashells, and people might buy them. My grandmother always said people would. I'll pay my way and yours too, and your cousin and I will get along just fine, I know it. Please ask me again to come with you."

In Freddy's eyes there was a flicker of something. It looked like pain, but if she felt like she was drowning too, or tumbling, she might be that same mix of happy and scared and shocked at how life could shift right under your feet from one day to the next. In the main, it was wonderful.

"Ask me again." She was thinking of the letter. Of the flicker in the movie house, bathing them in light. Billy Murray singing about Luna Park, it was going to be their song for the rest of time.

"Come with me," Freddy said finally. It was almost a question. She looked down at Bette's two hands holding her one. She looked up, met Bette's insistent gaze and added a smile. They touched their foreheads together as if sealing the pact. Freddy closed her eyes but Bette kept hers wide open, looking at their hands together. Like the Figure 8's first hill the feeling was a bit too much, but she liked it and could not talk herself out of it ever again.

"Ferris wheel!" Freddy said suddenly and broke away, running up the dune path.

When they were up so very high, overlooking the whole park and the lake and sky, the car swinging gently in the breeze, Bette thought all the things she could not say. I wish I could stay here all day every day, sleep every night at the Hotel Hanlan. The wheel whooshed downward and paused, and the swaying of the car intensified, a little too much like spinning, though different. Where will we live, how will we get there, promise me you won't get married, I love you, oh I love you more than anyone in the world. Freddy also seemed lost in thought. Was she dreaming of all the things she had described, re-imagining it all with Bette there beside her? Telling of Luna Park, she had taken on its voltage, and ever so faintly her Scots heritage had lilted in as she grew more excited, though when she sang she sounded American. Now she was silent, hands perched lightly on the crossbar. A long pale purple sugar burn snaked down the pinky finger of her left hand: Bette had never noticed it.

Back on the ground she resented the crowds. Let's go back to the secret beach and sit on the log and plan the when and the how of it. To go to a seaside paradise when the summer was nearly over seemed a strange choice, but they could settle in and spend the winter working at some job or other. Lorna would know where positions could be found, and it sounded as though a place to live was the easy part. And then to be there for the very start of a fresh summer. Everything could be decided later. She sensed that Freddy preferred to focus on the sweeter aspects when she spoke of it, not the silly details. Bette did not feel like sharing Freddy with the bumping, boisterous crowds just then and she was hungry. There had been nothing to make sandwiches with, and she hoped Freddy was not too disappointed. The Ferris wheel had made them both a little wobbly on their feet, and they held each other up for a dizzy moment at the exit.

Freddy tucked her hair up under her cap as always. As she did so, she said, "I want you to remember this, and repeat it all the way home to yourself, and every night at bedtime till we go," she waited for Bette to nod in agreement. "Repeat after me: Coney Island, is in the borough of Brooklyn, is in New York City, in New York State, in the USA. Amen."

Bette dutifully repeated it all.

"I should probably be off," Freddy said, glancing down the promenade. "I have to work a little bit earlier in the afternoons now, it's so busy this time of year."

Bette hated the thought of goodbye but she understood. Freddy rummaged in a pocket of her skirt and pulled out two red tickets. She held them out. "Here now, ride the Figure 8 before you go back. Once for you, and once for me." Bette protested but Freddy pushed them at her. "I have to go. I'll see you next Tuesday!" She leaned in and gave Bette a quick kiss on the cheek and hurried off, waving before she turned to run full-speed down the wooden walkway.

Riding the roller coaster without Freddy would not be the same; she knew she couldn't. She would save the tickets. Another day, when they could ride together. And then soon they'd have every day together and no more saying goodbye and mooning over phonographs and shell pictures in the long days between visits.

Coney Island

is in the borough of Brooklyn

is in New York City, in New York State, in the USA.

Amen.

When?

40.

He ran his plump fingers across her lap as she rowed, and Freddy fought hard not to spit. On shore, his old maid aunt waited for them. Freddy had seen the plain disapproval in the woman's watery blue eyes. She was nothing more than a common working girl, and Darius Peacock's passion for her was questionable. Everyone but Darius seemed to recognize this, and because Freddy cared only for the five hundred dollars, she was not offended by the old woman's quiet but obvious assessment of her character and prospects.

"I hope the rumours of another suitor are false," Darius said. "I think I have secured the right to non-competition."

"There's no one else," she said, letting the oars nestle into their locks.

"And no one hears your secrets but me," he purred. "Tell me what's in your heart, honeybun."

Freddy had to pull from all that she had learned at the pictures. It irked her to play coy, but she knew from watching pictures and girls at the park that it worked a charm. She wondered a little at his desperation where she was concerned. Surely a wife could be had in his own circle? He wasn't *awful*...

"I need a new dress for when I come to the city," she said with as much sorrow as she could manage. "I've been too ashamed to ask for the money you promised. And your aunt doesn't like me one bit. She thinks I'm beneath you...these tawdry clothes of mine don't help my cause."

Darius smiled broadly and patted her knees. "I've come prepared. I have half your dowry here today," he smacked his breast pocket, "and you will most assuredly have the other half on our wedding day. How about a kiss?"

On their wedding day? Freddy felt like smacking him across the head with an oar. Instead, she leaned in and closed her eyes, steeling herself. As his plush lips touched down on hers she willed herself to think of Mary Pickford, and though it was close to impossible—he had eaten a fried salami sandwich for his lunch—she made it through. His little flourish of tongue at the end notwithstanding, she had survived much worse.

Without a moment's pause, he pulled a narrow Bible from his interior breast pocket and handed it to her. "That's a lot of dresses in there," he grinned. "And don't trouble over Aunt Bonnie's opinions. She has no eye for beauty and thinks I should remain a bachelor." He dangled one hand sensuously in the lake as she rowed. "Do you think I might come with you dress shopping? I know a wonderful seamstress. She's married to my haberdasher. "

"Perhaps once *we're* married," Freddy said, rowing harder to shift the boat in the direction of shore. She glanced now and then at the red leather Bible in her lap. Two hundred and fifty dollars and not a penny of it would be spent on a dress if she had her way. "Till then I think I should remain a bit of a mystery to you."

"Coy mistress," he said with a smile. "We'll soon crush that habit out of you. Soon I'll know everything there is to know."

41.

She and Tess were sorting more negatives for digitization and playing a scruples game, and it felt good to be amused again. And sober. The mood between them had lightened. She would miss her terribly when she went off to Paris, but it was for the best. Wasn't it? For now they pummelled each other with half-sincere questions as they sifted through contact sheets and negatives.

What's more useful: love or money?

What if Edie Falco said she would grant you three sexy wishes?

What would your death-row meal be and why?

Say I offer you one thousand dollars cash: kiss my cousin?

Which one?

The waves of guilt after the bursts of laughter were lightening a little. She found herself smiling at worthy things and chuckling at corny jokes. Less aggravated by small talk, she could function in polite society again. The real problem was not that she couldn't live without Bianca—she would have to—but that theirs had been known as The Perfect Relationship to everyone around them. The looks of pure pity were hard to handle. How was she surviving, their eyes seemed to ask. When others broke up, they had turned to Joss and Bianca for the secret recipe for reconciliation. Nervous youngsters clutched hands on first anniversaries and asked how they made it work, not wanting the real answer. To give advice would have cast her as some premature yenta, and after all, they had only just survived the seven-year itch. By taking courses, learning a new language, taking a vacation…the way you'd handle any sort of death.

"…New York?" Tess was saying something.

Joss looked up from a contact sheet of photos she had taken

when Tess first became her assistant. "Pictures of you," she smiled, holding up the sheet. She had looked like the most beautiful boy in the world when she first walked through the studio door. People never believed that Joss didn't want to bed her beautiful assistant. That she hadn't at first opportunity. The twenty year age difference helped, she would remind them. The day Tess announced she had discovered a band called The Smiths in the vintage bin at the music store…

"I asked if you'd let me come with you to New York."

"This time…no." Joss tried to meet Tess's disappointed gaze. "When do you leave for Paris?"

"It doesn't matter," Tess sighed.

"Don't sulk, it gives you wrinkles," Joss teased. "I'm sorry. Can I think about it?"

"You're leaving tomorrow," Tess pointed out.

"I am?"

"Honestly…what will you do without me?"

Joss fought off a thought. "I have no idea. Maybe I'll just go to New York and stay there, and you can come meet me and have a full time career and keep me sorted."

"We'd build a little bungalow, if you and I were one,'" Tess sang out. When Joss looked at her for further confirmation, she added, "Dorothy Parker."

These were dangerous moments. When Tess, two decades younger, would cross into a kingdom where age mattered not a whit. She quoted Dorothy Parker and hummed Count Basie horn solos and generally carried herself like a creature out of time. Caught between dimensions in these interludes, a true steampunk. Other times, she was all youth and au courant arrogance. And it was all desirable, yet easy to resist on some level, because crossing into another realm, that of May-December, was not in Joss's plans.

"Movie break?" Tess asked, tossing aside a new folder of negs.

"If you make the chili popcorn, yes," Joss agreed, moving swiftly toward the cabinet where Bianca had alphabetized their sizeable DVD collection. She held up *The Way We Were* and Tess rolled her eyes.

"I'm more in the mood for *Sid and Nancy* right about now, but if you insist."

Joss knew *The Way We Were* by heart, and Bianca had once caught her mouthing the words to every scene.

"I don't know why you love that movie so much," Bianca had said, rather primly. "It's not a happy ending."

"I like how it ends," Tess called from the kitchen, yelling over the popcorn maker.

42.

She should not have taken the household grocery money and stayed overnight at the Hotel Hanlan, told the front desk clerk there that she was visiting her cousin, an aspiring rowing champion, which explained why she was travelling alone, which young ladies did not do without raising suspicions. She had come from Attica. Which part? The old money part, of course. The clerk sighed and suppressed a smile. The hotel was crowded for a Tuesday, and she nearly didn't get a room, but in the end a red-faced man in a hurry checked out early just as she was pleading her case. Oh, magic. It had seemed like a good way to practice derring-do and, to be fair, her parents had gone off to one of their occult conferences so what would be the harm being absent from an empty house? That was the logic that propelled her decision in any case, but things went poorly right after they went so wonderfully well. Had her sister not decided to waddle—in the heat—from her house to theirs to borrow some cinnamon—Bette would never like cinnamon again— the whole caper would have been a beautiful summer secret.

The missing grocery money was the least worrisome part of the scenario since money was forever going missing in the household. Ghosts, grandmothers who drank sherry, fathers who were fond of candy, and so on. Margaret, with her sudden, loathsome third-trimester urge to bake when she had never been fond of any kitchen had spoiled it all and tattled on top. Bette was not home in the evening and worse, she was not home in the morning when Margaret returned to inquire about her evening truancy. And in spite of being on the verge of childbirth, she had waited in the Titus family parlour, one eye on the balloon clock on the mantle, more deeply incensed by each fresh round of chimes. So that by the time Bette strolled in grinning, unrepentant even when caught, Margaret sported a very unattractive purple vein on her forehead.

"I was at Hanlan's Point," Bette said plainly. It was true and she saw no reason to deny it. Convincing Margaret not to report it to higher authorities (those named Irving and Felicia) would require more effort. "I was with my friend who works at the amusement park and decided to stay rather than risk the trip home after dark." There. Safety was always a concern. Morals, prudence, safety, all had value with Margaret.

"With that boy you rode the roller contraption with? Or someone *else*?" Margaret's fury remained stoked. It did not help in the least when Bette laughed. "I hope you know that you will be coming to live with me when the baby is born, Elizabeth. It's been the family plan all along. You will not disgrace this family or the Clackums either!" The thought of a disgraced Clackum sounded appealing (if uncomfortable) but Bette knew she had to gain control of her urge to fall on the floor laughing.

"That wasn't a *boy*," Bette said softly. "That was—is—Fredelle, a lovely girl of Scottish descent, eighteen years of age, a hard worker and a good friend to me since the day we met. A meeting you witnessed, to a degree."

Margaret was briefly stumped and said nothing. The mantle clock chimed and startled them both in the quiet. "What sort of a name is Fredelle?" she finally sneered. "Where did you sleep? Not in some ratty tent I hope, out of doors? I can't have you coming down with something when I most need your help, Bette."

"Let me walk you back to your house," Bette offered. "I will tell you all about it on the way."

Well, not all *about it.*

The version Margaret heard took two blocks and the boiling of a kettle. Rode rides, saw motion pictures, walked by the lake, good supper, early to bed in a clean lakeside cottage, farewell and see you another day. Margaret had never liked detailed stories anyway. It might not have been wise to add that she had no intentions of ever giving up her love for Freddy. Margaret liked vows to be stated inside churches only.

As soon as she stepped through the front doors of the Hotel Hanlan, Bette had felt the exaltation she imagined some people felt in cathedrals. She had no other hotel stays to compare it to, but it hardly mattered. Dressed in her best bustle and her favourite hat with its cascade of cornflower blue ribbons and one silk peony fastened to the brim, she felt she belonged there amongst the neatly stacked suitcases and highly polished dark wood floors. A man in a dark suit sat reading the *New York Times* in a luxurious leather wingback chair, smoking a cigarette in a holder. There was an elegance and serenity in the lobby that her home did not possess. And although her heart did not stop thudding until she had secured the room and paid for it and been lead to it by a bell-hop, it was excitement, more than fear, that made it pound so.

A crisply made bed, a washstand, a delicate oriental carpet, everything was in its place including a pen and a fresh bottle of ink on a beautiful writing table in the sitting area near the windows. She crossed the room to take in the view and caught her breath: they had given her a room facing the lagoon where regatta competitors rowed in hopes of recreating Ned Hanlan's glory. A lone man rowed up and down just then, as if to support the fable she'd spun for the desk clerk.

"Hello, Cousin," she whispered. What with the lie she'd spun involving the working boy Bill and his married aunt who also lived on the island, she was building quite an imaginary family for herself out here.

She ran her hand across the sleek bedcovers and marvelled at every detail. It was well before noon. She had come over on the

Bluebell very early, as soon as was possible. Had she not managed to book herself into a room, it wouldn't have mattered too much, but she was ecstatic over her success and looked forward to inviting Freddy up for tea and a look at the lagoon from a new vantage point.

It was disappointing to learn that Freddy would not be able to venture up to her room at the Hotel Hanlan. An employee of the midway, she was not permitted to visit guests or spend any time in the guest areas of the hotel or restaurant or at the dance pavilions. The rule seemed unfair to Bette, but Freddy was cheerfully accepting.

"I'll be welcomed anyplace I fancy in Coney Island." She was impressed by Bette's nerviness but less so by her extravagance. "You're impulsive," she noted as they walked along together. Bette winced slightly at the critical tone in her friend's voice but said nothing. "But you're here all day and night, which is lovely," Freddy added.

"Gives you a chance to see how quickly you tire of me," Bette quipped.

"Don't," Freddy said. She seemed keen to change the subject. There was a special program of brand new motion pictures at the theatre later that afternoon. Since Bette would be staying overnight, they could see the films then Bette could have supper and meet Freddy after she finished selling tickets for the evening program. A Canadian girl named Mary Pickford was in two of the films on the card, which they both agreed was proof that even girls from Toronto could make something of themselves. "She is the same age as *you*," Freddy pointed out.

"Let's go on a ride we haven't been on yet," Bette suggested.

"I'm not feeling so grand today," Freddy admitted. "Can we just ride the Royal Gorge? I'm not up for much."

Bette realized then she'd left the tickets for the Figure 8 at home anyway. On her dressing table, out in full view. It hardly mattered, since no one was home, but she was surprised at herself for forgetting when it was all she'd had on her mind for days.

Emerging from the scenic railway, they were surrounded by a bunch of rowdy lacrosse players. Though the boys whistled and hooted, Freddy seemed unflappable. She looped her arm in Bette's and pushed along till they grew bored and fell away to bother someone else. "There's a lot rougher types to contend with in Coney," she said darkly. "Lorna told me in a letter all about the Irish and the Italians, chasing her up and down the streets on her way home from working all day." Was she testing Bette? It was hard to tell. "Some of them think nothing of grabbing you right there in the daylight." They were nearing the theatre. Bette wished they could talk of something else, but Freddy was in a darker mood after the lacrosse boys. She surprised Bette by grabbing her by the arms and shaking her a little. "You'll have to be prepared to face these types, Bette," she said in an almost-growl. She glanced around and pulled Bette behind the Gem Theatre and continued to play the part of a menacing boy. "What'll you do, Bette, if someone grabs you? Like this?" She held Bette's hands tightly and pushed her about a little. It wasn't funny and she told Freddy so. But then Freddy smiled and returned to herself, not the faintest trace of villainy in her eyes although it had just been all over her face and in her movements.

"*You* should be in motion pictures," Bette said, laughing nervously.

"Should I? I thought you said I should be a singer?" Freddy still had hold of her hands, although gently now. Bette's heart began to squeeze as it had at the front desk of the hotel. Scared. Excited. Scared. Happy. Freddy was close enough that Bette could smell peppermint on her breath. A long moment passed. What should happen? Bette wondered. It felt like something might. Freddy was looking at her hard. Her eyes, whatever lit them now, made it hard to speak. But then she dropped Bette's hands and stepped back.

"Yes, you can handle yourself all right," she said. "Let's go before we miss the first picture."

In the dark of the theatre, watching Mary Pickford in *The Little Darling*, Bette pondered what had almost happened between them. Would such a moment happen again, and did she want it to or not? Freddy sat beside her, contentedly sucking on a fresh peppermint, beguiled by the action on the screen. A short picture called *Those Awful Hats* had everyone in the audience roaring with the laughter of recognition, and a few self-conscious women shyly removed their view-obstructing hats as the reel concluded. Bette should have enjoyed it more than she did, considering her antipathy for her brother-in-law and hats, but she had trouble concentrating. She sat through several more pictures and was relieved when they burst from the dark auditorium into the nearly blinding sunshine.

"I wish you could have supper with me," she said.

Freddy was in a peculiar mood. She didn't seem to be eager to chat, and Bette felt overcome with melancholy. Was it too late to go back to the hotel and collect her empty travel case and get her money back and go home? She could hardly bear the thought of sleeping all night on the island with her chum in such a bleak frame of mind. It wasn't at all how she'd envisioned the day or the evening. Supper alone wasn't appealing anyway.

They came to the saltwater taffy booth where Freddy knew the girl behind the counter. They exchanged a few friendly words about the crowds and the day and then the girl handed Freddy a paper bag. "Let's sit," she said to Bette, gesturing at a wooden bench facing the lake. She opened the paper sack and pulled out a candy-coated apple, the reddest red Bette had ever seen. "For you," Freddy said, smiling again. Would she ever be in the same mood for more than an hour at a time?

The candy was so sweet it made Bette's cheeks hurt but it was still slightly warm, too. She licked and stared out at the waves and from the corner of her eye saw Freddy chewing at her thumbnail. Nervous. Why?

"Did you ever want to say something, but it just wasn't possible to say it, Bette?" she asked, keeping her own eyes on the water. The sun moved into its less fiery afternoon position.

"I usually say what comes to mind, much to the disappointment of my family."

Freddy chuckled. "That must be a nice way to be." She stopped chewing her nail. "Maybe you could set me a fine example." Bette turned to her and they smiled at each other. The ease was back. Whatever had happened behind the theatre was gone.

"Say what you'd like to say," Bette coaxed. "I'm not going anywhere, no matter what you tell me."

"If only you meant that," Freddy said. She held up her hand before Bette could argue. "People say things like that, but they don't mean it, and then everyone's unhappy. Let's keep everything the way it is."

Bette sank her teeth into the softened candy shell on the apple. The combination of sweet and sour made her squint. It was good but it was unexpected, something to get used to and then crave constantly, like violet candies and salt licorice. When she finished melting it on her tongue and swallowed, she turned to Freddy. "If I were a boy, I'd kiss you," she said. There. She hadn't meant to say it, nor had she really thought it as words in her mind, but there it hung between them: the truth. She took another bite of candy apple and turned back to watching the water. Apparently Freddy had nothing to say back and it was an agonizing interlude. For the first time in her life, Bette Titus regretted being candid.

Finally, Freddy cleared her throat. "I have to go to work at the box office." Bette's heart resumed a sad tattoo of regret. She regretted having a room at the Hotel Hanlan. Her words. Everything except the pure pleasure of sour apple and sweet candy in her mouth as consolation. Freddy would go to work, and Bette could either leave the island, having wasted good money on a room she no longer wanted, a room her friend could not even visit because of stupid rules, or she could stay and suffer. Freddy stood up and yet she lingered. Bette wished she would just hurry and go, all their upcoming plans for Coney Island likely spoiled by a foolish confession she hadn't even known she wanted to make. Oh.

"Will you come meet me at the Gem at eight o'clock?" Freddy asked in a small voice.

"Yes," Bette replied. Relief rushed through her from head to heel.

"Eat supper," Freddy reminded. "Promise?" Bette nodded. "My friend Arthur works at the hotel restaurant. Make sure you sit in his part of the dining room. You can request it. He's lovely and old, with enormous ears, you can't miss him. And Bette?"

"Yes?" Oh, no, here it comes…

Freddy reached out and ran her thumb across Bette's chin beneath her lower lip, showed her the red smear of melted candy and then licked her thumb. "You might want to wash your face before supper." She grinned, and there was that dimple, and everything was restored. Again.

When Freddy had gone, Bette exhaled. Her thoughts racing, she went to the ticket booth and bought two tickets for the Figure 8 and marched up the ramp. She hoped it was terrifying and fast and that riding it could calm the giddiness she felt. The line moved swiftly as it was just before supper time. Like an expert she removed her hat, handed it to the ride attendant and climbed into the cart. She waited, dreading the intrusion of some stranger intent on riding, too. Was shocked when the operator shouted, "All arms in, all clear!" and the ride shot forward, the seat beside her empty. As she passed his platform, the operator looked down at Bette and winked.

Behind the Gem Theatre, Bette and Freddy swapped dresses in the dim light. Freddy looked wonderful in Bette's fancy dress hat, and Bette would show her *how* wonderful when they arrived in her room at the hotel. The plan to smuggle Freddy into her room had been hatched in her mind over supper. It was simply unacceptable to Bette that she could not share the luxurious thrill of her room with someone she cared for so much. Bending the rules, they strolled through the lobby. Nodded to the evening clerk as they passed and once out of view and earshot, giggled uncontrollably. Bette's hat was so enormous that it hid most of Freddy's face when she tipped her head at a certain angle. By the time they reached Bette's small suite, Freddy's neck was good and stiff, but they had made it upstairs.

"My," was all Freddy could manage. Someone had come in and lit the lamp on the writing table.

"We'll have a place as nice as this in Coney Island," said Bette. She turned Freddy to face the looking glass on the bureau so she could see herself, her beauty. If only there had been a way to capture her expression in a photograph. It was as if she had never seen herself. After a moment Freddy asked for assistance removing the hat. Clackum hatpins could easily have doubled as weapons, she observed, so long and deadly sharp. What a thought!

"Come see the view!" Bette took Freddy by the hand and pulled her toward the window overlooking the lagoon. The moon, although not full, lit the ripples on the water. Inspired, Bette pushed the chairs from the sitting area toward the window.

"We have to trade our clothes back," Freddy reminded her as she sat down. Bette turned off the desk lamp and let the moon and a lamppost in the courtyard be the only light in the room.

"Shhh! Let's just look at the water awhile. Pretend it's the ocean." They sat in silence for a few moments. There was laughter in the corridor as some people passed by on the way to their room.

A man laughed and said, "Just you wait!" and a woman tittered. Bette and Freddy looked at each other and smothered giggles.

"Why do you want to come with me to Coney Island?" Freddy asked when they had sobered. "It seems you have a nice life right here."

"I want adventure. With you." Bette remembered her earlier outburst about wanting to kiss Freddy and decided to be more guarded. Another round of awkwardness would be unbearable. The room was too pretty and the night too fine. Blunt honesty could ruin things, she was learning. "Why do you want to go to Coney Island?"

Freddy shrugged. "It's where they built America's first *real* roller coaster."

"And?"

"It's far away. It's what I've been trying to tell you, Bette. I need to get away." She had the frightened look Bette had seen when she first met her. The glancing-about nervous look of someone worried about something—or someone. "I can't tell you much. It's an awful story, and I won't say it aloud ever in my life."

"I think I know, Freddy. Is it something you'll ever be able to forget, once we're far away?" She was worried and took her hand. It was damp. "I need you, Freddy. Like nothing else in my life before. I don't care what you've done."

"You say you wish you were a boy," Freddy whispered. "I'm glad you're not." She stared out the window, her jaw set firm as if whatever was on her mind made her angry. "I have to go back to my cottage. We can't have this. Let's change clothes. Your room is lovely, Bette. It's nice to be here with you, but I have to get back. The other employees notice everything. That's another thing I won't miss!"

It would be a relief to dispense with the constant need to say goodbye. Bette switched the desk lamp back on and quickly scribbled something on a piece of hotel writing paper, folded it and set it on the table. They helped each other out of their dresses and slipped back into their rightful outfits. All cheerful business. Bette decided that Freddy should keep the hat on to camouflage her face till she was safely out of the hotel. It didn't really match what Freddy wore, but it didn't matter. "I can't go back with it on," Freddy protested.

"Throw it in the lake," Bette said matter-of-factly. Freddy frowned. "Leave it on a bench, then. I really don't mind. Here," she took the note from the desk. "You wrote me a note, and I've written one to you. Read it tomorrow and tell me what you think next Tuesday, all right?" Freddy grinned. She liked it when Bette was cheeky and mysterious. She nodded and slipped the note in her dress pocket.

"What will you do tomorrow morning?" Freddy asked as she stood at the door.

"Besides think of you?" It slipped out. She scolded herself inwardly. "I'll likely ride the Figure 8 a time or two. Once for me and once for you."

"You should write poetry while I'm up on stage singing," Freddy teased. "I won't see you before you go back to the city, but next Tuesday, same place as always."

In her pocket the note Bette had written said *Please kiss me.* They stood at the door pretending to admire the pretty room from a new angle. Bette reached out to caress Freddy's cheek and the girl flinched, jumping back a little. Her eyes were wide with fear, but when she saw that Bette's hand had moved with gentleness she clasped it to her face. "Sorry," she murmured. She closed her eyes, embarrassed. *I want to. I can't chance it.*

"It's late," Bette said, breaking the lull.

"Next Tuesday, then," Freddy said brightly.

One day I'll buy you a dress to match that hat, Bette thought as she watched Freddy make her way down the hotel corridor to the tiny elevator. She heard the iron gate squeak open, then shut, then the grinding sound of the cables easing the suspended box down a floor at a time. Someone must be getting on at the floor below; Bette stood listening in the hall. At the far end of the corridor there was a door that led to the staircase. She heard the frantic sound of someone running in boots. Now Freddy appeared in the staircase doorway, headed down the carpet back toward Bette as if someone was chasing her. What had she forgotten?

"Hurry!" she said, pushing Bette back into her room. She closed the door and bent back the brim of her massive borrowed hat with one hand, took Bette's chin in the other and brought her lips to Bette's lips, full on. As if she had any idea at all how to go about it, which she seemed to. Maybe from watching motion pictures? And to Bette's complete astonishment, she too knew what to do and did it, kissing back as if one of them not being a boy hardly mattered, at least not just then.

"Let's lie down and spoon," Bette whispered in Freddy's ear. She had never expected the night to take this turn. It was just about as thrilling as the first ride on the Figure 8, only it was just the two of them now. Everything made such sense. Freddy took her hands and led her to the big bed. They both paused to remove their boots, and then clambered up on the bedspread, stretched out and, to Bette's complete if fear-filled delight, continued kissing.

Not being a religious person, Bette did not fear going to hell as they kissed and caressed. But she did feel as if someone had opened a giant door and pushed her through it, slamming it behind her. If she never emerged from that room at the Hotel Hanlan again it would be fine with Bette. Had she all the money in the world they would just stay there, kissing and hugging and spooning and holding each other tight till the sun came up and went back down again. Nothing she had ever known felt this wonderful. Freddy was nervous too, her hands shaking as she pulled ribbons from Bette's hair.

"I want to see it flowing around your shoulders," she said, tugging it free. "I want to touch you."

Would they live like this in Coney Island, Bette wondered? In a beautiful room with a window overlooking the ocean—Freddy said it was right on the ocean—holding each other every single night after a full day of rides and adventure? It seemed impossible to imagine. It seemed perfectly possible. Her head was as discombobulated as if she had been on a spinning ride.

"I never want you to leave," Bette whispered. "You're everything I need."

"I have to. Norma will notice if I'm not in my bed. And I'm not who you think."

"Just stay till right before the sun comes up."

"I could get in all kinds of trouble…" Freddy could see she was losing the "battle." She curled up tight against Bette and murmured, "If you insist."

"I do," Bette replied, still reveling in the mixture of complete calm and wild panic in her belly. "I do insist. Always will. Touch me again…"

43.

Those passionate kisses gave Freddy kick, and she stamped around the island with a smile on her face that made everyone, Norma included, suspicious. It was too soon in the season to be a smile prompted by summer's end. And anyway, nobody working on the midway really wanted the summer to end unless they had another sweet deal on the horizon. Maybe she did, Charlie suggested, trying to pin down the source of her joy. Could a mere kiss elicit such delight and determination? But it wasn't just one kiss, and it was also the promise of more such kisses, and touches, stolen far away from here, that put the swagger in her gait. But could she trust completely in a life based on kisses? Were there other people living such lives?

His note, delivered by post, was brief and to the point. *I see what you are up to, plotting. You will marry me—or no one. Come to the C hotel Saturday, or I will go and see your little friend and, she might not care for you so much by the time I'm done with her.*

Freddy waited till Norma went out to do her show on the midway, then took out the dented tin peppermints box where she kept her money. In addition to the two hundred and fifty dollars given to her by Darius Peacock, she had painstakingly saved one hundred and seven singles. It occurred to her that it would be easier to just leave on her own, with less money, and send Bette a letter from the USA. A letter saying what? Come meet me, or I'm sorry for changing plans? One thing was obvious: she could not risk Bette's safety. Was it even safe for her sweetheart to venture out to the island on her own? He was clearly watching them, or had someone else on the job. But who? No one liked him enough to become an accomplice, she reassured herself.

Don't come back to Hanlan's, she wrote, her hands shaking. Then crumpled up the note. There was no way to explain the danger of returning alone to Bette. He might snatch her on the ferry over, or worse, at the dock before she ever came across. Or lure her elsewhere, pretending he had a legitimate visit with Freddy all planned.

Marry Darius Peacock, get the money, and run away, she told herself. How hard could that be? She longed to have someone to ask for advice. Norma would have been the most sensible choice of advisor, as she was clearly not afraid of Knapp. Her suggestions would be logical, the cool-headed counsel of a spinster. Her gut told her to marry no one and run for New York before it was too late. But the extra money from Darius would mean that she could send for Bette sooner…

It's not safe to come to the island just now, she wrote. *Will explain later. I love you, dearheart,* she added, *and no matter what, I always will. Wait for word from me.*

Indian Road, Charlie had said. He did not know the number but said the house was large and had an iron statue of a cat on the verandah. Why write a note, she reasoned, why not just go across the lake and go to her house and ask to speak with her? It might be safer to send Charlie in her stead, in case Knapp was inclined to follow her. He kept saying he was leaving Toronto, then continued to linger. Norma had chased him off a second time, and Charlie had warned Freddy that Knapp had been spotted near her cottage. His menacing note indicated he was still close at hand.

Taking tickets and making change, she longed to visit Bette at her own house, to see the place where she slept and went about her days. But the island was, to some extent, a safe haven, and as long as Knapp didn't know where Bette lived, Freddy felt certain she would be okay. As the day wore on, her spirits flagged. Something told her not to go to Bette, to let her be and not drag her into this mess. The only way to do that was to obey Knapp's command and go to the city.

44.

From the moment she jumped down from the blue shuttle outside Laura's apartment building on West 93rd, she'd been consumed by a childlike remorse. The trip was impulsive, another escape from working. She had packed a small knapsack, her cameras and her sleeping bag. The front door lock gave her a hard time, but she persevered. A glorious solitary week ahead: she was getting in.

The apartment was stuffy, and she opened the immense windows. She cracked the door on the bright green retro fridge and found a pitcher of water with a bloated slice of forgotten cucumber at the bottom. In the freezer: a pound of good espresso and a bag of vodka-filled candies. The armoire was bursting with clothes, shoes, hats; the closet, too. She sat on the end of the bed and watched the curtains billow in the late afternoon breeze. For a long moment she was out of time: free of her name, her profession, Tess, her relationship with Bianca—she floated there on the end of the bed on West 93rd as just herself, devoid of identifiers and attachments. Even Laura was absent from her thoughts, a minor miracle. It was how she imagined devoted meditators felt all the time—out of time and free.

She should call Bianca when she was settled in. It was by no means a major effort to do so, but still she resented having to check in. Call me when you get there. Call me when you leave. Call me. It was what couples did, but still she could not shake the feeling of grudging. To not call was to provoke an argument later. They were not big fighters, but when Bianca became strident with her code of how to be, Joss became surly as a child.

Call and get it over with, she urged herself, still not remembering there was no one to call. Laura had an abundance of CDs, and she rifled through them, avoiding the phone. Stevie Wonder. Paul Simon. Carly Simon. Rickie Lee Jones. Soon "Rainbow Sleeves" floated through the flat. She was helpless against the memory of Laura singing in the shower one morning. One long, erotic morning, and all this fall-out...

"Hi babe," she said as cheerfully as she could into Bianca's voice mail. After all, she was where she wanted to be. The curtains continued to undulate and horns honked below. "I'm safe and sound."

And then, hanging up, she realized she had forgotten to disconnect Bianca's cell.

45.

It was Bette's careless "loss" of her hat—one of Clarence's finest creations—that proved to be the real spark for her troubles. Margaret had noticed her bare head upon entry, said nothing, let Bette walk her home and then a day later, loudly reported its loss to their parents as proof positive that Bette had been up to no good at all and was on the road to ruin at Hanlan's Point with her *friend with whom she had spent the night, likely amongst vagrants and thieves.*

Audacity. Attachment. Devotion. Excessive. Unhealthy. Childish. *I miss you.* Your sister needs you now more than ever. Listen. Listen to me. Are you listening to me? Grandie. *I miss you.* Crazy. Influence. Devotion. Attachment. Girls. Childish. Stunt. Antics. Responsibility. Grandie. Lunatic. *Luna Park. Luna Park.* Are you listening? Make her listen to me! *It was worth it.* Your daughter. Restrictions. Curfews. Immoral. Unhealthy. Excessive. Devotion. Your sister. The baby. Selfish. Love? Not love! Never love. I told you, Irving. I said. Disturbance. Forbidden. Attachment. Forbidden. Prohibited. *Don't forget verboten.* Mock me? Don't mock me. This serious matter. Dr. Thomas. In the eugenics book. How dare I? Facts. Ask Dr. Thomas. Her sister. The baby. Someone has to help. *Can't make me.* Married. Lunatic. *Luna Park. Luna Park.* Unmarried. Time limit. Someone. Dreamland. That damned phonograph. Damn that woman. Yes, your mother. Enough indulgence. Remain home until married. Unnatural devotions. *Don't forget errant, wanton or, for good measure, insubordinate.* Listen to me. Are you? Make her listen to me. *Luna Park. Try and stop me.* Disgrace! Perversion! *LOVE. Wait for me.*

46.

She walked along the shore as far as the trees would let her and sat in the sand, far from her secret beach. This had been as close to home as anyplace ever had, and she would miss it. The wild woods and the lighthouse, the rushing sound of Lake O at night. They should have been two young girls together out here, giggling and carefree. For the summer entire, not just a piece of it.

I love you, she wrote in the sand with a long stick. She would say the words in her ear someday, the first next chance she had.

Under her bed at the cottage, a packed bag with her tin of money tucked inside. She had explained to Norma her plan to elope the next day and apologized for not much warning on the matter. Do you love him? Norma had asked, and Freddy hadn't been able to answer.

I love you, she whispered now to the lake, where a swan bobbed solitary and keening on the waves. They were supposed to travel in twos. This one, large and thus likely a male, was not at all pleased with his bachelor status. He roared and squawked as a gull flew too close and Freddy understood his outrage.

There were too many things they had not yet done together. Sleeping under the stars on a beach was one, taking the train to Niagara Falls was another. Braiding each other's hair, laughing along to Ada Jones records while sharing a cream soda on a hot summer night in a room in Brooklyn. Her dream of Coney Island did not seem as magical without Bette along for the adventure. Nothing seemed quite right without her involved now. Hollowed out and wrong. Their interactions had been simple, and yet so potent. Like nothing she ever felt with any boy or man. Some would say that was the fault of Knapp, but Freddy knew in her heart it wasn't his roughness that had turned her heart to feel such passionate friendship with Bette. It had something to do with Mary Pickford. With beauty. With the Figure 8 ride on a hot June day at just the right moment in time.

47.

There were at least a dozen women milling in the hallway, dining room and kitchen when Bette came groggily downstairs in her dressing gown at seven in the morning. Two days had passed since the familial explosion and subsequent ban on further trips to the island. She had not been expecting a crowd when she slipped from bed after a restless night of bad dreams and galloping thoughts. Some of the women busied themselves painting placards. Mary Agnew supervised another younger woman as she cranked the mimeograph machine. More pamphlets, more literature for the cause, sonnets for and about the downtrodden. The chances of a serene cup of coffee were nil amidst such chaos. *Goddamnit.*

"I beg your *pardon?*" Mary Agnew was aghast as usual. Bette quickly realized she had expressed her annoyance aloud. Oh well. Smiling, she headed back up the staircase.

"Elizabeth!" Her mother's voice cut through the din of the hen party. "Get dressed and come back down. We'll need your help today at the Junction rally." She turned to Mary Agnew and smiled. "She has excellent lungs for shouting."

"I'm told," Mary sniffed.

The carnal fumes from the nearby abattoirs mixed with the thick August heat. The day was sunless but no less suffocating. The shouting of slogans into the megaphone her mother insisted that she carry at the front of the matriarchal mob made her hoarse in short order. The endless, angry day moving from one factory to another recriminating, lamenting, cajoling, all forms of disapproval at top volume. Bette had no idea what they were against or for. She knew only that her throat hurt and this was the most malodorous form of repentance ever conjured up. Her father might disapprove of her forced involvement, but after joining in the chorus of "no more amusement parks for you, young lady!" he had slipped off on one of his meditation retreats. No ally there. It broke her heart.

But Bette wasn't particularly worried about the kybosh on Hanlan's, since she had every intention of breaking free. She had a letter for Freddy already written and kept an eye out for the sight of Charlie passing by the house. Reading on the front porch with a view of passersby was still permitted although there were plans, as Margaret had warned, to put Bette into full service once Baby Clackum arrived. Provided she could get the letter to Freddy before Tuesday, all would go well. Her embroidered satchel was packed and stowed beneath her bed, ready for departure. It contained another letter, this one addressed to her parents in the way of an explanation. One day she would be back, it said, but since they had raised her to have a plan for life and to believe in destiny, she had no choice but to follow the call of the universe etc., etc. The chains of marriage were not for her; surely her mother could understand the lacking appeal of domestic oppression?

The thought of the packed satchel kept Bette going as the women marched up and down past the various packing plants and tanning factories of the Junction. A policeman on the beat eyed them suspiciously as he passed. The women were all beautifully attired and clearly too engaged to be classified as loiterers, but their placards *could* poke an eye out. In the right hands, everything was a weapon. Inventing his concerns made Bette chuckle, and yet again, there was Mary Agnew standing by with her eyes narrowed.

"You're not at all like your lovely sister," she said so that only Bette could hear. "You're quite *different*."

"I shall only take that as a compliment, Miss Agnew."

"Mrs.!" snapped the old bird. Her placard was drooping in the heat. ADIES ARE F R ORKERS RI TS it read.

Someone had brought a picnic basket along, but every other hot wind brought with it the aroma of entrails, offal and fear. The only protestor to accept a sandwich was an extremely tall, thin girl whom Bette suspected had come along more in hopes of a meal than the promise of an uprising. She wondered what Freddy would make of all this stamping and chanting in the name of workers' rights.

The first spats of rain were cool and welcome. Bette lowered her megaphone and tilted her cheeks to catch the droplets. The rain came faster and faster; a deluge soon filled the gutters. Many of the women had rushed to find shelter under a maple tree. A clap of thunder inspired Bette to open her eyes and look around. She stood alone and drenched in the middle of the road and knew her mother would be angry.

"You're a sensualist, Bette," the tall thin girl whispered when she finally joined the others under the canopy of leaves. It was nice to feel admired, though disapproval and wrath were inevitable once her mother had a chance to scold her. The storm showed no signs of easing off. The best that could be said for it was that it rinsed away some of the stink of animal sorrows: there was no breeze that wasn't full of wet. Placards drooped and some of the women made noises about needing to get home to take washing in off clothes-lines. What revolutionaries, Bette thought nastily.

"Our work isn't done yet!" Mary Agnew cried out when some of the protestors tried to slink off. "We've still got to make our way down to the ferry docks and confront the con artists who've corrupted Miss Bette, here!"

The other ladies looked at Bette, and she looked directly at her mother. Was it one of Mary's customary uninvited outbursts or a definite plan, with its inspiration in her own mother's admission of recent events?

"Another more clement day, perhaps," Felicia said, turning away from Bette's enraged gaze.

"I QUIT the REVOLUTION!" Bette shouted into the megaphone before setting it down on the ground and marching back into the downpour. She folded her arms across her chest and stomped as hard as possible along the road so that spray from the puddles flew up on either side of her. Faintly she heard her mother insisting that she re-join the group, calling her name, but she would not oblige, and she marched faster and more angrily. In which direction she had no idea; rain blinded her as did humiliation. Nothing was sacred: her mother clearly thought that every experience could be recounted, shared and directed toward The Cause, however pathetically. Pleasure was corruption, independent action was randomly punishable. Really, deep down, Bette's mother and her placard-waving chums were just very bored married ladies who'd spent too much time in over-heated lecture halls. She would show them what a real revolutionary looked like!

By the time she got her bearings and reduced her stomp to a clop, the rain had also reduced its passion to a light but decidedly chilly drizzle. She was cold and hungry and would have given anything at all to walk through the door of her Grandie's house (it was still hers, *they* had done nothing to deserve it) and smell a Lancashire hot pot bubbling away in the oven. Such smells had died away before Grandie herself slipped off, but Bette still longed for the reassuring aromas that had once emanated from that kitchen. She could come home weeping after being teased at school and be instantly cured by a bread and butter pudding, wake from a nightmare to find that Grandie happened to have whipped up a soothing pot of potato soup in the middle of the night. Grandie had spent hours teaching her to cook. She had tried to replace the tastes and smells herself by following a cookery book, but they never tasted quite as good and Bette knew why. Her brother had been right: Grandie was a witch of sorts and just then she could have sorely used her wisdom as well as a meal from her magical cauldron.

The house smelled only faintly of the damp ink and paper from the mimeograph machine and stale cigar smoke. Tears began to well up hot and bitter. Her dress and boots and underclothes were soaked, her whole body shivered and ached. Knowing that Grandie's old room was no longer the same hardly mattered. She went to it on instinct, straight to the bed which her mother had at least left as it was, and climbed beneath the quilts in her sopping cold clothes and muddy boots. Like a small child she burrowed and burrowed till some warmth could be found, and then she cried for as long as she could. Eventually a clean, strong feeling came over her, followed by need of a nap. She found a dry spot on the pillow for her cheek and was falling into a deep sleep when she smelled onion cooking. There was no smell like it, no person she associated it with more. It grew stronger, more glorious, and yet she could not make herself get up and run to the kitchen to see who was cooking it. Her body was stone, and the allium lullaby continued till she was floating away from her wet clothes, that house, the rotten day.

48.

Laura had always lived a vagabond actress's life with few posses-
sions, but she kept her small book collection in New York. Joss ran
her fingers along the spines of a half-dozen plays till she came to
Saint Joan by Shaw. The note on the bed had instructions. *Go see
the statue at the end of my street. Jeanne D'Arc lives on West 93rd, did
you know? It's where I go when I need to ground myself. Sorry to have
missed you… XXX.*

The statuary was nearly buried in the trees, but there she was,
her sword raised high. Joss sat at the base of the eternal virgin's
statue and closed her eyes, hoping that some of her revolutionary
spirit would rub off. The sun dappled her jeans, danced across her
knuckles. Her camera was back in the apartment, shoved in a closet
for safe-keeping. Buried under layers of scarves and shawls and
dresses Joss had never seen her friend wear. Her New York clothes.
Did she have a whole other set in Los Angeles? A self for every city?
A lover in every quarter?

Two tourists appeared with cameras and asked if Joss would
oblige them with a snapshot. They were a tweedy pair, keen on seeing the statue from every angle—and she could not resist ordering
them to pose this way and that. They could have no idea that her
portraits had hung in galleries. This was the USA, after all. Here
she did not matter a fig. Finally they wandered off. Joss resumed
her quiet meditation of nothing at all until her stomach growled,
signalling lunch.

Tomorrow she would camp out for theatre tickets. The plan
called out for a trek to Zabar's. She was feeling up for the battle
that was the frantic Jewish deli. In the mood for a duel over which
kind of potato salad and how many shaved pastrami sandwiches. It

was a few blocks away, and she would be faint by the time she got there, but she was keen to be in motion, surrounded by the pleasing blast of upper Broadway. Noise was what she craved. Noise and mayhem. She was saving Coney Island for her final day in the city. Hoping in some slim way that Laura would show up and agree to go with her as she had before.

49.

The feeling of suffocation and no escape was so intense that she fainted for a few seconds, came to and tasted blood and fell away again. She was engulfed in a blackness and knew she could never see Bette again, that it would be best to just struggle alone. Her head ached. A blow to the side of her face. The light would always find Bette, she reasoned. The taste of her own blood choked her anew, and she blacked out again. There was no freedom from this, and she would not, try as she might, escape it with Bette at her side. Their dreams had been childish, and dangerous to Bette. The choking sensation was relentless, and running for a door was pointless, she was caught and would never be free, not even in her dreams. Pain blazed through her, indifferent to her youth and softness. Everywhere she tried to turn her face there was a smear of blackness and hatred, blinding her. She sang to herself and rocked till she fainted again. Something smashed down over her head. The ceiling was falling in, she decided. To his wrecked mind, this was love.

50.

Wake her? I've tried. Try again. We have to tell her. I tell you I tried to wake her for tea this morning. She hates tea. Sick people do not drink coffee. Did she not wake when you changed her clothes? She opened her eyes and looked at me. And? Did she speak? Not really. What does that mean? She spoke the way she did as a child, remember? The special language? Yes. I'd forgotten. I'd like to write some of it down. It doesn't matter now. We have to wake her and tell her. Why? She'll need calming. She needs to know. Not right away. Urgency won't change anything. Why is she sleeping so deeply? I need to go to Margaret. I'll stay. If she wakes? I'll wait for you to get home before I say anything. Promise? I promise. NO coffee, she's sick. Yes, Felicia. Dr. Thomas brought a bottle of soothing serum. In the drawer beside the bed. Oh? This morning, when you were reading. Did we ask for it? He knows she needs something. How does he know that? I have to go, Irving, Margaret isn't feeling well. All right. Bye, love. Bye, love.

Bette? Keep sleeping, Bickie. But listen, my darling one. There's been a fire.

51.

Sleep without aid of booze was even more elusive in Laura's big, plump bed. She thought of Tess going off to Paris and felt sorry for herself. Tess would invite her to come visit, but it wouldn't be a good idea. Tess needed to break free. Joss's mother had warned her to go when she was young and in love, and she hadn't listened. She would never know what it was like to hold hands across a table in the Marais with a perfect romantic feast laid out. And forget Italy on her own. She'd never sip an Amarone in the vineyard where it was made. She knew these things now. Why are you so negative? She could hear Bianca's voice. Ironically, the refrain *Why are you so negative?* caused more tears than any vacation photo or randomly discovered slip of handwriting had. Was being realistic a sign of negativity? If so, she was turning into her father and so be it. At this, she laughed and pictured herself buying cigars and pepperoni sticks and anything else a fella could chomp on. Some things she just knew. She should call him soon.

At 6:00 a.m. she climbed from bed, threw on her sweats and raced across the park with her bag of Zabar's goodies to join the queue for tickets to *Mother Courage*. Got on line and nodded amiably but not too amiably at her neighbours. Pulled out Laura's tattered copy of Elizabeth Smart's *By Grand Central Station I Sat Down and Wept* and pretended to read. Judging from her place in the crowd, she would get tickets. Unless it was one of the show nights when a lot of comped celebs came out. She would not rest until the pale blue tickets were in her hand. Each person who succeeded was rewarded with two, and there she was, alone, a single rider. By no means would it be difficult to divest herself of the free ticket. If she were enterprising, she'd sell it and buy herself a nice steak dinner someplace. She really was turning into her father.

The rules for lining up for the Public Theatre productions in the park had changed a lot since 9/11. The friendliness in the crowd was the same: the woman next to her held out her hand and introduced herself as Peggy. She was there with a man she described in a whisper as her *reluctant boyfriend*. Then she introduced him, loudly, as Queen Gary. The man was only mildly annoyed by this billing, and she shook his hand too.

"You *are* gorgeous," he told her, squeezing her shoulders. Her skin tingled where his long, perfumed fingers had touched down. No one had touched her like that since Hank. "We'll all watch out for each other. It's what Meryl would want." He winked and knelt down to smooth out his expensive blood red sleeping bag. His eyes were dark, nearly black, and she felt she could see right into him and vice versa. She wondered briefly if her efforts to become bisexual should not be redoubled. Not that Queen Gary was interested or up for a full re-examination of his own orientation. What was the matter with her lately?

"You're a million miles away," he teased, giving her another gentle squeeze.

"Yes," Joss said. "Where I belong."

"Oh darling, don't let's be ominous all day. Save it for tonight. It's what Bertolt would want."

52.

He finally woke her on Thursday at noon. It broke his heart how fresh and happy she had looked at first blink, like her child self from long ago. Fleeting: she asked what day it was and, upon learning the day and the time, leapt from the bed in a temper, a string of foul words flowing from her mouth. He wasn't even sure he knew what a number of them meant, or where she had discovered them. Shouting with her still-sore throat, she scrambled into her robe: she'd been poisoned, tricked, sabotaged! She would have no more of their meddling, their bossing and judging. More cursing as she sprinted to her room in search of street clothes, shoes and, unbeknownst to her father, the packed satchel. They would not receive the touching farewell letter now, the villains! Her heels thundered a floor above as she moved from cupboard to washbasin. Every so often she gave a holler of indignation. The sound of the worktable covered in jars of shells overturning punctuated her primping session—she had brushed and pinned up her hair quite beautifully when she stormed back to the first floor.

Her father made fresh coffee to the best of his ability. The pleasing aroma of it made her pause as did the pleading look in his eyes. One last coffee, then, she decided, letting him usher her into the dining room. In addition to setting out her coffee cup and saucer, he had laid out the newspaper on the dining room table. Irving's hands shook terribly in his lap when she sat down across from him and looked down at the headline on the *Globe*.

FIRE ERUPTS AT HANLAN'S POINT

Yesterday. While I slept. She read the article beneath the headline. Young ticket taker overcome by…young ticket taker killed…

going back for unsold tickets and money…Figure 8 roller coaster destroyed…

Coffee sprayed Irving's face as she drove her clenched fist through the cup and saucer with a howl of animal rage unlike any he had ever heard in his life. Even during séances, nothing like that sound. He tried to grab hold of her, but she moved like a dervish, all bleeding fists and fury. The only option was to block the dining room door to keep her from fleeing the house. But now she stood absolutely still, as if in a sort of trance, and made no sound at all. The newspaper was soaked in coffee. Broken bits of cup and saucer—the pieces not embedded in her flesh—littered the otherwise immaculate dining table. She regarded the mess with vague recognition. He noted the blood dripping from her injured hand but thought better of moving or speaking just then.

Destroyed. Yesterday. *While I slept…*

"While I SLEPT!" She was on him with her fists, slapping and punching, wrestling with all her might to get hold of the doorhandle.

"We only learned of it this morning!" He grabbed for her hands, desperate to reduce the number of landing blows.

Without warning, she fell to the floor at his feet and sobbed quietly. He had read the article himself and the young girl who had been burned to death was not named. He knelt down. "It might not be your friend," he said, touching her hair. "Might it be another girl?"

"I have to go and see," she said, as if addressing the floorboards.

"Perhaps tomorrow," he suggested.

"NOOOOOOOOOOOOOOOOOOO!" She sat up and screamed at her father with refreshed outrage. "You let me sleep! How could you let me sleep?" Fresh angry tears. Now she hammered herself with her fists.

He sighed. Reached across and stilled her punches. "Go then." He prayed it had not been her friend, that there had been another girl working when the fire ripped through the Gem Theatre, the roller coaster, the stadium, the hotel…the whole point a disaster zone. He wondered if he should go with her. It might be dangerous or even impossible to reach. But he knew she wouldn't like company, especially just now. She blamed him for letting her sleep through her sickness, brought on by wet clothes and mental over-exertion. For other things, too, undoubtedly. You could forget how delicate she often was when she lost her temper. She was gathering herself up now, preparing to go to the island, which, according to the newspaper, was a smoking wretched mess. The amusement park all but gone, the hotel gutted in spite of efforts on the part of a bucket brigade to save it.

She regarded her bloodied hand with amazement, plucked a piece of china from her palm. There were spatters of blood on her dress. She should change, wash her face, look wonderful to charm the gods and let Freddy be all right. No, just go. Hurry! She thought of Freddy saying it: *Hurry!*

The satchel lay on the dining room floor. He righted her chair and sat looking at his mother's embroidered bag. She had gifted it to Bette years before. It had housed dolls, then knitting and strangely, a collection of large rocks at some geologically obsessed stage. She had never been anything but her own girl, he thought, opening the clasp. Now the satchel seemed to have been put into more traditional use as an overnight bag. A chemise, a small cribbage board, one bar of soap, stockings, a boy's cap and a letter addressed to Freddy. The friend. *Don't*, he told himself. And so of course, he did. Every word. The habit of betraying her which called itself loving concern was hard to break.

I have had enough of missing you. Of everything but you. My mother and father are imbeciles, will never understand. They've all planned to entrap me with care of my sister's child. Some old maid aunt role for a fate? So I am coming to be with you till we can get away as planned. It will not be your worry where I sleep or what I do to keep busy. I can sleep under a tree or behind the Gem Theatre! Anywhere closer. I need to be near you till such time as we can go to Coney Island. I am so happy, Freddy, and have been since the first day we met. My soul requires your proximity and you were right: our lives will never be the same if yes or if no. I said yes, and will always say yes, but I am coming early. Don't be angry with me or feel rushed. I'll get a job in the hotel kitchen and make you smuggled sandwiches for supper. Nothing is impossible for us. You are the only being I believe in. Wait for me by the Figure 8 on Tuesday. Always, B.

He must go after her, prevent her from running away. But why? So he could sit her down and tell her they were selling Grandie's house? They had decided to leave Toronto, and she could either live with Margaret and Clarence or come with Irving and Felicia to the country where they planned a free-thinkers' farm retreat. Away from the city with its incessant automobile noise.

Wait and trust, he decided, cleaning up the mess. He tucked her letter to her friend in the satchel and quickly took the bag upstairs to her room to hide it. Felicia was with Margaret, who was labouring right then. The less she knew, the better off everyone would be. She knew of the fire. For now, that was all anyone knew.

53.

Queen Gary was the first person she had ever encountered who snored elegantly. And did so for crisp, thirty-minute intervals from which he woke looking refreshed and peaceful each time. He fell into these slumbers four or five times in succession before waking with finality and a loudly exclaimed, "Lord!" Once he had patted his face with a damp scented cloth extracted from a drinks cooler, massaged his jaws and taken a sip of something mysterious from a Thermos, he proposed a game of cribbage.

Joss had not played since she was a child and shyly admitted as much.

"It'll all come back to you," Gary said with a movie-starlet smile. "Trust me."

She proceeded to whip Gary's ass without apology five games in a row, and he accused her of being a hustler. Then she imitated John Voigt in *Midnight Cowboy* to his deeper amusement. "I'm a hustler!"

"Movies!" Gary shouted and clapped his hands. "I live for them. Too bad I'm dying!"

Joss fell silent. Gary was having none of that and poked her in the ribs.

"Let's talk about Meryl," he suggested, slugging again from his Thermos. "Spirulina and marijuana smoothie," he explained as he declined to share. "How many times have you seen *Sophie's Choice*?"

And on it went, their two-hour Streep Movie Inventory, till the announcement that the tickets would be handed out momentarily, and that the crowd was to maintain order throughout. "As if there'd be a punch-up for *Mother Courage*," Gary sneered as they edged closer to their quarry. "Although you never know, these days. I won't miss the human element of life. Oh, here come the vultures now!" He referred to the people who, refusing to wait on line for hours on end, hovered looking to purchase a ticket. Peggy peered down from behind huge dark glasses and murmured, "What do you think we'll get for them this time?"

Gary looked at her with wide eyes and shook his head. Joss leaned closer to invite explanation. Gary relented. "I've been selling my tickets for medication money. Fourth day on line. First day dressed as myself."

"He was Jane Fonda in *Klute* yesterday, you missed something special," Peggy added. It became obvious that they waited for tickets, both sold them, and that Gary, in spite of being encyclopedic about Meryl Streep, would not even be seeing his idol in the play. His joke about dying had not been a joke at all. Unlike Bianca, he was choosing to fight.

When the man at the box office handed Gary his two free tickets, he paused for a few seconds. "Enjoying the show?" he asked, knowingly.

"Yep, very much," Gary said. He turned to Joss and blew her a kiss as he went to leave with his tickets.

"Wait," she said. "Here." She held out her two just-acquired tickets to Gary as Peggy looked impatiently on.

"No," Gary said. "I can't."

Joss shook the tickets at him. "You and Peggy. For all those hours you've waited. Or sell them if you want, I don't mind."

"*Cry In The Dark*?" Gary asked. "Thirteen times."

"Four," Joss said with a shrug, pressing the tickets into his hands.

"Meet me back here at seven," Gary whispered, handing one back. "She doesn't even like Meryl. Or Brecht."

"Deal," Joss smiled, excited by the promise of seeing him again.

The first time she had lined up for tickets, for *The Seagull*, she had been with Laura. And it had been a perfect night for camping out.

Joss had lied about Laura not being there. It was an old habit, a reflex. She lied about having coffee with her in Toronto, covered up their dinner dates, too. Now Laura had surprised her and come home early from LA. They'd packed a six-pack of bottled water, potato chips and sleeping bags and headed down to the park at 10:00 p.m. with the other die-hards. The police had allowed the line to form in the park and then, at 1:00 a.m., had shuffled the entire queue out onto Central Park West without a single squabble breaking out. Joss loved New Yorkers for many reasons, but their ability to obey unspoken rules was by far the most charming quality.

Much like her new friend Gary, Laura was good at sleeping, and their conversation had halted after the decampment to Central Park West. But the happiness Joss felt just sitting beside her on their cardboard mat and sleeping bags was beyond compare. Joss nursed a childish fantasy that Laura would wake up and look around and realize that, after all these years, they were meant to be together. Who else would be game to sit up all night keeping vigil on Central Park West? Acting sentry while she slept?

In a window high above Central Park West a woman typed on an old school typewriter. No laptop light illuminated her face. A pool of yellow electric sun spilled over her shoulder instead from a stand-up lamp behind her. She typed furiously, then sat completely still, as if waiting for something. Joss was reminded of the heron on the lagoon. She wondered what she was witnessing: a private memoir unfolding for the first time, or the fifteenth painful rehashing of an epic? It might have been a letter to her mother or a cookbook in progress. Or perhaps the woman was a famous poet—did poets use typewriters? She had always envisioned a quill or fountain pen in service of verse. Whomever and whatever she was spying on in those moments, it felt incredibly intimate and somehow perfect for the night. Laura had rolled over on her stomach and curled her fist under her cheek like a girl.

The young stockbroker camped out next to them on a thin towel offered Joss a sip of Jagermeister from the bottle.

"How long have you been in love with her?" he asked quietly, nodding at Laura.

"Does it show?" Joss declined the bottle.

"From across the park," he said with a drunken smile. "But I think she's learned to live with it." He flashed her a kind smile and put the cap back on his bottle.

They stayed quiet after that, till Laura and the stockbroker's girlfriend woke up. A group decision was made that Joss and Rory would go fetch coffee and snacks, while Laura and Tina spelled each other off for bathroom breaks.

At the corner store where they loaded up on sandwiches and cups of coffee, Rory admitted that he had no desire to go to work the next day. He had come to New York from a small town in Colorado, and he wanted to go back. His job at Cantor Fitzgerald was killing him, he confessed. Tina wanted him to quit and open a rafting business back home.

"Why don't you?" Joss had encouraged him.

"She just seems a bit rash, is all," he said, paying for the snacks and waving off any effort on the part of Joss to chip in. "Everything she proposes is risky."

They made a happy foursome and took turns taking pictures of each other triumphantly holding up their free tickets when the happy hour arrived. Rory did call in sick, with the three women all around him smothering giggles. And they would never see each other again, not even that night. Their seats were across the theatre from one another, and no effort was made to keep in touch or meet up for drinks after.

When the Twin Towers fell a few days later, all Joss could think of was how Rory had hated that job and yet simultaneously felt the suggestion of living a dream might be rash. Safely back in Toronto going about her business, Joss cried inconsolably and prayed that Rory had called in sick that September day too. Laura, thank god, had flown back to LA on the tenth. Joss was afraid when she couldn't get through on the phone.

"I'm sure she's fine," Bianca had said gently as they watched the news. It was likely the most honest moment they had ever shared.

54.

The stink of scorched wood and charred canvas drifted over the harbour; silver tendrils of smoke still rose from the devoured skeletons of roller coasters. The sweet scent of the lake was overtaken by winds carrying wet ash from the efforts of the Nellie Bly tug. Before even reaching shore she could see and smell the destruction. It was necessary to shut her ears to the comments of gawkers riding the ferry out for a good look at the latest fall-out of a wayward spark in a wooden kingdom. Their heartless curiosity was nearly unbearable. Talk of insurance and arson and none of it mattered till she clapped eyes on Freddy Montgomery and knew that another girl had been taken away from someone else.

There was so little left. A chubby man with a cigar clamped in his teeth spoke to four other men who wielded notepads, their fountain pens flying as he extolled the virtues of change, the necessity of an upbeat attitude. She could hardly bear to look up and around at the collapsed buildings. Few structures were spared the black bruises of fire or the ravages of water.

The Figure 8 was nothing now. *We'll go to Coney Island, it won't matter. No crying.* She saw the destroyed heap where the girl had died; a constable and a fireman talked solemnly, pointing in various directions. Girls died every day. *Not mine.*

For safety's sake the largest of the ruined buildings and structures had been roped off or blocked by various makeshift methods, with signs warning trespassers of consequences. Where were the worker's cottages, she wondered? No one would be working because there was nothing to work at, no crowds to please save for the prurient nosey parkers.

Stay calm! You need to find Freddy in this mayhem. Irrationally, she stood there remembering the smell of an onion cooking as she had fallen asleep. The comfort it had offered seemed so ridiculous. Childish. The hypocritical recriminations of her parents flooded in her thoughts, her friendship with Freddy soiled by remarks of limited intelligence, the envy of her sister who could not go anywhere herself. Mean thoughts: she hoped the baby cried unceasingly and drove her sister mad. Bette would not be there to soothe it, feed it, push it around the block in a pram like some nurse...

"Bette," the voice said. It was more of a gasp than a greeting. She turned to see Charlie, not in his usual dandy's attire of suit and trousers and hat, but in coveralls and boots. Uncovered, his red hair was like a flame on his head. His bloodshot eyes had none of their usual mischievous light. "Oh, Bette," he said, shaking his head. Her fear escalated. He had been crying, he shook his head, he wore no hat—she began to shake as she waited for him to go on. "It's a fiasco," he said, opening his arms to indicate the mess.

"Yes, yes," she barked impatiently, grabbing his sleeve, "but FREDDY?"

"Gone," he said, and Bette thought she would faint. There wasn't a single breath of air available in the universe. She covered her mouth with her hands and gave a soft howl. Charlie took her in his arms and held her tightly, rocking slightly. His clothes smelled of fire and smoke. After an interlude he loosened his grasp and looked down at her crumpled face streaming with tears. Bette continued rocking, keening a little under her breath. The pain was unimaginable; the fear made truth made the gutted feeling worse, not better.

"She'll be fine," said Charlie. "She's a smart one, she'll get away some day." He took a cigarette from the front pocket of his coveralls and smoothed it before lighting it.

"Why would you phrase it like that?" Bette was stunned by his cavalier speech. An urge to vomit overtook her although with nothing in her stomach, nothing came. She had never liked red-headed men, she reminded herself. It was essential to get away from this one. Only now he had hold of her arm.

"Wait, Cookie," he said, using her pseudonym. The wheels turned behind his red-rimmed blue eyes. He understood her reaction now. "She left. Saturday, days ago. You didn't know? She said she was going to see you soon—" He swore softly and exhaled cigarette smoke. He moved to embrace Bette again, but she pushed him roughly away.

"Stop playing games, Charlie. Where is Freddy?"

"Gone *away*," he said. "Getting married to a Bible preacher. Norma over at the arcade said she went pretty willingly, too, took all her things with her." He spat. "Thank God it wasn't the other one. I never liked him. She worked for his father out in the country someplace. Something wrong about him. He knew her since she was a kid fresh off the boat. Well you don't choose a woman when she's still a child! At least it wasn't him that took her."

"No," Bette said. "The fire. I read it in the paper, and you mustn't lie to me another minute." She lunged at him to deliver a good punch, but he caught her fist mid-air.

"Let's walk over and see Norma," he suggested, staring her down. She could see he wasn't lying, and her legs buckled under her. Again, he had lightning reflexes. "Norma's booth is one of the few that made it through the fire. It doesn't even look like it was in the same place as everything else! Come now."

The Shoot 'Em booth was indeed intact and untouched by fire or water. The lady Charlie called Norma loomed over them. Bette was surprised to see a woman in charge of a game of skill.

"Bette was wondering where Freddy might be," Charlie said, picking up a rifle and handing it to Bette. He took one for himself and aimed at a row of wooden ducks that began moving as soon as Norma pulled on a lever. The ducks moved up and down till Charlie's shots knocked them over.

Norma looked down at Bette and gestured for her to take a shot at the ducks. Although she had never held a gun previously, it felt somehow natural to peer down the barrel of it.

"She left days ago, dear."

Bette pressed the trigger and took down a blue duck as it floated upward on a stick. Norma and Charlie gave each other a look.

"Who with?" Bette asked, lining up a yellow one this time.

"A fellow who's been here a few times. I'd have run off with him, too—he's a good-looking gentleman. Big fella. Snappy dresser." This time both Bette and Charlie took their chosen targets out. "But a rich type who thinks he can make a lady do whatever she likes. He had his eye on Freddy a long time. All summer."

Bette knocked down three more targets. Norma whistled through her teeth and held out her hand till Charlie gave back the pellet gun. She held out her other hand till Charlie paid her for both his round and Bette's.

Bette set down the gun. She felt sicker than any ride had ever made her feel.

The theatre where they had watched motion pictures. The roller coaster. The hotel. Burned to rubble. The rich man she knew nothing of and Freddy went willingly. NO. NO. NO. NO. NO. NO…

"You want me to walk you back to the ferry, kid?" Charlie asked.

She would never come to Hanlan's Point again and wasn't sure about leaving. Not just then. The idea of being escorted to the ferry made her desperately unhappy. She thought of Freddy boarding the boat without her. NO. NO. NO. She had pictured them riding away together so many times it seemed already to have happened. But she had left with someone else. A Bible preacher? It made no sense. Was everything a lie? Everything was a lie. She could not bear it. Her mind began to work without her permission. You said, Freddy. You said and promised and touched me when we were alone and NO, NO, NO. She longed for Grandie's arms around her.

"Sweetie, you might need a doctor, you don't look so well," said Norma, leaning over to collect Bette's abandoned rifle. "Charlie, take her. She doesn't look right."

"I'm fine," Bette said. "I'm going to go for a walk."

"I'd take you all the way home, kid, but I promised the boys on the clean-up crew..." Charlie looked flustered. The tips of his ears were as red as his hair.

Bette waved him off and smiled at them both as if to reassure. They could not possibly understand the depth of her anguish right now. It seemed best to smile grimly and get away. She felt like ripping her own features off her face, removing all traces of the face that had been kissed and would now live in solitary confinement, madness...

The secret beach was where she wished to be. Just for a few moments alone. There was no reason to go home, and no other destination that called. She didn't know where Freddy was and could only hope she was safe. Had he taken her away to make her dream of Coney come true? *NO, goddamnit.* She thought of his hand over Freddy's that day, his strange, unfriendly manner. No. Better to think of the feeling between them on the Figure 8 that first time, all the times, or here on the beach, in the theatre, up in the hotel room which no longer existed.

Had any of it been real? She could not even climb back up over the dune and run to ride the roller coaster to bring back the feeling. Was Coney Island even real and were they ever really going, together? There could be no going without Freddy. Some pacts were sacred. Weren't they? Or were they not at all? Who would know about their special love, smashed in an afternoon's choice? A very bad feeling began to swirl in her. It wasn't new, but it was bigger than before. She sat down on the log where Freddy had told her all about how it would be and what they would do there. She blinked and faced the lake, which was so calm it hardly seemed like the same body of water. A man appeared, rowing hard across the smooth surface of the water. His grace was soothing. It must be an exquisite feeling to be strong like that, she thought, watching his arms like pistons. The rowers usually stuck to the lagoons but not this one. She guessed Ned Hanlan could row wherever he liked. All the way to Rochester if he wanted, now that he was dead.

Freddy was all right someplace. Safe. She cared nothing for Bette and never had. NO, NO, NO. No one knew the man she went with except that he was good looking. Willingly, they said. Would he let Freddy wear her cap? Perhaps she didn't need it now. No longer in hiding. Kissing someone else. Worse: laughing about Bette as a childish memory. Or never telling a soul because they were the only two such kissers. And they had touched each other. Would she tell her Bible preacher about that? There was nowhere to go now, Bette knew. No place that would allow for a love like that, like theirs. It did not occur to her to try to find Freddy. To run and beg. All was loss and her heart could not bear it and would not lug it around for a lifetime. She would go to Grandie. Trust her parents and their oddball beliefs were right: you could find each other again. She would not live out her life pining for another night in a pretty hotel. Those lips and arms and eyes had been perfect, and she would settle for no others. Would not be made to settle.

It tasted awful. She wondered how Grandie had stood the flavour and kept it down. Bette held her nose and downed as much of the tincture as she could. Wishing she had some water to drink to subdue the bitterness. Such a pretty name, such an ugly flavour. She had left her satchel behind, but had not forgotten the laudanum bottle from Dr. Thomas. He was so helpful. Always lending a hand. Cotton candy would chase away the taste nicely, but she didn't have any. Her father would always be able to find her wherever she was. They could hold a séance if they missed her. Grandie. She missed her so much. She slid down to sit on the damp sand with her back pressed against the log and sipped again, shivering. Freddy would not place her hands on Bette's shoulders again or sing in her ear. She didn't want to. She had not meant what she offered. Or had, and couldn't give it? There was nothing to look forward to. Only a fool would stay on to find that out. Bette's mind swam around looking for a way out of the blurry cave. Willingly? No, not likely. She must get up from the sand and find Freddy. Walk. Get up and walk. Where did she ride to, on that boat with that man no one liked? There was no roller coaster boat. No hotel island. Everything grand had burned away except *kiss me*, and she had run away without saying goodbye. *Why?*

55.

Streep was brilliant in *Mother Courage*, a roaring air-raid siren of a Brechtian mama. Gary had obviously sold his ticket: he failed to show. Instead, Joss sat silently rapt with strangers on either side of her. The cast of a popular TV comedy show caused raised eyebrows as they filed past toward reserved seats. At intermission, Susan Sarandon glided by Joss's elbow on her way to the ladies' room. The weather could not have been more perfect. Joss was exhausted as she made her way back to Laura's apartment after the show. Three encore curtain calls for Meryl Streep, Kevin Kline and company. Waiting around afterward for a glimpse of La Streep wasn't without its appeal, but it seemed too lonely a thing to do solo. Would anything get easier?

She could not help but think of how differently her previous evening at the Delacorte Theater had gone. Letting herself into the tiny apartment building, she was awash in guilt for having deceived Bianca so skillfully. So long ago. Why? Why did it matter now? She could feel a tidal wave of shame coming and knew it would only be a matter of time before she hit a liquor store or bar. Get control, she warned herself as she climbed to the fourth floor, past the opera singer who never went to bed and the seeming aviary in 305.

After seeing *The Seagull*, she and Laura had dragged their weary bodies home but stopped at a wine shop on the way. "I want to drink expensive champagne with you. Just once," Laura told her as she grabbed a bottle of Pol Roger from the display fridge.

"Any other fantasies?"

"Don't," Laura warned her. "Don't spoil it."

Nothing about the night had been spoiled. Her kiss was even more devastating than Joss remembered. She drank her full share of champagne and never said a word about any of it to anyone. Not even her sponsor, Berta, would learn about the champagne slip. In the morning Laura had brought her a cup of coffee in a huge blue mug and sat on the edge of the bed.

"You're going back to her, right?"

Joss sat up. This would mark the second chance to be with Laura, and she was terrified. It seemed easier to hurt herself than to hurt Bianca.

With silence for an answer, Laura stood up again, wiped her eyes. "This never happened. And by the way, I'm getting married."

56.

You have to understand—you can't come where I'm going. He said it himself this morning, Why not bring your little friend along, why not go get her just for me? And my heart went cold. It's one thing to have lived through this for myself, another to drag you with me. He's a sick man. He took all the money I had and set it on fire right in front of me. What sort of madman does that, when he could have spent it on whiskey or new shoes or train tickets to New York? He says we'll go there one day, but we never will. Will you know to go there and wait for me? Can you feel me trying to reach you? It's not safe for me to write to you, and Charlie is over on the island. He always adored you, always helped us. I know that if you go, you will hate me for not being there. I had to run, but he caught me.

Forgive me for never being able to tell you of these things, to warn you. The nightmares I have known cannot be shared aloud. There are so many good things I wanted you to know about me. All the good things that are me, not the awful things I have seen and done. I had a barn cat at the farm named Sparky, a big fat tuxedo boy I used to smuggle pieces of trout to when I had the chance. I was kind, Bette, I was a good girl before I had to do this cruel thing and leave you without a word, to save both our lives…

57.

The B train issued a violent screech as it rounded some unseen bend in the track, and Joss listed sideways. As the train stopped and its doors slid open, a number of people, including a sullen young guy with tinny headphones, flooded out of the train and onto the platform at Broadway and Lafayette. The man across from her stared straight into her solar plexus. From somewhere within his jacket pocket he'd produced a small carton of macaroni salad. She wondered if he might begin to eat it with his fingers, but he reached up and quite jauntily plucked a gleaming silver fork from the band of his fedora. She hadn't noticed the fork till now and wondered how she could have missed such a thing. He ate with great concentration for several moments, savouring each mouthful, closing his eyes at intervals to mark the depth of his appreciation. And then, without warning, he glared right at Joss, as if to silently berate her for staring at *him* the whole way down the track. His eyes were fierce. After a few seconds' paralysis, Joss looked away, fully admonished.

"That's right," the man said, loud enough so that she and anyone nearby might hear. "Let a man have his breakfast in peace, goddamn."

At Grand Street the car all but emptied. Without so much as a glance, the old man stood up and shuffled out, dropping his emptied salad carton to the subway floor as he exited. The doors closed and Joss saw him gazing back at her as he licked the fork clean with long feline laps of his tongue. She knew better than to read into anything she saw in New York. In the years that had passed since 9/11, nothing so small and eccentric was considered worthy of analysis. Observation, yes: it paid to keep your eyes open, though even that had lost its efficacy. Your world could end in a hospital corridor, on a bike path, in the aisle of a SuperHouse department store, buying light-bulbs. She'd read about that last phenomenon in a *New York Post* piece while waiting on line for an Americano. She supposed she should be grateful to have made it out of the coffee shop alive.

The train cooled in the absence of bodies, and she relaxed against the seat. A still-significant portion of the ride lay ahead, and her eyes devoured the outdoor view as the train hurtled over the Manhattan Bridge and then over top of neighbourhoods she would likely never drop down into. She gawped as if she might one day visit them, as if they would welcome her, but some part of her knew that neither thing was true.

The weather was holding nicely, throwing late-August sun over the streets below the train. Burnt-out cars littered one block, club-locked sports cars the curbs of another. Every so often there was a glimpse of an ancient past in the upper facades of the whitewashed buildings that flew by. The curve of an old movie house marquee, a guardian gargoyle left on the cornice of an apartment house, some whisper of a time when stonemasons delighted in their work. Everything whipped past at breakneck speed as she peered down. The full ache of the Stillwell ride hit her. It all hurt more somehow on sunny mornings. She wished she could be one of those passengers content to read thrillers or stare at their own shoes or, more amazingly, to sleep deeply then rise magically at their appointed stop. She loved to look and ride and hurtle along, feeling New York shift above and beneath her. In her next life, she hoped to be a New York pigeon, capable of seeing it all.

A multi-generational family of Puerto Ricans clambered onto the train at DeKalb and followed the human tradition of sitting beside her in spite of a vast array of unoccupied seats further down the train. They carried flags and coolers and lawn chairs and shrieked at each other with such affection and focus that Joss half-considered fleeing the train in an effort to leave her throbbing loneliness behind. Someone carried a roast chicken, the warm buttery smell of it a minor but insistent torment. Now, she thought, go now. But the doors closed and Joss knew, watching this family, that they too were heading for Stillwell Avenue station, and that she must not abandon her mission. She had wanted this voyage for as long as she could remember. Not just to be in New York, but this particular ride to the end of the line.

58.

Charlie found Bette face down in the shallows and ran to get one of the constables from the dock. No amount of shaking or shouting would rouse Bette. He should have known, he told the policeman, there was something about the way she had cried, he ought to have stayed with her, God help us all if it's that easy to break in two on a sunny day. Sad because her friend went away but, come now, there would *be* other friends. The cop shook his head, and they asked Charlie did he know where the girl lived and how did he know her. How simple it had been to hand her an advertisement and promise her a perfect day. His job, after all, was to make sure pretty girls came across the water to have fun. A barker's job was to bring the crowds. Keep them coming. Not lure them to heartbreak.

When he and the policeman stepped off the ferry on the Yonge Street side of the water there was a police wagon waiting there, and the ambulance for her body. For a moment Charlie's heart skipped: was *he* in trouble? A suspect in Bette's death? Had someone seen him go into that gentlemen's café in the alley off King Street? But the other two policemen only wanted to talk to the first cop. They stepped away for a few moments, but Charlie was told to wait. The police all shook their heads, and the first one came back to where Charlie stood smoking a cigarette and trembling.

"Do you happen to know anything at all about a young woman who worked on the island, a Miss Montgomery?"

"Yes sir. That's Freddy—Fredelle. Bette's friend. She ran off with a guy nobody really knew only a few days ago. She used to sell tickets at the theatre and she sold candy, too. Why?" Charlie wished the sun would ease off being so bright when everything was turning sour. The thought of the police knocking on Bette's family's door to tell them what had happened was already too much.

The constable began taking notes on a leather-bound pad. "My colleagues here have just come from the Clyde Hotel where a young female, name of Montgomery, was found unconscious, half-way to dead. They're looking to talk to anyone coming across who might have known more about the girl's past. Her character. They'll want to talk to you at length, of course, since you seem to know a thing or two. Who was the fellow you said she left the island with?"

"Well sir, there were two who fancied her. Hard to say which fella was worse? There was one who was real bad news—"

"Bit of a coquette, was she?"

Charlie bit his lips together. "Didn't you just tell me she was nearly killed? Half-dead when you found her?" His face reddened to match his hair, he was so angry.

"These little girls," the cop said, "they know exactly what they're in for."

"Watch it," Charlie said.

"Watch what?" the cop sneered.

"Just … watch it." He smoothed his hair with his hand and made a move to go. "You've got my house number."

"Yeah, I got it," said the cop with a disapproving nod.

"Is she going to be all right?" Charlie asked, ignoring the piercing eyes of the other constables.

"As all right as they ever are," the officer shrugged. "With all due respect to your lady friend there, she's going away to rest for a good long time. There was a guy found hanged in the room across the hall from hers, beaten black and blue. That's some kind of a lovers' quarrel."

"That's not possible," Charlie insisted. "She was obviously defending herself! She worked hard, two jobs day and night. It wasn't any of her doing!"

"People are disappointing, what can I say? They can lead many lives all at once. Try having my job for a week, you'd see." The cop lit a slim cigar and shook his head.

"This is all a misunderstanding," Charlie said softly. This was not a perfect day, and he wanted everything to go back to the way it had been before the damned fire.

"Well, here's one thing we know for sure," said the constable, spewing smoke. "She owed one Darius Peacock five hundred dollars, and that money ain't nowhere to be found."

"That's the guy!" Charlie cried. "There's no way she would owe him that kind of money. He sold Bibles, I think..."

"Yeah, well that's a *lot* of Bibles. Naw, they had another *arrangement*, and she reneged upon it," the cop said. "It was Peacock who called us to help get his money back. Said he saw her going into the Clyde with a paid paramour, if you take my meaning."

"She had no such associations, Mister. She was best friends with the gal who drowned. A good girl."

"You think the dead girl knew that Miss Montgomery was supposed to marry Mr. Peacock for the price of five hundred bucks?"

Charlie frowned into the sun and considered lighting another cigarette. He felt weary and sad, and heartbroken for both girls. "Not likely, no."

"But two girls, they tell each other everything, don't they? All their secrets?"

Charlie thought of the young fellow he caught peering into Freddy's cottage the one afternoon and shuddered. The man had had a knife sticking out of his pocket. "I don't think Freddy was feeling safe enough to tell all her secrets. Maybe not even to a friend. What did the fella look like that they pulled down from a rope at the hotel?"

"German kid, blond hair, farm boy build."

"That 'kid' was after Freddy all summer. Wouldn't leave her

alone. And he was a good five years older than her, which makes him a man." He paused and thought a minute. "He was far too strapping to be beaten up by a woman. And he sure didn't seem the type to despair and hang himself. Where's this Peacock fellow?"

"People do all kinds of things," the cop said slowly. "When they're angry, women can be pretty damned strong. Any reason she might have been angry with him?"

"She knew him from before, that's all I know, and she never looked happy to see him when he came around. He dogged her."

"Did the other young gal know him? Have an opinion about him?"

"Listen, Mister, I'd just be guessing at this point. I wasn't privy to their private conversations. Would you mind awfully if we went to the young lady's house and got on with telling her parents? I feel just sick about them not knowing."

The cop shrugged and waved one of his cronies over. "Officer Lawrence will take you to the Tituses. You can show him the house, and he'll take it from there."

59.

His spiritual beliefs seemed to abandon him the moment the police officer began to apologize for the purpose of his visit. Charlie stood back, eyes averted as the gloriously handsome figure of Irving Titus crumpled on his front stoop. It had been enough to lose one child, and now hearing of the death of his youngest daughter, his world cracked open and nothing but darkness poured in. There was nothing reassuring about all he had studied. Reincarnation would be of no use as a comfort, for she was gone, his child and best friend. They had known each other for lifetimes, but now she was lost in the underworld. He blamed himself, and Felicia too for not having kept her safe. Too busy with our heads in books, he scolded himself as Felicia beckoned them to come inside. Upon hearing the news, Felicia's shocked reply was, "You have a very poor sense of humour."

Left alone on the sidewalk, Charlie heard the lady of the house begin to scream her outrage. He lit a cigarette and wandered across Indian Road to where a new house was being built on a vacant lot. A working boy raised his cap as Charlie passed by, and Charlie shook his head. All of life marching on as someone's heart shattered two doors down.

60.

By the time the train pulled into Stillwell station, she wished she could find a special telephone to the dead, to call Bianca and apologize for not loving her as much as she deserved to be loved. If only such a phone service existed. The lines would be lit up day and night, with no shortage of customers.

61.

The hotel room door had flown open with such force it created a breeze, and it would have been the last thing he felt before Darius Peacock pulled him off her. She was badly bruised and bloodied, as she had made the mistake of telling Knapp she planned to marry and there was nothing he could do about it. She had not mentioned that Darius was on his way to the hotel to collect her. Darius had picked her up on the island, but there was this one more meeting with Knapp she had felt compelled to have. She'd made up a story about meeting a friend at the hotel for luncheon first. But after agreeing to her plan, Darius Peacock had followed her.

As he held Knapp's arms pinned back, Darius shouted questions at her. "Is this your lover?" She shook her head. "An assailant?" She shrugged. "WHO is this?" Darius had screamed, yanking back Knapp's arms so that he winced and whimpered. "Do you love this man?" She slipped from the bed and gathered her clothes around her, shook her head no, hoping the hotelier would not be roused by the commotion. "Strike him," Darius ordered. "Prove to me you hate him and strike him. I think I know who this devil is to you."

At the moment when Knapp laughed, everything in the room went silent.

"You find this funny?" Darius said between his teeth, yanking harder till a cracking sound erupted from Knapp's left arm. His usually cherubic face was contorted with fury.

"I will kill you both," Darius promised. "Strike him."

Freddy could not bring herself to hit Knapp with her hands, as she knew the effort to be futile. His body was hard as granite from hours in the fields. She picked up a candlestick from the side table and tested its weight in her hands.

"Not with that," Darius instructed. "You might kill him. I want the pleasure of the deed."

Knapp began to struggle and Freddy panicked. Picked up a parasol and swung its hooked handle as hard as she could at his face. Before he could laugh again, for it had not hurt, she wound up again and smashed it all the harder into his throat. His genitals, which he could not cover with his hands, were next.

"Good girl!" Darius cried out as she continued bashing her tormentor with the wooden end of the umbrella. He wept now as she attacked him over and over, stabbing at him with the poker end of the parasol, batting him with it with a strength that surprised no one in the room who knew what she had been through at his hands. Darius Peacock was a man of his word, and he soon rescued Knapp from her battering and began to administer his own blows. He held Knapp at a remove with one hand and punched with the other. Urged Freddy to pack her things and go, and wait for him across the hall in Knapp's room.

She did as told and cowered in one corner of the appointed room, fully aware of the thumping that signified a murderous, relentless beating.

Then all went quiet and she waited. Darius slipped into the room where she waited and looked at her with pity. "You pathetic creature," he began, moving toward her with the candlestick. "Come, come to me," he whispered as she buried herself in a corner of the room, hands up in pale defense.

"Please," she said, weeping.

"You're no good to me now," he said quietly. "All banged up and used. But let me tell you, he will never bother you again." He reached out and caressed her swollen jaw and she winced. "I was never here today, understand me?" She nodded. "I will call the police from a phone box claiming to have happened upon a suicide when collecting a debt, and you will wait right here, on the floor, as if still incapacitated by your late friend in the next room. Only, remorse has led him to darker deeds. You'll be free eventually. The bones will mend and your bruises will heal."

Tears spilled down her face as she realized what he had done. Knapp was dead, and there would be terrible trouble. But Darius Peacock, wealthy and a true Christian, had done her a good turn before turning her in. Her tormentor was gone forever.

62.

Stillwell. She had finally made it. She wondered what a view of the ocean cost down here. Even Nathan's Famous had been gobbled up by a condo tower, gathered in a sleek embrace of steel. It looked somewhat crazy as the ground floor business of the ritzy residence. A kind of sacrilege everywhere she turned. Someone had warned her that a lot had changed. She had nothing to compare it to. She had dawdled and missed her chance to see its final heyday.

Joss made her way along, trying not to think about all that was missing. Instead of the notorious Russian flea market, a fussy little over-priced deli. Coffee shops without a shred of Mom-and-Pop energy. There was nothing Diane Arbus would have wanted to photograph, not now. All the grit had been scrubbed away, replaced by gleaming towers, glass and steel reflecting the ocean. In an effort to honour the past, the condo buildings were named after the former amusement parks. Dreamland Adult Living. She wondered if the people nesting there had a clue?

But the Cyclone was there, tucked between moderate towers. Somehow it had clung to the piece of earth it had claimed since 1927. She would delay riding it for a little longer, then ride as many times as she could stand to. The only other ride that had stuck it out was Deno's Wonder Wheel, also incorporated into a residential tower's immense courtyard. She felt like crying, both from the realization of a lifelong dream and because there was such a sadness to the place. Or maybe it was her regret-filled grief playing tricks, making everything raw, ridiculous or somehow sad. It wasn't Bianca's fault she had been a coward all her life.

Maybe some oysters at Nathan's first. A hotdog, after all that's what a person ought to do, right? She doubled back to the famous eatery. It had been a few years since she'd been on a roller coaster, but she knew that riding with an empty stomach was not advisable. Or was it the other way around?

An androgynous young woman with some sort of radio sat at the sole table outside the hot dog stand. If she wanted to sit down to eat in the sun, she would have to share with her. Joss sat down, not asking if she minded, and unpacked her lunch.

"I've got all day, sweetheart," the girl said with a wink, turning the radio down. Great. The only nut-cake in the place, and I have to choose to sit with her, she thought. Be kind, Joss, try at least. She glanced over at her and smiled politely. She had gorgeous soft brown eyes. She sort of reminded her of the film actor Robert Downey Jr., perhaps what he'd been like as a boy. There was a beautiful duality to her energy, both girlish and boyish. She reminded her ever so slightly of Tess. When the girl didn't say anything further, Joss took a bite of her hot dog and tried to people watch. There weren't a lot of passersby considering what a beautiful day it was. But she could feel the young androgyne looking at her.

"Is there something you'd like to ask me?"

Joss sipped some orange soda to ease the dryness in her throat.

The girl laughed and began cranking the radio. As she did so she turned up the volume. It wasn't the sort of music you'd expect a kid to listen to, but it suited the location perfectly. Something very old, the singers strident and sincere.

"What sort of radio is that?" she asked, pointing. It was unusual looking. When she cranked it Joss thought of the ancient gramophone Hank had had in his studio.

"Solar," she said, taking one of Joss's French fries. Her audacity somehow fit the moment. "You like this music? I chose it for you."

"Meet me down at Luna, Lena / Meet me at the gate / Meet me down at Luna, Lena / I'll be there at 8 … "

Now Joss felt quite deeply disturbed and decided to move along. She didn't need her day derailed, and the young woman's unusual choice of song was alarming.

"Have a lovely day," she told her, gathering up her litter.

"It's a perfect day," the girl grinned. "Enjoy the rides."

Lucky guesser, she told herself as she headed away from Nathan's. Maybe she looked like a thrill seeker. And anyway, why else would you come to Coney Island?

63.

Scrubbed, groomed and morally sorted, she re-entered the big bad world of June sniffing the air like a pointer on the hunt. Only she was no dog. Precious years of her prime might have passed, but she was still a looker, a real tomato in the new parlance. Not to mention an excellent example of moral rehabilitation, a credit to her sex. Not bad for a former vagrant, possible accomplice to suicide and *occasional prostitute*. The latter ridiculous charge still irked her. Why not then: occasional murderer, occasional bank robber—had they no idea how silly they sounded?

After breakfast and morning vespers, Freddy stood on the sidewalk gazing up at the reformatory windows crammed with a row of envious faces. The red brick building had played too large a role in her life, and she ought to have sprinted away, but something held her there on the corner. A deep fear unlike any she had known, and that was saying something. She pretended to review the piece of paper in her hand. Think of the arrangements, the promises made. Run! But her legs stayed stock still. Upon her third and final release from P. Miriam Woodyard's Reformatory for Wayward Girls and Ladies it was understood that she'd spend three nights at the Women's Christian Temperance Union dormitory. Her beloved sister Elizabeth would then come to collect and take her, via motor car, to a town less tantalizing, one with fewer temptations and plenty of God-fearing bachelors. And, until Freddy hit the street, this had seemed like a perfectly reasonable, almost believable arrangement.

The slight lapse in administrative custom could not be helped. *Elizabeth* wasn't able to come to the city until Wednesday. Freddy's emptied bed was needed right away, and none of the matrons could spare the time to personally escort her to the WCTU dorm on Gerrard Street. The Christian Temperance ladies were busy in their own right. It had been a hectic month; moral turpitude was on the rise.

Although never married herself, Miss Woodyard rejoiced in her role as a spiritual shaper and keen cultivator of the qualities that produced fine wives and upstanding spinsters. The city depended on her expertise, especially now. Because she took her esteemed position very seriously, she turned out dozens of successful graduates of her strict program each year. Little mention was ever made of the ones who did not pass muster. They simply remained, as Freddy had this second time around, behind the walls of Miss Miriam's, indefinitely, washing porridge pots and murmuring vespers, lusting after the postman or, in some cases, each other. The truly incorrigible, unstoppable ones got thrown in the nuthouse, or, very rarely, back into society via the back door, only to find themselves back at Woodyard's Reformatory.

To be released now, at last: Freddy was lucky and knew it. She was a three-time offender, and this was her last chance at the good life. At any life outside reformatory walls. The next stop was a permanent spot in the nuthouse, and she had NO interest in that fate. For no reason she could fathom, she now enjoyed the full confidence of her jailors that she could and would find her way in the world. No former charge of the home was ever supposed to leave alone, free and on foot, but in this case Miss Miriam felt confident that what had been promised would be done. This one was bright, pleasant and sufficiently remorseful (now) where her past conduct was concerned, the type who'd appreciate the gift of Miss Miriam's trust. The sister Elizabeth's letters were remarkably well written, shimmering with Christian faith in her long-lost sibling. There was also the matter of a hefty packet of cash that came in from an unidentified businessman who may or may not have contributed to

Freddy's third fall from grace. He had taken her out for supper, his wife had found out, and after a series of bad investments he decided to accuse Freddy of seduction and fraud. Edwin Collins Sr. had given her two dollars for a cab ride home to her rooming house, and when she declined to let him accompany her, his scorn at her haughty virtue was immense.

And so now she waved goodbye to all the girls and ladies crowding the windows and headed away from the building she'd called "home" on and off for eight long years. In her mind she always referred to it as "The Prison."

On the day of her liberation she possessed: one scuffed suitcase, the outdated dress she was wearing, a change of undergarments, an old red leather Bible, an overcoat and ten dollars cash, the customary bursary awarded for unwavering good behaviour during internment. No real fortune, but her upstanding (if imaginary) sister had promised a solid, immediate marriage in Freddy's near future. Trouble was, Elizabeth didn't actually exist. The letters from Elizabeth to Miss Woodyard were written by Freddy herself, mailed back to the home by the obliging handyman, Tipp. It only took two lengthy evangelical epistles to Miss Miriam to ensure her own freedom: not bad. Eavesdropping on Miss Miriam's dictated reply to the first of these letters facilitated further correspondence. Her strict adherence to routine meant that she could always be found in her atelier, dealing with her mail in the sixty precious minutes before lunch. Never a moment wasted, idle minds the devil's playground and all that.

While ten bucks wasn't much of a dowry, it stood for having something when she was used to having nothing. Temporarily rich, scared half out of her wits and trying to do the right thing, she headed west instead of east, south rather than north. Instead of rushing toward three nights of temperate Christian sleep, followed by the kind of rural cure Miss Woodyard favoured, she hurried toward the lake. Fresh air is fresh air. The suitcase and overcoat were bothersome, but she'd manage.

She wanted three things and in this order:

an ice cold Honey Dew,

a red hot loaded down with fried onions and hot mustard and

at least two rides on the Sunnyside Flyer.

The delicious thing was: she could have all three. The ten bucks was burning a hole in her pocket. A girl who had been brought into The Prison after her told her all about the then-new park on the shores of Lake O. She had even ridden the Flyer.

The Honey Dew was icy cold as promised. Gorgeous orange gulps numbed her throat as she washed down not one but two red hots slathered in onions and mustard, consumed right in front of the scandalized vendor. Ladies never ordered the fried onions, his furrowed brow said. When she licked mustard from each of her fingers, he glared into the middle distance, aware of every lurid tongue-lap at un-gloved flesh. Her gloves lay wadded up several blocks away.

Belly full, suitcase and coat checked at a handy storage kiosk for a nickel, she was off to the Flyer. Even waiting in line for a turn was a thrill, especially when she reached the loading dock. Here she could see the recent riders coming home. Whenever a train *screeeeeed* to a stop it delivered fresh packs of faces, all of whom look tousled beyond repair. Most were giddy with pleasure, laughing loudly and slapping each other's shoulders or embracing as they chuckled with relief. One or two might be seen fighting tears or running green-cheeked for the exit ramp.

Freddy's first ride was deluxe. A seat to herself—this hardly ever happened—she must be on some kind of a run! She was thrown roughly sideways in the cart as the train raced around curves and plunged down hills. Her hips slammed into tin plating, her elbows cracked against wood. Oh, glory! When her backside rose up from the bench on the notoriously dippy dips, Freddy's breath caught and stayed caught till the end of the ride. There was no seat companion to reach out and grab her arm to keep her down, keep her from becoming airborne. She chased away thoughts of another time, bit her cheeks to keep from crying. Love was for fools. She was out for herself now.

The second time around she was paired up with a young man in a light blue suit and straw boater whose father bullied him as they waited in line. An older brother clearly favoured by the father smiled through the relentless attacks on his young brother's masculinity, his lacking sense of fun and his fairy's fear of throwing up in public. Now nestled in beside this potentially nauseated seatmate, Freddy realized his face was the exact same colour as his jacket: ice blue. Teary-eyed, he clutched the safety bar and seemed to expect nothing less than a very violent death. The knuckles of his quite beautiful hands were ivory white. Disgusted, his father gave him a final withering over-the-shoulder look as the ride lurched forward. As the train rumbled up the first incline Freddy was sure she heard the young man say something in Latin. Something about *fortuna*.

As much as Freddy wanted to comfort the poor thing—he couldn't be more than thirteen or fourteen, tops—her own ecstasy was more important. Hard won in ways this rich kid could never fathom. The first hill was everything: the slow jerky climb as titillating as the swooping drop. Mental and physical preparations were essential if every precious second was to be fully savoured. Just before the downward rush, Freddy closed her eyes and thought: Please, kid, don't puke on the only decent dress I own. Then she screamed till her throat burned, joined by her seatmate whose near-choral wails of fearful rage might have been mistaken for screams of happiness on the ground below. On terra firma again he turned to Freddy, gave a little bow and thanked *her* for not throwing up on his favourite suit. He then flounced down the midway away from his father and brother. She'd have wished him luck in the world, but he looked like he'd be just fine.

Freddy boarded the Flyer twice more for good measure.

She'd had ten bucks and now, with only a dollar and a half left of her "dowry," Freddy had, at least in Woodyardian terms, gone fully astray. She hadn't meant to muck up—she never meant to—but the Flyer was even more wonderful than she'd dreamt of and more perfect than even that. All those nights murmuring "the dippiest dips" into a pillow—her thrill seeker's prayer—all the dreams of speed, ascent and gut-flipping descent became real that afternoon and, frankly, she wasn't about to stop when something felt that good. It reminded her of Bette and the love she could never regret no matter how many Bibles they threw in her path.

She was sorry to have to stop riding, but she'd learned her lesson about any man's offer of a free ride. Treats never came without strings. Sure, she could linger around till some chump invited her to join him on the Flyer, thinking he'd protect her from the big, bad, AJ Miller-designed machine. But freedom tasted too good, and her past mistakes, the ones that landed her three times at Woodyard's, still haunted her.

Stumping along the boardwalk with the rest of the free world, she was too happy to give in to panic over a lack of funds. She tripped down to the beach and collapsed in a heap, her pale complexion taking a beating from the sun. She longed to remove her boots and stockings and sink her toes into the sand but made do with dragging her fingers through it instead.

The object was small, glittery and hard, and when she took it into her lap, careful to make sure no one was looking her way, her breath caught. Somebody had lost a very big engagement ring. She knew from her stint as a counter girl at Eaton's that this was no piece of costume jewellery. Diamonds. Glancing about herself again, she slipped the ring into her dress pocket and continued playing in the sand for what she imagined was a suitable interval.

Dusting sand from her skirts, she headed back to the Flyer to witness the excitement of the other riders. The diamond could not be cashed in here, so she reminded herself to keep an eye on the time. To her amazement, she saw her former seatmate, he of the ashen complexion, lining up for a second turn, this time by himself. Freddy gave a short bark of laughter. Out of the corner of her eye she noted a man moving toward her, hat off and purpose clear. She was not at all tempted, and so moved swiftly out of the path of his advance, away from her beloved Flyer and down the boardwalk. She had a diamond to pawn and a New York train to catch and Union Station was a helluva hike in heavy reformatory-issue boots.

64.

There was no line-up when she arrived at the entrance to the Cyclone. No tickets, just cash fare, three rides for twenty-five dollars. Did she want three rides? Why not? The man taking the fares was decrepit. He didn't smile when she handed him the money, and he grunted something about take your hat off lady or you'll never see it again. She wondered if he'd been working the ride for a long time. When she refused to surrender her camera bag, he shrugged and muttered, "Everyone's an expert."

Joss gave another younger guy her Yankees cap and climbed into her seat. The last of the old wooden coasters, it rattled her teeth as it began the first upward climb. The ocean air was a thrill of its own. Up, up, up over the once-was playground…

She screamed like a child, and it felt so good she didn't care if people on the ground were frightened for her. Seated alone in the car she had to work to hang on and twice felt certain she would meet her end, smashed on the tracks like you heard people were. Half the fun of riding was the unspoken fear that today would be the day a cotter pin would fly loose or a wheel would rip off, something simple that would end in disaster. You took your chances up there, and now she was flying, her teeth clenched, every bone in her body shaken for all they were worth. She screamed with pleasure and did not realize she was actually weeping. Tears were pouring down her face, but the bliss was so exquisite she was already planning to ride again, immediately, maybe ten more times if she felt like it. It was orgasmic, it was better than any feeling in the world, and the Cyclone made good on its reputation. The only other person riding on the same train was a man who opted for silence and gave her a slightly pitying look when they screeched into the loading bay.

"Again?" The operator asked, bored. She had waited all her life for this ride, and his boredom was an affront.

"I'll come back," she said, climbing out. Her legs were rubbery and she staggered down the ramp.

She was waiting at the bottom of the exit gate. Joss would have to be firm and ask her to stop following her around.

"Was it perfect?" the girl asked. Joss nodded tersely and tried to walk past. She held up her hand. "Don't be afraid. Let's go ride the Wonder Wheel."

Joss snorted. "I would like you to leave me alone."

"Oh, I'm going to. I promise. But first we have to ride the Wonder Wheel." She held out her hand and Joss stared at it. Refused to take it, but did concede to walking along beside her since it was clear she wasn't going to take no for an answer.

"My treat," she said as they went to the ticket booth. Joss protested but again, her stubbornness was overt.

"Swinging or non-swinging?" the carny asked when they pushed through the turnstile. You funnelled yourself to the desired gate, but the man apparently liked saying it. The girl turned to Joss.

"You can only do swinging. There's no point in riding it if you go in the baskets that don't move." She had decided to just let her guide the experience. Why not? Maybe she was a serial killer and there was no avoiding her fate, hundreds of feet in the air where no one could help her? She could just hear Bianca's disapproval! You did what? With whom?

The ride looked and felt ancient. The age of it made it seem like an entirely foolish decision, and as they slowly moved forward everything about the Wonder Wheel made her wonder all right: would that door stay shut? What exactly did swinging cars do that the others did not? She glanced over at her seatmate. The bench was slippery, there were no restraints, and this kid next to her was beautiful but nuts.

"Hold my hand," she said. She shook her hand at her when she refused. "You have to."

"I don't have to do anything," Joss said nastily. There was a limit.

"This time, today, you have to. Hold my hand."

Joss took her hand and looked out the side of the basket, avoiding her soft brown gaze. The girl's hand was smooth and dry, warm and strong. It was surprisingly reassuring.

"Close your eyes," she said softly. "Then count to three, then open them again."

She was reluctant for all kinds of reasons, but there was some relief in blocking out the oppressive towers of condos; everywhere she looked she saw the greedy mad world that had devoured the place they had once called Sodom by The Sea. The playground was long gone and she felt depressed, not delighted. She closed her eyes. Did she really have to count? The girl squeezed her fingers gently to let her know she did.

"One. Two. Three."

The Elephant Hotel glimmered in the summer heat in the distance. It literally was a hotel shaped like an elephant, and it was wood, and it would burn down easily when the time came, but for now it was insane and glorious. One roller coaster after another, a field of them as far as she could see, and turrets and towers that were painted white and pink and baby blue. Everything was in place: she could smell the hot sugar on the breeze, she could see the beach, the ocean sparkling, rivers and rivers of parasols and hats below, there were hundreds of people stamping up and down the boardwalk sunning themselves, promenading—

The car lurched forward out over the pavement far below, and she thought she might die from terror. The girl held tight to her hand even though she really would have liked to grip the seat and not her fingers. Or risk it all and try to take a photo. The swinging was intense, the ride was mad but then she realized so was she, seeing things that weren't there, screaming for all her life, the rocking, swaying basket that looked like it had last been maintained in another era. The girl was laughing beside her, squeezing her fingers and enjoying it all. Could she see what she was seeing? Steeplechase was there and Luna, beautiful Luna Park was there, and she wept at the sight of it, she had tears pouring out of her now and what was happening, what was happening to her mind? If she let go of her hand would the rides disappear, would she succumb to this extremely weary feeling that was sweeping rapidly through her, taking her over? It was night. There were lights twinkling on ropes, on wires, everything twinkled so beautifully; the day had turned into night somehow, but it made sense, it was stunning. The car lurched forward again, and she screamed and cried. She could see it all, and she did not want the ride to end.

"It's okay," the girl said. "You can let go now."

65.

They stood side by side in the studio staring at the print on the wall. Joss had flown home from New York the evening before. Tranquil as she rode the ferry back to the island, she knew she would not sleep. Before setting into work she cleared every empty wine carton and bottle from the house, resolute. She opened windows and lit a stick of cedar incense, went to the stereo and fiddled till she tuned into a big-band radio station in Rochester that Tess had turned her on to. She edited and printed and re-printed until dawn, then slid it carefully into an empty vintage frame she'd had leaning against the wall for too many years. Tess had come as soon as she called. Something in Joss's voice and the early hour had panicked her soon-to-be-former-assistant. Two cups of black coffee sat untouched on the desk near them.

Now Tess was trembling. She wasn't cold. A late summer heatwave was rolling in, and the studio at the back of Joss's cottage was a sauna, even with the French doors open. "This is the picture," she said at last.

"It is indeed *a* picture," Joss teased, but she did not feel jokey inside.

"You know what I mean. Who is she?"

Joss shook her head. "I met her at Nathan's Famous. Near the Coney Island Cyclone roller coaster."

"We need to put a name to that face. You're going to sell this for a lot of money."

"I never got her name. And there is no way I'm selling this one. She's all mine." Tess reminded Joss that she always took down the names of her subjects. And of all the photographs to not have a name for, and to refuse to sell? Because this was *the* picture. The one that made all of the other excellent photographs look almost soulless, a destination ascended to, slowly and without any swagger or certainty, yet not an accident. Selling it, sharing it, wasn't about the money. It was about being known again.

"I have been known," Joss said, remembering the warm dry hand in hers and the view of the ocean sparkling beyond the miles of rides. There would never be another such perfect day, and she was okay with it. She had a Muse that would last forever, and it wasn't Laura.

Tess wanted to know what had happened with the girl in the photo. Something Joss wasn't rushing to discuss. Joss had no response when nudged. The girl was twenty, tops. A young woman with the body of a greyhound and the distressing eyes of a seer. The emanation of the photo was as stirring as its composition.

The girl leaned against the wooden entrance ramp to the Cyclone, her peculiar eyes fixed on something just outside the frame, her blurred fingers cranking the solar-powered radio… *Meet me down at Luna, Lena, meet me at the gate*… A half-smile on her lush lips, she was pretty and handsome in one stroke. Blue jeans from another time, the denim worn to perfection. Dream jeans. The soft grey t-shirt she wore read as silver in the print, and Joss leaned in to point at the faded blue number 8 on the bicep of the girl's right sleeve. "I never noticed that when I was shooting her," she said.

"Bullshit, you notice everything when you're shooting. Really?"

"This was different. I breathed differently when I looked at her."

Tess looped her warm arm in Joss's and gave her a sideways hug. She peered at the photograph some more and shook her head in amazement. The girl was not only a new direction in Joss's whole style, but there was something eternal about her stare. In spite of her indirect gaze, you felt seen back in sly periphery. She would never grow old, she would always be this very perfect, knowing moment in her life, with a washboard stomach and lean long arms and Joss's

lucky number on her sleeve. Eight nominations for photojournal-
ism prizes in the early years, eight fellowships, the number of times
she had quit smoking this summer, the exact number of times she
had been to New York before she met Bianca. Tess knew all these
things and remembered them. The photograph would come to rep-
resent Joss's imagination, the whole drive of her vision, and here
they were standing around doing nothing about it. The studio was
tight with the quiet realization between them. This was *the* picture.

"Where are the others? The sheet? Should we call the agency
or wait?"

"There are no others. I took this one and came home. She
wouldn't pose for more."

"You took one photograph? And this is what came out? That
never happens. We both know." Tess began to re-arrange things
on the desk. She had something on her mind, and she was slow to
spill it. The photograph had transfixed them both in different ways.
They were going through very different crises at the same instant.
Joss wanted to call Laura, but wouldn't. Because Laura had never
looked into her the way the tomboy gamine at Coney Island had.
She never would, and Joss was suddenly, shockingly fine with that.
Tess was watching her think all of these things, and her own crisis
deepened. Joss could feel the anxiety in her old friend, and she
turned and put her hand on Tess's shoulder. For the first time in an
hour, she looked away from the photo of the girl.

"What is it?"

"I'm not going to Paris," Tess said finally. "Something came up."

Joss gasped, dropped her hand. "What could possibly 'come up'
that would keep you from living out a dream?"

"It wasn't my dream," Tess said with a smile. "It was always
yours."

Joss turned back to face the girl in the picture. "This is my
dream."

ACKNOWLEDGEMENTS

Thanks to The Toronto Arts Council, The Ontario Arts Council, The Canada Council for the Arts, and the individual patron saints who kept the wolves from the door during an interval when I could not work.

Thanks also to Artscape Gibraltar Point for an inspiring retreat space, and Antje Duvekot for the beautifully triggering song "Coney Island."

Early research was conducted at the City of Toronto Archives, and Sally Gibson's book *More Than an Island* provided so much fuel for the imagination.

My love and thanks to my family and friends for cheerleading skills nonpareil, and to the wonderful team at Tightrope Books for all their hard work.

Lastly, eternal gratitude to Timothy Findley for conversations about life, roller coasters and writing that are with me still.

Permission to use Sonnet XXVII by Edna St. Vincent Millay was obtained through the Edna St. Vincent Millay Society in the United States.

ABOUT THE AUTHOR

Marnie Woodrow is the author of two short story collections and the acclaimed novel, *Spelling Mississippi*. She is also a playwright, an editor, and a creative writing instructor. She lives in Hamilton, Ontario.